D1402401

THE WEDDING AGREEMENT

A Strictly Business Novel

ELIZABETH HAYLEY

A SIGNET ECLIPSE BOOK

SIGNET ECLIPSE
Published by New American Library,
an imprint of Penguin Random House LLC
375 Hudson Street, New York, New York 10014

This book is an original publication of New American Library.

First Printing, May 2016

For more information about Penguin Random House, visit penguin.com.

ISBN 978-0-451-47554-1

Printed in the United States of America
10 9 8 7 6 5 4 3 2 1

Penguin
Random
House

To Shauna and Sarah
We couldn't have done this without you

Chapter 1

Case Study

Cass grabbed hold of the bowling ball and strutted confidently up to the line, unfazed by the fact she was sliding a bit as she pulled her arm back and threw it forward, releasing the twelve-pound burden from her hand. Then she spun around quickly toward her group of girlfriends, who were craning their necks to peer around her.

"I thought you said you bowled a couple of months ago," Lauren said as Cass heard the ball land in the gutter with a loud thud. Quinn's eyebrows raised, and Simone bit her bottom lip.

"I did," Cass shot back quickly, surprised by the question even though she'd knocked down only a total of six pins in the last three frames. "I just forgot to mention it was on a Wii." She let her eyes dart quickly to where Alex was seated toward the end of the group. His eyes twinkled with amusement, but he didn't open his mouth. "Fine, the Wii game wasn't my best performance either."

This time Alex clearly couldn't resist. "Best performance? My seven-year-old daughter's got more game than you."

"First of all, I'm pretty sure Nina's got more game than *you* too," Cass snapped back with a smirk. "You couldn't pick up a chick in a henhouse." Her comment elicited a roar of laughter from Scott, Xavier, and Tim, and a soft chuckle from Alex, who'd become used to Cass teasing him. "And speaking of games," Cass said, her eyes darting to Lauren and Scott, "when are you two going to stop playing musical wedding dates? You've been engaged for months. Have you guys decided on a day yet or what?"

Lauren shrugged. "We're between a couple places. Both venues have Saturdays in April open, so it'll probably be then."

"April? That's, like, over a year away," Cass protested. "You guys drag your feet doing everything. Scott had the ring for, like, five months before he even proposed, and you didn't have the engagement party until two months later."

"Whoa, wait a second," Scott cut in. "I was all set to ask Lauren to marry me, but then my impulsive older brother had to go and propose to someone he wasn't even dating at the time."

"Well, when you say it like that—" Tim started.

"How else can I say it?" Scott joked. "See what I get for being the polite sibling and not stealing your thunder?" Scott settled back into his seat and slid his arm around Lauren. "Not everyone can make life decisions as easily as they can pick what to order at a drive-through," he added on a laugh.

"You act like I proposed and we rushed off to have

Elvis marry us in some Vegas chapel or something. I knew what I wanted," Tim said, giving Quinn a seductive glance that he didn't try to hide. "Besides, we put a lot of thought into the actual wedding. So much thought that we even managed to convince Mom to come. And we all know she couldn't stand the sight of me for the better part of the past decade." Tim's smile had a way of adding a bit of humor to an otherwise sensitive subject. His struggles with addiction had caused a rift between Tim and his mother that no one thought could be fixed. Not even him.

"Tim's right, Laur," Cass insisted. "Quinn somehow managed to help repair a severely damaged relationship, *and* they planned an entire wedding . . . all in, like, seven months. It can't be that difficult."

Tim rose to take his turn, and pushed up the sleeves of his shirt. He released the ball with ease and turned back toward the group as the ball sped toward its targets. "In all fairness, *I* didn't plan much of anything." Cass rolled her eyes as every pin fell. Tim trotted over to take a seat between Quinn and Scott, who shifted slightly to make room for his brother on the row of beige plastic seats. "Quinn took care of all the logistics, and I just gave my two cents when it came to all of the fun stuff like food tasting and picking the band."

Cass had a feeling that Tim had had more of a hand in the wedding planning than he'd let on, but she didn't question him. "Well, as a bridesmaid, I think I should have a say in some things, Laur."

Xavier stood, holding two empty pitchers. "Enough wedding talk for me. I'm going up to get us a refill."

"Well, as the bride, I think you shouldn't," Lauren said, ignoring Xavier's departure completely. She kept her expression even, but Cass could tell she was holding back a laugh. "We're just taking our time to make sure we're both okay with everything. Planning a wedding's a big undertaking. You'll find out if you ever get married."

Cass stuck out her tongue at her friend. Though Lauren's comment would have offended most twenty-eight-year-old women, Cass understood Lauren's intended meaning. She wasn't saying that Cass couldn't find anyone to marry her. It was *Cass* who had chosen the bachelorette life years ago, opting to put her career in public relations above having a family. And she didn't keep her intentions a secret. She'd had boyfriends in the past, and every one of them was more than comfortable with her choice. After all, how hard is it to convince a twenty-something-year-old guy that you're not looking for anything serious? "Fine, fine," Cass finally said. "But just for the record, I haven't seen this much thought go into planning a wedding since Kim and Kanye tied the knot."

Scott shook his head. "Would it make you feel better if we promise not to name any of our future children after one of the cardinal directions?"

"Yes," Cass said simply.

"That's a shame," Simone chimed in, "because I always thought South Jacobs had a nice ring to it."

Alex sat up a little straighter. "If you ask me, marriage isn't isn't worth the hassle. I've done it once, and I don't plan to do it again."

Cass had been wondering when, if ever, Alex would give his opinion. The tense relationship between him and his ex-wife, Tessa, was no secret to anyone in the group. For that reason alone, Cass couldn't blame him for never wanting to walk down that road again . . . or, in this case, that aisle. That's why, even though Alex was thirty-three, Cass had no reservations about the casual sex the two would have every so often. She knew it would remain just that.

"Too many people focus on the trivial details like dresses and flowers and cake," Alex continued. "None of that shit matters—"

"Cake always matters," Cass interrupted, as an attempt to bring more lightness back to the conversation.

Alex leaned forward, resting his forearms on his thighs as he averted his gaze from the group and focused his attention on the beer he held between his hands. "None of it matters in the long run," he repeated, this time more to himself than to everyone else listening. "The marriage is what matters, and when you don't give a shit about *that*, who cares if you have roses or"—he gestured wildly with his hand as he looked to everyone for help—"or . . . what's another type of flower?"

Scott answered immediately. "Tulip, gardenia, calla lily, peony, lily of the—"

Tim shook his head and grabbed Scott's arm. "You're not helping."

"Right, sorry," Scott said.

The rest of the group had already erupted with laughter, including Alex, who needed it more than anyone. He wasn't sure why he'd gotten onto his soapbox, but he knew he needed to get the fuck off it. "It's fine," Alex assured Scott before draining the last of his beer. "Now let's just focus on the game. For Christ's sake, the girls are only seventy-four points behind us, and there are only three frames left. I'm worried we might not cover the hundred-point spread." That earned him a hard punch to the arm, courtesy of Cass. "Ouch. That actually hurt a little," he said, surprised.

"You know, you'd make a much better professional boxer than you would a bowler."

"Clearly," Cass replied, tossing her blond hair over her shoulder with a smirk. "Someone better tell Laila Ali I'm coming for her."

"She's retired," everyone said, almost in unison.

Cass glanced around at the group in disbelief. "How did you *all* know that?"

There were some shrugs and some replies of "I don't know."

"Well, okay, then. I guess Laila's safe from the wrath of Cassidy Mullen."

"I bet she's thankful for that," Alex joked as he stood to take his turn.

The guys ended up covering the spread, which caused the girls to demand a rematch. And that was how most of the night continued, with the group of friends doing what they did best: joking, drinking, and talking about nonsense until they were laughing so hard Alex could feel tears forming in the corners of his eyes. Finally, after one more game, the night started to wrap up.

"We should probably get going," Scott said. "I have some patients I need to check on at the hospital tomorrow morning before I head over to the satellite office, and Lauren has an early appointment coming in too."

"God, you guys are so old," Tim joked. He was actually six years Scott's senior. But as a chef, Tim rarely had to get up early, so he seemed to take every opportunity to poke fun at his little brother when he'd skip out before the rest of the group. "Anyone want to go to that place up the street that lets you cook s'mores at your table? They're open until midnight,"

Tim asked the rest of the crew after Scott and Lauren had left.

Quinn didn't give anyone a chance to respond before she grabbed Tim by the arm. "We're going to take off too. And don't worry," she added. "Someday I'll fill you in on what it's like to be married to a fourteen-year-old."

Alex chuckled. "You might not want to say that too loudly in a public place."

"Oh right," she said, her face reddening.

After a few minutes, the rest of the group headed out to the parking lot.

"So, how about you?" Cass asked Alex once Simone and Xavier were in their cars. "You have an early morning too?"

Alex didn't have to try hard to interpret Cass' meaning. They'd gone home together enough times over the past year or so for him to know exactly what she was asking. "Not early enough that I can't have a late night."

"Good answer," Cass said as she climbed in her car.

Alex grinned as he unlocked his door and hopped in to follow her. Cass' apartment was closer, so that's where they headed. And within fifteen minutes of leaving the bowling alley, they were fumbling up the stairs to her apartment. Though her door was only steps away, Alex couldn't stop himself from backing her up against the wall when they reached the landing outside her apartment. He used his hips to pin her to the hard surface as his lips found hers, moving slowly but with a need he knew Cass would recognize immediately. His hands roamed her body, his fingertips lightly grazing the soft skin under her shirt. Already he ached for her, so he finally released her long enough to let her move toward the door. But Alex couldn't break contact for long. He nestled his cock against her denim-clad ass as she searched for her keys. Just as she found them and slid the correct one into the lock, Alex abruptly stopped trailing his lips up the back of her neck, and his body tensed.

"What's wrong?" she asked.

"Are your neighbors always that loud?"

Cass acted like she hadn't even registered the heavy metal music and raucous laughing rumbling from next door. "Sometimes."

"That's bullshit. Want me to say something?"

"Now? Are you kidding me? Right now I want to be making our own noise."

That was all Alex needed to hear. About a minute later, after removing his jacket and unstrapping his service weapon, he was rocking his hips against her as he tasted the cool mint of the gum that still lingered on her mouth. He stayed there, letting his tongue move softly over hers for a bit longer while he ground against her. He allowed himself to enjoy the taste of her before his tongue left her mouth and worked its way down her neck with quick nibbles.

She laughed, the vibration of her throat humming against his lips.

"Suddenly ticklish?"

She squirmed below him. "A little."

Alex slid his hand under Cass' shirt and toward her back to undo her bra. She arched in response. "Mmm, sexy *and* helpful," he said, popping the clasp and moving his hand back toward her chest so his fingers could toy with her nipples.

Cass let out a breathy sigh. He stayed there for a few moments, letting her enjoy his touch. He loved how hard her nipples got between his fingers and how her soft moans increased in intensity as his hands moved over her skin. Cass gripped his back through his T-shirt, which she then pulled over his head in one quick jerk and tossed to the floor beside them. "Pants off. Now," Cass said, catching Alex by surprise.

He gave her an amused grin as he stood up, his cock noticeably tenting the fabric of his pants. "You're bossy when you're horny." She didn't answer, though he could tell she was biting back an insult. Slowly he kicked off his shoes and socks before moving his hands to the button of his jeans and letting them hover there unmoving, curious about how Cass would respond.

She squirmed on the couch for a moment or two as Alex brushed a hand over himself to grip his cock through his pants. "Let me show you how this works," she finally said, sitting up to pull her shirt over her head and let her bra fall down her arms to the floor. Then she leaned back onto the couch, popped the button of her jeans, and shimmied them down her legs until she could kick them off completely. "You show me yours; I'll show you mine," she said, letting her hand skate down her torso until her fingers slid under the sheer fabric of her thong just far enough to give the elastic a sharp tug until it snapped back into place.

But Alex had gotten a glimpse of what was beneath. And what he saw made him grow even harder. It's not like he hadn't seen it before—her smooth skin just begging to be stroked—but it made him ache to be inside her, feel her stretch around him. This time when his finger touched the button of his jeans he didn't hesitate. He removed them immediately and stood over Cass, his cock pushing out the fabric of his black boxer briefs. He knelt down to get a condom from his wallet and ripped the foil with his teeth. Then he reached down to remove his boxers and slide the latex over himself. He was so fucking ready. "Your turn," he said, gesturing to the small piece of material covering the area on Cass that Alex wanted most.

Once Cass was as naked as Alex, he settled between her legs once more, enjoying the sensation of them wrapping around him as he guided himself inside her. He started slowly, wanting to feel every inch of himself move in and out of her. He also knew how much it teased her, the gentle grind against her. Cass ceased licking his neck to whisper "Faster" in Alex's ear, a request he was always happy to comply with. He sped up and the two quickly found their rhythm, their heart and breathing rates increasing with every thrust. Alex could feel Cass tightening around him, bringing him closer to release.

"God, Alex," Cass let out as part of an exhalation.

He could tell she was getting closer, and put his hand up to tangle in her hair, pulling gently as he increased the speed of his hips even more, working them both toward their much-needed release. At last he felt her clench around him, her body pulsating around his cock as she released a throaty moan and a few soft curse words. He let her ride out her orgasm before concentrating on his own, which came a few moments later as he pumped inside her hard and fast.

He pulled out of her after a few seconds and headed to the bathroom. By the time he got back, Cass was already in a baggy T-shirt and flipping through the channels. "You going to hang out for a bit?" she asked. "I'm sure one of the eighteen *Fast and the Furious* movies is on somewhere."

Alex laughed, but it was the truth. He'd watch

those movies anytime they were on, and everyone knew it. He thought about taking her up on her offer. There was nothing that appealed to him more at the moment than a movie and waking up curled around a half-naked—or fully naked—Cass. But before he could open his mouth to reply, Cass opened hers. Except it was to let out a slow yawn. Though it was hard for him to admit it, he knew it was in both of their best interests to get some rest. He gave her a small smile before he started collecting his clothes from the floor and dressing. "I actually have some work I should probably get done before I go in tomorrow morning."

"All right," Cass said, pulling her hair up into a loose ponytail as she walked Alex to the door so she could lock the dead bolt behind him. "Drive safely."

"Always," he replied with a smile. "And I'm going to stop by next door and say something about the music. You'll never be able to sleep with that going on."

Cass playfully rolled her eyes, but Alex didn't care. Protecting people close to him was something ingrained too deeply in his personality, and he couldn't shut it off.

"You want me to wait here in case they jump you?" she said teasingly, but he knew the offer was sincere.

"Nah, I'll be fine. If they start getting rowdy, I'll flash my badge and gun. That usually settles people down." He shot her a mischievous smirk before she closed the door behind him. Then he headed down the hall toward the noise. A loud bang of his fist on the door caused the music to cut off and a shaggy-looking kid to answer the door.

"Can I help you?"

Alex quickly appraised the person in front of him. He was most likely a college kid. Alex wondered how he could even afford to live in the building until he saw the Tag Heuer watch on the kid's wrist. *No doubt about it; someone has Daddy paying the rent.* "Yeah, man. Would you mind turning the music down? Some of us have early mornings."

The kid looked at Alex a second, probably trying to assess whether he should do as he was asked or not. "Sure, man. No problem."

Good answer. Alex was often thankful for his bulky frame. It kept people from trying to fuck with him. "Thanks. Have a good one." Alex didn't wait for a reply as he turned and started toward the elevator, wondering if there were any better sleep aids than bowling and hot sex.

Chapter 2

Assault

Alex grabbed a spatula out of the bin on the counter and flipped it up in the air before pointing it at Nina, who was seated on the barstool. "Banana or chocolate chip?"

She took a sip of her apple juice. "Daaaad," she replied, drawing out the word as if it had two syllables, "you know I want both."

Alex smiled back at his daughter's grin, which, since yesterday, was missing another tooth in the front. "That's my girl." He shook some of the pancake mix into the blue glass bowl and filled the measuring cup to the correct line with water before dumping it in. "So, did the Tooth Fairy come last night?"

Nina's smile broadened and she tucked a wisp of her soft brown hair behind her ear. "Yeah!" she said excitedly, withdrawing the five-dollar bill and two ones from underneath the countertop.

Alex gave his daughter a look of surprise. "Seven

dollars is a lot of money. You think she gave you that amount because you're seven years old?" he asked, pouring one large circle of batter and attaching two smaller ones to make the shape of Mickey Mouse on the pan.

Alex turned around and watched Nina put a finger to her lips, pulling on her bottom one as if she were pondering the question she'd just been asked. "I don't think so. I only got five dollars when I lost my first tooth, and I was six then." She furrowed her brow for a second and then spoke again. "You think if I leave her a note and tell her she forgot the other dollar last time, she'll leave it for me?"

Alex chuckled and leaned against the countertop, his hands on the edge of the cold granite. He couldn't lie to himself. A part of him loved that he'd given his daughter more money when she'd lost the tooth at his house than when she'd lost her first one at Tessa's. The ex-husband inside him smiled at the thought that he'd unknowingly one-upped her. But the much larger part of himself—the father in him—felt a pang of guilt at his daughter's question. It was just another example of a time when his and Tessa's trouble communicating caused confusion for Nina. Alex sighed heavily before returning to flip the pancakes. "It's not polite to ask anyone for money, Nina, even the Tooth Fairy. I'm sure she must've just forgotten how old you were—you know, with all the kids' houses she goes to each night."

Nina seemed to accept this answer as the truth, letting the topic go and quickly replacing it with another. "Okay," she said simply. "Can we have that coconut syrup we had last time?"

Alex picked up the pan and brought it over to Nina's plate, sliding her cartoon-shaped breakfast onto it. "You know, you have quite an extensive palate for a little girl."

Nina had already pulled one ear off the pancake and shoved it into her mouth, getting chocolate on her fingers in the process. "Thanks," she said, though Alex knew she probably had no idea what his comment even meant.

The two spent the next ten minutes eating and talking about what to do for the day. Nina wanted to feed the ducks at the pond around the corner, and Alex suggested that they stop by the mall later in the day so she could pick out a gift for herself with the money she'd gotten from the Tooth Fairy. Alex had just put the last few bites of his fourth pancake into his mouth when he heard his phone ringing on the other counter. He chewed quickly, wiping his mouth on the way to check his phone. *Who calls before nine a.m. on a Sunday? No one I want to talk to, that's who.* He rolled his eyes as he saw the name on the screen: *Don.* He swiped his finger along the bottom of the screen to answer, and swallowed the rest of the pancake that was in his mouth before speaking. "Walker."

"Morning, Alex. Sorry to bother you."

No, you're not. "It's fine. What's going on?"

"We got a guy we're looking at for the Abner case. We're gonna need to take a look at this before we arrest him."

Alex heard himself sigh, but quickly tried to cover it with a cough. He hated how his job with the FBI could interfere with his time with Nina, but there wasn't anything he could do.

"Sorry. I know it's the weekend, but you know what a big break this is."

"I know, I know." Alex pinched the bridge of his nose and squinted, turning away from Nina and heading toward the family room. "It's just that I have my daughter until tonight and . . ." Alex let his voice trail off. "Never mind. It's my problem, not yours. Is the afternoon okay?"

"Should be fine. We have our guys surveilling his house now. If he goes anywhere, we'll let you know."

"Sounds good. Thanks, Don." As he hung up the phone, he thought about how his next phone call would suck way more than the previous one.

Surprisingly Tessa didn't give him too much shit when he'd asked if she could come pick up Nina a few hours earlier than she'd planned. She'd agreed to get there by one instead of after dinner, and Alex was grateful for it. The few hours left still gave him time to take Nina to the duck pond and the mall, so the two got ready quickly and headed down the street with a bag of bread.

Nina seemed to be understanding of her father's work schedule, but he still felt horrible. It wasn't the first time their weekend together had been cut short because of his job, and he was again reminded of the effect that the divorce had to have had on her. She was a seven-year-old girl, not a basket of rolls to be passed from person to person.

But Alex tried his best to push aside the guilt he felt, at least while Nina was still there. The last thing he wanted was for the small amount of time they had left together to be polluted by negative feelings. And, thankfully, he was able to do that. They went through a half loaf of bread, tossing it into the pond as far as each of them could throw. After the mall, they'd headed home for lunch. They'd just finished eating the grilled cheese Alex had made for the two of them when the doorbell rang. "Why don't you go finish packing up your things upstairs while I talk to your mom?" Alex said, lifting the plate from in front of his daughter.

"'Kay," Nina answered, quickly bounding toward the stairs.

As Alex walked to the door, he mentally prepared himself for the person who'd be on the other side of it.

"Hi," Tessa said, as soon as he pulled the wooden door open for her to step inside.

"Hey, thanks again. Don called and—"

"You don't have to explain every time, Alex." She moved to the stairs, looking up toward the sound of Nina stomping around above them. "I was married to you for four years, remember?"

Unfortunately.

"I know how it is." She folded her arms across her chest and pressed her lips into a thin line, averting her eyes away from his.

Alex stayed silent. He knew that look. It was the same expression Tessa wore right before she'd come clean after Alex had confronted her about her infidelity. After about thirty seconds he couldn't take it anymore. "Oh, just spit it out, Tessa. What is it?"

Tessa brought her gaze up to his and moved a strand of her strawberry blond hair away from her eye. "Pete's starting a prepackaged-meal company, and I'm going to help him pitch it to some gyms this summer. We'll be gone for about eight weeks, traveling around the country and even overseas. It's a great opportunity for us, Alex. Pete's put a lot of effort into everything. He's even come up with the recipes himself. It's not just shakes and protein bars. It's real food, like—"

"Save your spiel for your international tour," Alex spat. "I don't give a shit about Pete's cooking skills.

The only thing I care about is that you're taking my daughter during the part of the year when I normally get to spend the most time with her. You can't even do this. Part of our custody agreement stipulates that I get to have her for three weeks—"

"That's not what I meant," Tessa said, shaking her head. "I didn't mean Nina's coming with us. She can't. It'll be way too much traveling for someone her age. Summer is Nina's vacation. I wouldn't make her come along on some work trip."

Alex scratched the back of his head and narrowed his eyes. "Oh," he said. "I thought you were telling me I'd see her less, not more. I'd love to have her for the whole summer."

Tessa hesitated a moment, biting her lip. "I'm going to leave her with my parents, Alex."

"You're going to leave *my* daughter with *your* parents? Who live in Jersey?" Alex was livid. "I just said I'd love to have her for the summer."

"Loving to have her and actually being able to have her are two completely different things. Your work schedule is crazy. Look at what happened today. You can't tell me this is a rare occurrence. Who are you going to call when you need someone to come pick her up suddenly? My parents? They live three hours away."

"I'm aware. Nina's going to love spending over six hours in the car every time it's my turn to have her, by the way. Not to mention how that cuts into our ability to do things besides play license-plate bingo."

"You're acting like I'm taking Nina from you. You'll see her as often as you do every summer."

Alex ran a hand through his thick, dark hair. "Jesus, Tess, you're missing the point. I'm Nina's father, not some stranger you pay to babysit her for a few hours while you go out for the night."

"I'm not saying you're not her father. I'm saying my parents are both retired. They have the time for her. Time that you don't have."

"I have time for my daughter."

"Okay. What exactly do you plan to do with her while you're at work five days a week?"

Alex scoffed. Tessa clearly thought she'd stumped him. "The same thing she would've done if you weren't going away. Summer camp. I'm assuming you still work at Pete's gym a few days a week and would need to send her just like you've done every other summer. I'll drop her off before work and pick her up on my way home each day."

Tessa rolled her eyes but didn't disagree that a day camp was a valid solution. "And what about when you get called in to work unexpectedly at night or on a weekend? What then?"

"I'm perfectly capable of handling anything that would come up while you're away."

"And what would be your idea of handling it? Dragging our seven-year-old daughter to work with you so you can introduce her to some of the murderers and pedophiles you hang out with?"

"Oh, come on. That's completely ridiculous. You're being irrational, and you know it."

"Well, then what? Tell me, Alex. What do you plan to do when you have to go in to work suddenly?"

Alex searched his brain for an answer, but he couldn't find one. His sister had kids of her own, and she lived about forty-five minutes away. The chances that she wouldn't be carting her three boys around to practice or a doctor's appointment when he called were slim to none. He knew from experience. "I'll figure something out," he finally said. "I always do."

"Like you did today?" Tessa's green eyes glared at him, begging him to admit what he already knew. He didn't have an answer.

And just like that he felt the fight drain from him. He couldn't argue with that. As much as Alex hated to admit it, Tessa had been granted primary custody of their daughter for a reason. Alex had been a single guy with a demanding and often unpredictable career. Not exactly a suitable situation for a young girl. At least in the eyes of a judge. At the time Alex had promised himself he'd become more stable, eventually try to get fifty-fifty custody. That was almost four years ago. And his living circumstances hadn't changed. Deflated, he peeked around the banister and glanced up the steps, making sure that Nina wasn't on her way down. "Does she know yet?"

"Not yet. I wanted to talk to you first," Tessa said quietly.

"Well, mission accomplished." Alex let out a disgusted laugh, but tried to cover it with a real smile when he saw Nina bounce down the stairs.

"Ready, sweetie?" Tessa asked.

"Yup."

"Give Daddy a hug and a kiss good-bye."

Nina wrapped her small arms around Alex's waist tightly. He knelt down so she could give him a kiss on the cheek.

"Bye, Daddy," Nina said quietly.

Alex kissed her forehead softly and stood up, watching her as she walked toward Tessa's car. It wasn't until the SUV was down the road and out of sight that he finally responded. "Bye, baby," he whispered.

* * *

Cass sat at her desk, looking at the papers splayed out in front of her, trying desperately to see a way to spin the nightmare before her in a positive way. *How can I turn a stalker who was caught digging through a woman's trash and stealing her underwear into someone with a successful restaurant?* At least he was acquitted—that was something.

The ringing of her cell phone interrupted her thoughts of the large muscular man asking his female customers if they preferred Victoria's Secret or Frederick's of Hollywood. She hoped her bosses appreciated the miracles she worked every day and would eventually reward her with a corner office. Sooner rather than later. Cass glanced at the phone screen before answering, a smirk lifting her lips. "Mr. Walker, to what do I owe the pleasure?"

"Not sure. But I bet I can think of something," Alex quipped.

"I'm sure you could. Okay, stop trying to get in my pants—I'm working. What's up?"

"You're separating business from pleasure? Has hell frozen over?"

Cass couldn't help but laugh. "You're a real comedian today."

"I try. Okay, down to business: are you going to Scott and Lauren's housewarming Saturday?"

"Of course."

"You want to go in on a gift with me?" Alex asked.

"Ah, so now we arrive at the real reason for this call. Let me guess—you want me to pick out a gift and put your name because you're too lazy to go out and get anything. Right?"

"Are all women in a conspiracy to give me a hard time lately?"

Alex's voice was light, but there was a slight agitation infused that made his words come out more clipped than he probably intended. "What happened now?" Cass questioned.

"What do you mean?"

"You know what I mean. Who else is giving you a hard time? Because I gotta tell you, I don't like sharing the role of resident ballbuster with other women. It makes me feel dirty."

"You love feeling dirty," Alex joked, clearly trying to change the subject.

Cass wasn't having it. "Spill it, Alex."

He let out a loud sigh. "Tessa's giving me shit again. She wants to travel around the country this summer with that asshole, selling tofu and protein shakes or some shit. She plans to leave Nina with her parents instead of with me. I got to hear a whole speech about how I can't even handle having Nina for a weekend, let alone a couple months. I know she gets pissed about my sometimes-erratic work schedule, but I'm a good dad. Nina should be with her father, not her grandparents."

Alex let all the words out in a rush, as though he'd been holding them in for so long that, once given the opportunity to break the dam, he couldn't contain the flood. Cass felt horrible for him. She'd met Nina a few times, and it was clear that the father and daughter had a special bond. "When did she tell you this?" Cass asked.

"Sunday, when she picked her up."

Well, that explains the tirade. "Have you talked to anyone about it? Maybe seen a lawyer?"

Alex groaned. "I haven't even wanted to *think* about it, let alone talk about it. But I did give my lawyer a quick call, and from the brief conversation we had, I could tell he didn't think it looked good for me. Tessa's going to cite the times she's had to pick up Nina early or I've needed to reschedule because of work. And since the judge will have no reason to prevent Nina from spending the time with her grandparents, fighting this in court will just end up being a waste of time and money. Not to mention the fact that I don't want to put Nina through a custody dispute over two months' time. It won't go my way. I just know it."

"You don't *know* anything." But Cass didn't quite believe her own words. Alex had been married to his job for the entire time she'd known him. That was something Cass could relate to and didn't fault him for. Cass had known for most of her life that her primary goal was to be successful in whatever career she chose. Her mom had been a homemaker, and while she had always seemed to enjoy taking care of her family, Cass always wondered if it was as rewarding as her mother always made it out to be. Surely her mom had had dreams—goals she'd wanted to accomplish besides raising three ornery girls. She'd gone to college with hopes of a career, but once children came along, her mom had put getting a job outside the home on hold. And that hold became permanent. Cass respected people who raised children more than she could ever put into words, because that life was absolutely not for her. She liked playing with her sisters' kids, but also deeply enjoyed being able to give them back after a few hours. Cass was the first to admit that she was selfish with her time. And unlike her sisters, who were working moms, Cass wasn't willing to give up what little free time she had so she could chase a toddler around at a Gymboree class and attend parent conferences. Liking to take things at her own pace and do what she felt like, when she felt like it, was a character trait she'd always had. So much so that even settling down with a man caused her to break out in hives. And listening to the stress Alex was dealing with didn't sway her opinions in the least.

"I know enough," was all Alex offered in response, and Cass had nothing much else to say.

Consoling depressed men in domestic disputes was not her forte. So she elected to change the subject instead. "Should I get something pretty for the house or a bottle of expensive booze?"

Alex snorted. "Clearly they're both enamored with pretty things. Go with that."

Cass smiled as she thought of her friends. "Pretty" was putting it mildly. They were definitely one of the most sickeningly attractive couples she'd ever seen. "Pretty, it is."

"Okay. Thanks, Cass. I owe you one."

"You can repay me after the party. But it's going to take more than once." Cass smiled, hoping returning them to their shared language—flirty banter—would help Alex's mood a little.

And as he laughed, she knew that it had worked. "You're on. Schedule me for back-to-back appointments, then."

"I'll pencil you in. See you Saturday."

She ended the call and reclined in her chair, unable to keep her thoughts from how there'd be much more than a penciling in on Saturday.

Chapter 3

Undercover

Alex stared at the phone in his hand, willing it to stop ringing so he didn't have to answer. He couldn't believe Don was calling him again . . . two weekends in a row. And this time on a Saturday. He couldn't call Tessa to get Nina early again. It would only validate her accusation that his schedule interfered with his relationship with his daughter. Not to mention that since Tessa's birthday was tomorrow, he had Nina for just one day. He couldn't let Tessa think that he'd wasted his only day with his daughter by working.

Finally he slid his thumb over the bottom of his phone, exhaling the breath he must have been holding. When Don quickly confirmed Alex's suspicions that he would need to go in to work for a few hours, he hung up and began dialing his list of potential babysitters. His first phone call was always going to be his sister, Christina. *Family is family, after all.* But Alex wasn't surprised when Christina said she was over two hours away at his nephew's AAU basketball game. *Why do her kids have to be such good athletes?* Alex immediately moved on to a few other people who had watched Nina in the past—an elderly neighbor who had a granddaughter about Nina's age, the mother of one of Nina's friends. He even called Xavier, who'd had Nina over once when he was babysitting his niece.

But when none of them were available, Alex started to panic. He glanced at the clock, taking note of the fact that he had to leave in less than forty-five minutes. *Think, damn it.* He knew Lauren and Scott would be getting ready for their housewarming party, and it wouldn't be fair to dump a child on them in the midst of all that. Nearly out of options, he almost considered asking the man who peddled bootleg porn in the apartment complex down the street. Surely he'd have time to watch her.

But Alex knew there was only one person left whom he could legitimately ask. Before he could change his mind, he clicked on Cass' name and hit Call.

A groggy voice answered almost immediately. "Hello."

"Hey, sorry to bother you. It sounds like I woke you up."

Cass yawned. "You kind of did."

"Oh, well, sorry again. Although if it wasn't almost noon I might feel worse about it."

"Not all of us have real responsibilities. Rough night."

Alex laughed, wondering but not wanting to ask what that meant. "Well you might be in for a rough afternoon too."

He waited a few seconds for Cass to speak again. When she did, her voice sounded more alert than it had only moments before. "What does that mean exactly?"

"I kind of need a favor."

Cass was silent.

"You can say no." Alex thought for a second, exhaling a defeated sigh. "Actually, you really can't. Well, not unless you're okay with Tessa castrating me with a rusty butter knife." Alex rubbed his hand across his scalp. "I need you to watch Nina for me. It'd just be for a few hours. I could drop her off at your place on my way in to work, and you guys could just meet me at Scott and Lauren's house later."

"You need *me*"—Cass sounded incredulous—"to watch Nina."

"Yeah, I do. I know it's not really . . . your thing. But I have no other options. I called everyone else before you—my sister, Xavier, a neighbor, Nina's friends' moms. If anyone else could do it, I wouldn't have called you." He realized how that sounded, but it was too late to take it back.

"Did you check with the woman we saw on the metro that time? You know, the one who was singing that Kelly Clarkson song and wearing a beaded necklace as a shirt. I bet she'd provide hours of entertainment for little Nina."

Alex hesitated, unsure of what to say. He did feel slightly bad that Cass was his last call, but he knew kids weren't her thing. And she never tried to hide that fact. "Cass, listen. I—"

She let out a laugh, relieving Alex of any need to apologize. "Relax, Alex. I'll do it."

Alex's body released all the tension it had been holding, and he exhaled a sigh of relief. "Thanks, Cass. I owe you big time."

"It's really not that big of a deal."

"It is to me. If there's anything you ever need, just ask."

"Well, now that you mention it," Cass said slowly. "I could go for that thing you did with your tongue that night after we left that party at Simo—"

"Are you really bartering sexual favors in exchange for the care of my seven-year-old daughter?"

"Well when you put it like that . . ." Cass paused for a second. "You know what? On second thought, I'm actually okay with it. I'll just put it on your tab."

Alex rolled his eyes but couldn't hold back the grin that spread across his face. Cass was saving his ass. The least he could do was give her some in return.

Cass and Nina sat across from each other in Cass' living room. Despite having been around Nina before, this was the first time Cass was alone with her. "Are you hungry?" Cass asked.

"No. Daddy made me lunch before we left." Nina's voice was soft but steady. Considering that she was in the home of someone she barely knew, she didn't look overly uncomfortable. Cass wished she could say the same for herself.

"Are you thirsty?"

"No. I'm fine."

"Do you want to watch TV? Play a game? Go to the park?" Cass was firing questions at the poor kid like she was a murder suspect. She wasn't ordinarily so awkward around kids. Her sisters both had children, and Cass had babysat them on occasion. It shouldn't have felt so strange for Cass to spend a few hours with a little girl.

"What do you want to do?" Nina asked, her head cocked slightly to one side.

Pour myself a drink so I can relax, Cass thought. The way Nina was looking at her made Cass feel like it was crucial to answer the question correctly. Cass had never felt such pressure. "I want to make brownies."

Nina's eyes lit up, letting Cass know she'd said the right thing.

"You want to help?" Cass prodded.

"Yes!" Nina jumped up off the couch and smiled widely.

"Let's get to it, then. I'm pretty sure I have everything we need."

Nina followed Cass into the kitchen. Pulling a dining room chair in behind her, Cass told Nina she could stand on it, as Cass began gathering the ingredients and preheating the oven. She plopped everything down in front of Nina and read the directions. For the next few minutes, the girls worked side-by-side, with Cass reading the steps on the back of the brownie box and Nina carrying out the instructions. Cass gave the mix a few extra stirs to make sure everything was fully combined, spread the batter into the pan, and put it in the oven.

Turning back around to face the little girl, Cass saw Nina's eyes drift toward the bowl of brownie batter. "You're not going to make me eat the leftover mix alone, are you?" Cass asked.

Nina shook her head vigorously, picked up the wooden spoon, and licked it clean. Cass couldn't help but smile at her. Nina really was a cute little thing. She had Alex's dark brown hair, with big brown eyes and porcelain skin. It was a good thing Alex worked for the FBI, because he was going to have his hands full keeping the boys away once Nina hit middle school. Having a firearm was going to come in handy.

Nina got what she could with the spoon, but when that was no longer yielding enough results for her, she resorted to swirling her finger around the bowl to collect the chocolate. When she was finally finished, Nina had done a better job of cleaning the bowl than a dishwasher would have. Too bad she hadn't been as successful keeping herself clean.

Cass let out a small laugh. "You have chocolate all over you face."

"Oh." Nina's expression dropped a little as she looked down at her hands, covered in batter. Her eyes began frantically scouring the kitchen for a napkin. "Sorry. I didn't mean to make a mess."

Shit. Cass hadn't meant to sound like she'd been scolding Nina. "You didn't make a mess. I usually get way messier when I bake. You must cook a lot."

Nina offered a tentative smile.

Cass pulled her cell phone from her back pocket. "Here. Let me take a picture of you to send to your dad."

"Oh, um, oh-okay." Despite the hesitancy of her words, Nina brightened at the mention of sending a picture.

"Say 'brownies,'" Cass urged as she positioned her camera to snap a photo of Nina.

"Brownies," Nina said through a wide grin.

"Got it." Cass turned the phone around to show Nina. "You look adorable."

Nina blushed slightly at the compliment, which made Cass smile. She sent the picture to Alex and then wet a paper towel to help Nina clean up.

They had just finished washing the bowl and

spoon when Cass' phone dinged with an incoming text. *Looks like she's having fun. You didn't put pot in the brownies, did you?*

Cass laughed, causing Nina to look up at her. "Is that my dad?"

"Yup. He said it looks like you're having fun."

Nina smiled broadly before walking into the living room, seemingly more comfortable in Cass' house now that they'd bonded over brownies.

Cass stayed in the kitchen and replied to Alex. *People are capable of having fun in my company without being high. I believe you've enjoyed yourself a time or two.*

She then went into the living room and found Nina pulling a coloring book and markers out of her backpack. "Is it okay if I color?"

"Well, that depends," Cass said. "Can I color too?"

It seemed that Cass had said another thing right, because Nina nodded excitedly and got out an extra book for Cass. As Cass picked out a green marker to begin coloring a picture of Ariel, her phone dinged again.

How do you know I wasn't high?

Cass snorted, causing Nina to look up at her. "Is that my dad again?"

"Yeah."

"What did he say?"

Cass fumbled for a reply since the truth wasn't an option. "He said we'd better save him some brownies." Cass had never been more thankful that her job required her to think on her feet.

Nina looked pleased at that and resumed coloring Cinderella. "Tell him we can't make any promises."

A smart-ass after my own heart. Cass quickly typed

out a message telling Alex to leave them alone—they were busy coloring—and that they'd see him later.

And that was how the two girls spent the afternoon: coloring, talking intermittently, and eating brownies. Cass couldn't remember when she'd had a better day.

Chapter 4

Publicity

Everyone had been shocked when Cass showed up at Lauren's housewarming with Nina. Cass was trying not to be offended, but her friends weren't making it easy.

"So wait. Alex needed a babysitter for Nina . . . and he called you?" Quinn questioned.

Cass crossed her arms over her chest. "Why is that so surprising? It's not like I'm some homicidal maniac. I'm a successful, responsible adult, thank you very much."

Simone looked over at Nina, who was sitting on Scott's shoulders eating a hot dog. "She looks happy, so it couldn't have been too much of a train wreck."

"Seriously?" Cass yelled indignantly. "Why wouldn't she be happy? I'm a great time."

"At least that's what the bathroom wall at Mickey's says," Simone said, causing Quinn and Lauren to burst out laughing.

"Screw you, guys," Cass muttered as she walked toward Scott. *How did this guy make it through med school thinking it was safe to let a little girl sit on your shoulders and eat a hot dog? Didn't he ever see* Field of Dreams? "Hey, guys."

"Hi, Cass." Nina was beaming as she sat on Scott's shoulders, causing Cass to no longer have the heart to make him put her down. She'd have to settle for watching them like a hawk.

The backyard of Lauren and Scott's new house was packed with friends and family. Cass found it easy to mingle among the crowd, but she never strayed too far from Nina. She had a fleeting thought that she was being a bit of a helicopter babysitter, but Alex had entrusted his most prized possession to her and she didn't want to fuck it up. They'd been there about two hours before Cass began wondering where the hell Alex was. Tessa would be there soon to pick up Nina, and Cass didn't think she'd respond well to Nina being at a party when Alex wasn't present. But that concern was shot to shit when Cass heard Nina yell, "Mommy!" and saw her barreling toward a petite woman with Nina's large eyes. Cass had to admit the woman was striking.

Cass felt her eyes widen as she looked around for someone, anyone, who was better suited to meet Alex's ex-wife than she was. Thankfully Cass saw Scott and Xavier walking toward Tessa. Scott sent a brief wave to Cass—a kind of "I'll handle this" gesture—and Cass was immediately grateful. Despite that, she felt herself edging closer to them, curious to see how the exchange was going.

"Hey, Tessa," Scott greeted.

"Hi, Scott. Xavier. How have you guys been?"

"Doing well," Scott replied. Xavier nodded in response but mostly seemed content to let Scott do the talking. "How about you?" Scott asked.

"Can't complain. This is a beautiful house."

"Thanks. We like it," Scott said with a smile.

"And I hear congratulations are in order. I almost fainted when I heard you were getting married." Tessa giggled at her own joke, which Cass found annoying.

"Yeah, well, when you meet the right girl, you gotta snatch her up."

Tessa smiled in reply. "Where's Alex?"

Before Scott could get in a word, Nina burst out, "He had to go to work. I got to spend the day with Cass. We had tons of fun. We made brownies and colored and came here, and I ate hot dogs."

Tessa had looked down at her daughter as she spoke, but raised her head sharply to glare at Scott once Nina's words registered. "What does she mean, he went to work?"

Scott shoved his hands in the pockets of his khaki shorts. "He got called in but didn't want Nina to miss the party, so—"

"So instead of calling me to come and get *my* daughter, he left her with someone I've never even met? I've only even heard that name a handful of times. This is so typical of him. Just last week he tried to guilt-trip me about leaving Nina with my parents for the summer, and then he pulls this?"

Cass watched as Nina lowered her head and stared at the ground. She clearly realized that her words had gotten her dad in trouble. Cass felt horrible for her. Without sparing a second thought as to what she was about to do, she ran over to Quinn, grabbed her hand,

and slid off the engagement ring. "I need to borrow this," she said, before shoving it on her own finger and rushing toward Tessa. She slowed her approach when she got close, trying to catch her breath. She quickly stuck out her hand toward Tessa. "Hi. You must be Tessa. I've heard such great things about you. I'm Cass, Alex's fiancée."

Cass had never had four heads whip in her direction so quickly before. And since she was prone to impulsive displays, she found that fact quite surprising.

"His . . . fiancée?" Tessa looked shell-shocked. As did Scott and Xavier.

"Yup. He just asked me last night, actually. But we were waiting for the big announcement until after the housewarming. You know Alex—he's not one to steal anyone's thunder. I thought you might think it was weird for him to entrust Nina to me, so I figured it was better if you knew I wasn't just some random girl." Cass knew she sounded like a blathering fool, but she couldn't help it. She was hoping if she spoke quickly enough, Tessa wouldn't see what complete and utter bullshit it was.

"I don't . . . no offense, but I've only ever heard your name mentioned in passing. If Alex was so serious about someone, why wouldn't he tell me?"

"Does he often talk to you about his personal life?" Cass hadn't meant the question to come out as bitchy as it did, but she couldn't help it. Who did this woman think she was, doubting their fake engagement like that?

"Well, no, but I thought he would have mentioned if he were planning on getting married."

Cass plastered on possibly the fakest smile of her life. "Maybe he wanted to make sure I'd say yes first."

"Maybe." Tessa sounded completely confused.

Nina, on the other hand, looked ecstatic. "Do I get to help plan the wedding?"

"Of course," Cass replied. *Shit*. She really hadn't thought this lie through. Her focus had been saving Alex from completely blowing his chances at spending his summer with Nina, but now she realized the mistake she'd made. Nina looked so excited—she'd no doubt be hurt when she found out it was all a sham. Cass refused to dwell on that thought though. She'd already told the lie, and now she had to see it through.

"Yay!" Nina exclaimed as she lunged toward Cass and threw her arms around her.

Thank God I let her make brownies today. Cass had no doubt Nina's reaction would be different if they hadn't had such a fun day together. At least she'd done something right.

"Congratulations, I guess," Tessa said as she offered a small smile that looked more like a grimace. "We've got to go. Tell Alex I'll call him tomorrow. Let's go, Nina." Tessa took the bouncing little girl's hand and hightailed it out of the backyard.

Xavier and Scott slowly turned toward Cass. She offered a sheepish smile in response.

Scott shook his head before muttering, "If you get married before Lo and me too, I'll never hear the end of it." And with that, he walked away.

"I hope you're really good at your job," Xavier said with a smirk. "Because you're going to have some major damage control to do."

Cass squared her shoulders and looked at Xavier with all the confidence she could muster. "I'm fucking phenomenal at my job." And she was. She just wished she'd asked Alex if he *wanted* to be a client before she'd taken him on.

Alex scanned the pairs of familiar eyes that had been trained nervously on him since he arrived at Lauren and Scott's. "What?" he asked cautiously. "Why are you all staring at me like that?" He tossed his beer cap in the trash and leaned against the rail of the deck before taking a long drink.

Lauren elbowed Cass in the ribs, causing a loud squeal to escape from her. "Tell him."

Cass glanced from side to side at her friends, like she was waiting for someone to speak so she didn't have to.

No one did.

Alex's eyes stayed fixed on Cass as he spoke. "Better just to come out with it. You know I'm trained in interrogation techniques."

"Fine," Cass replied. "It's not even that big of a deal."

Out of the corner of his eye, Alex noticed Xavier biting his lip. "I know it isn't anything with Nina. You said you guys had a nice afternoon." Alex put his beer down on the deck railing and moved it between his fingers. Then he let out a long sigh. "Tessa said something to you, didn't she?"

Cass spoke softly but her voice exuded the same confidence it always did. "Well, yeah, but it isn't—"

"Don't tell me it isn't a big deal. It is to me." Alex could hear the anger that now laced his words. "It's bad enough Tessa's always laying into *me*. But now she's bringing my friends into it?"

Cass kept her voice steady, but Alex could sense her hesitation. "I was going to say that isn't why everyone's acting weird. Tessa's comment to me," she clarified. "She *did* say that you had a lot of nerve giving her crap for leaving Nina with her grandparents, who at least Nina knows well, when your only option is to leave her with a virtual stranger. But it was what I said in response that you may have an issue with."

Alex looked at her curiously. "What did you say in response?"

"That I wasn't a stranger."

"You're not." Alex looked confused.

"I said I was your fiancée."

Alex looked desperately around at his friends for a hint that this was some sort of joke. But he didn't find one. When his eyes found Cass again, she nearly winced. "My what?" he asked, his voice rising. "Please tell me I just misheard you—that you did *not* just tell my ex I got engaged to someone she hadn't even met until tonight."

Cass remained silent.

Alex threw his arms in the air. "Oh, this is fucking great. So now my ex—who already thinks I'm an unfit parent—also thinks I found a new mother for our daughter."

"I'm not Nina's new mother. That's insane," Cass said.

"I fucking know it's insane," Alex nearly yelled. "You know what else is insane? You!"

Alex ran a shaky hand through his hair and plopped his elbows onto the deck railing. As he collapsed his head into his hands, he caught a glimpse of Scott ushering the guests on the deck into the house to give Alex and Cass some privacy. In his anger, he'd forgotten anyone was even watching. By the time Alex had calmed down enough to turn back toward Cass, they were alone.

"Alex, it just came out. I wasn't really thinking. It'll be fine," she said casually. "Let me explain."

"Explain, then." Alex's eyes bore into Cass' before he began pacing. How could Cass act so nonchalant about what she'd just done? "What reason could you have for telling Tessa I was engaged?"

Cass sat down on a nearby chair, obviously feeling a sense of ease about the situation that Alex found impossible to understand. "Because there wasn't any other option at the time," she replied simply.

Alex strode toward her, feeling the anger pulsing through his body. "No other option? Really? How about *not* saying we're engaged? You could have tried that."

"If I didn't say we were engaged, then Tessa would just have more ammunition on you—another day when her unreliable ex couldn't even make time for his only child. Just one more tally mark to add to her 'times Alex was an undependable dad' list. This way Nina was just spending quality time with someone her father trusts enough to marry." Cass turned one corner of her lip up, clearly amused with herself. "You should be thanking me."

"Thanking you? You've got to be fucking kidding me. On what planet should I be thanking you for creating another whole new mess of problems that I now have to deal with?"

"I think you're overreacting."

"Am I?" He could feel himself ready to explode at any moment, but he knew that would only make things worse.

"Yes," she said calmly. "You are." Then Cass let out a long sigh, and Alex saw her expression shift.

She looked contrite. "Though I'll admit that I didn't think this through, I think that it's actually turning out to be a pretty decent plan." She uncrossed her legs and leaned forward, resting her forearms on her thighs comfortably. "It's all about perception. And I'm in the business of perception. Don't forget that," she said, lifting her eyebrow slyly.

Alex sighed heavily and then groaned at the realization that it was doing no good to get so worked up. What was done was done. There was no turning back. "Perception," he repeated. Though he sounded incredibly unconvinced, he'd finally relaxed enough to take a seat next to her. His voice sounded much calmer now, but it still held the same cynicism as before. "What other way is there to perceive our 'engagement'?" he asked, using air quotes to emphasize how ridiculous it all sounded. "I mean, other than as a gigantic lie—and one that will come out eventually. You know, when we don't get married and all."

Cass thought for moment. "Engagements fall apart all the time. Ours won't be any different. We just need to let Tessa think we're engaged long enough for her to decide Nina can stay with you while she's away. You needed a person to spend time with Nina when you can't. Here I am," she said, pointing to herself.

With no choice but to hear her out, Alex sat back down next to Cass and let her continue.

"And Nina would have a positive female role model to hang out with while her mom's away."

"Yeah? Who?"

Cass gave him a shove. "Glad to see you got your sense of humor back. I mean, it wasn't anything to brag about to begin with, but it's better than the anxiety you've been throwing around for the past ten minutes."

Alex almost released a laugh, but the gravity of the situation just wouldn't allow for it. So he gave her an eye roll instead.

Cass continued. "You know what I'm saying though. Tessa's out of bullets. We just have to keep up the charade long enough for Tessa to leave for their trip. Once she's gone, she'll be too focused on Pete the Protein Peddler to worry about your relationship status. Plus, it'll be too late to do anything about it even if she wanted to." Cass shrugged as if the whole thing was no big deal. "That's when we let our fake relationship fall apart, just like all of the real ones out there," she said, obviously pleased with herself. "Totally believable. Not to mention, you have the added benefit of proving to Tessa that you're able to handle Nina for extended periods of time by yourself. That'll go a long way in court if you want to fight for more custody in the future."

Alex had to admit that the plan wasn't half bad. Except for one thing. "What happens when we have to break the news to Nina that we aren't getting married? She's been through enough the past few years, and she really likes you. This will just hurt her more."

Cass put a hand on Alex's shoulder and rubbed gently. "I'm not going anywhere," she assured him. "We were friends before our engagement—"

"*Pretend* engagement," Alex corrected her.

She rolled her eyes. "*Pretend* engagement. And we'll be friends after it. I mean, I know that doesn't happen often, but it *does* happen. I'll still be in Nina's life, so in that regard, Nina won't notice a difference. The only adjustment will be that we won't actually get married. And she'll get over that. Right now she's just excited about the wedding. She's seven years old,

Alex. She probably doesn't even have a complete understanding of what a wedding means. She just wants to pick out dresses and tiaras and other shit nobody cares about." Cass paused for a moment and adjusted her position so she could see Alex's face, which was now directed absentmindedly on the backyard. "She'll be disappointed for a little while, but she'll get over it."

Alex let out a long breath. "You really think so?"

"Sure. Kids are resilient. If you want, we can break the news to her right after we tell her Santa isn't real. Even a canceled wedding can't compete with that bombshell."

Alex let his head flop to the side so he could look at Cass, knowing she would recognize the defeat written across his face. "If you leave now, you might be able to make it to Oz in time to get a heart."

Slowly she reached out to take his hand and wrapped her fingers around it. "I promise it'll be fine. It's more important that Nina has her father than a wedding."

Alex knew that was the truth. He would do whatever it took to have his daughter in his life as much as possible, even if it meant planning a pretend wedding with the heartless creature sitting beside him.

"What?" Cass asked when Alex still hadn't said anything.

He inhaled a long breath before finally speaking. "Cassidy Mullen, will you pretend to marry me?" This time Alex couldn't hold back the laugh that surfaced. And once he started, it was difficult to stop.

"Yes! Yes, of course I'll pretend to marry you!" Cass yelled, throwing her arms around Alex and jumping onto his lap for a kiss. "I can't wait to start planning our fake wedding." She put a finger to her lips as if she were thinking hard about something. "But I think you need to get me a ring first."

Alex stared at her intently before replying, still shell-shocked about what they'd just agreed to. "Fine," he said. "But I hope you like Cracker Jacks."

Chapter 5

Conspiracy

It had been nearly a week since Cass had ambushed Alex with her proposal, and she'd barely spoken to the man since. Now that she thought about it, sending him the "Congratulations on your engagement" e-card had probably been in poor taste, but she didn't know how else to restore some much-needed humor to their situation. She could own the fact that she'd acted impulsively, but Cass still didn't think her decision was a bad one. What better way to get Alex's ex-wife off his back than to fake-plan a wedding with a successful businesswoman?

But as she pulled open the door to Mickey's Bar and Grill, nervousness hit her almost as hard as the music from the blaring jukebox. She stepped inside the local bar and let her eyes surreptitiously roam the room in search of her friends. Catching sight of them, Cass hesitated. They were sitting around a table, sharing pitchers of beer and laughing. Alex looked especially relaxed, and she suddenly found herself wondering if her presence would put a strain on his happiness. *Get it together.* These were her friends—she'd known the girls since seventh grade, and the guys had infiltrated their pack seamlessly when Lauren hooked up with Scott. She had no reason to feel awkward. Taking a deep breath and squaring her shoulders, she approached them with the confidence she prided herself on.

Simone was the first to notice Cass. "About time you got here. Where've you been?"

Cass decided Alex's tensing and sudden interest in his glass were a figment of her imagination. Or at least she'd pretend they were. "Ugh, got caught up with a client. I swear, I don't understand why people hire a PR agency if they're not interested in what we have to say."

"I don't know how you deal with that crap all day. Trying to find ways to make some people look good to the public has to be exhausting," Lauren said.

Cass grabbed a glass and poured herself some beer. "It's not that much different from what you do as a psychologist, when you think about it. You help people uncover their strengths so they can feel good about themselves. I uncover their strengths to make *other* people feel good about them. Though you do have the added perk of being able to medicate them."

Lauren laughed. "I can't prescribe medication. I'm not a doctor yet."

Cass tilted her head in Scott's direction. "I'm sure this one can get some samples for you to pass out. You can hook a few people up."

"Speaking of hooking up," Quinn interjected, "how's the wedding planning going?"

Cass didn't miss her sly smile. "I'm assuming

since you're looking at me that your question wasn't directed at Lauren."

Quinn shook her head slowly.

"Not sure." Cass shrugged. Deciding that she wasn't going to suffer in the spotlight alone, she jerked her thumb toward Alex. "I'm still waiting on a proper proposal from this one."

Alex huffed out a laugh. "You're going to be waiting a long damn time."

"Now, now, that's no way to talk to your future spouse, Snookums."

Alex allowed his middle finger to respond for him.

Scott leaned forward and rested his forearms on the table. "Seriously though. What are you guys going to do about this whole thing? I mean, you can't just take it back. It makes you look bad to be engaged one day and single again the next."

Alex sighed and sat back in his chair. "We're not going to take it back. We're going to just . . . let it run its course."

"Run its course?" Scott furrowed his brow. "It's not the flu. You told your ex-wife *and* daughter that you were getting married. You—"

"I actually did *not* tell them that. She did," Alex asserted as he pointed a finger at Cass. A finger Cass very much wanted to bend backward until it snapped. "And like you said, it would make me look bad to back out of this farce right after Tessa found out about it. I don't need to give her any more ammunition to use against me. So we're just going to go with it."

"How are you 'just going to go with it'?" Simone asked. "A wedding involves tangible things: dresses, flowers, a venue, a ceremony."

"A ring," Quinn added.

"You mean I can't keep borrowing yours?" Cass asked with a smirk.

"Not if you value your life," Quinn responded. Tim draped his arm over his wife's shoulders, looking ridiculously pleased at how much the ring obviously meant to her. They were so cute, it was nauseating.

Alex rubbed a hand over his face. "I know. Nina already asked me when she could pick out her dress for the wedding." He seemed disgusted by the idea.

Cass' ego took a hit. "Listen, being engaged to me can't be *that* disturbing of a concept. I have a lot to offer a fake fiancé."

"Like what?" Simone asked, looking genuinely curious.

Cass' eyes widened. "You do realize you're supposed to be on *my* side, right? You should be listing my finer points."

Simone seemed to rack her brain, her silence signaling she'd come up empty.

"You're just bitter because you're the last single girl at this table," Cass huffed dramatically, causing the others to laugh. "It'll all work out. I mean, some people are engaged for years before they actually go through with it." Cass turned her head slowly toward Lauren.

"Fuck off," Lauren muttered.

"We just need to keep up the charade long enough for Alex to get Nina for the summer. Once Tessa leaves, Alex and I can break up quietly, and it'll all blow over. We just have to go through with some of the tangibles to sell it effectively, but we're both pretty good bullshitters. We got this."

Alex looked up at her with narrowed eyes. "Since when am I a bullshitter?"

"Oh, come on. Are you seriously telling me the FBI is full of Boy Scouts? You guys lie all the time."

"You have no idea what my job entails."

"Please," Cass scoffed. "I've seen *Criminal Minds.* Sometimes you have to lie to catch the bad guys. No one's blaming you." Cass knew she was baiting Alex, but she couldn't help it. He was acting like she'd harvested one of his kidneys while he was sleeping. She had only been trying to help him. And she *would* help him—as soon as he got his head out of his ass.

"Blaming me? I help get violent criminals off the streets. Why would I ever think someone was blaming me? Have you lost your mind?"

"I don't know. You tell me. You're the one who's supposed to be good at reading people."

"Uh-oh," Simone interrupted. "I sense an annulment on the horizon."

Cass snorted out a laugh. "Like I'd involve the church in this sham. It'll be a civil service all the way."

Alex stared at her for a second before releasing the tension he'd been holding. "You're totally fucking with me, aren't you?"

Cass nodded. "And I'm clearly really good at it. We won't have any trouble convincing people that we're a couple."

Cass was relieved to see a small smile tilt Alex's lips up at the corners. This was who they were: a pair of ballbusting friends who legitimately enjoyed each other's company. If they were ever going to pull this off, they'd need to work together and keep their friendship intact. Cass may have never been interested in a serious romantic relationship, but she was a damn good friend. Alex was going to need to have a little more faith in the fact that she'd never let him down.

Alex took a long drink of his beer before putting it back on the table. "Okay, fine. So you want to marry me, or what?"

"Nina, Mom's here," Alex yelled up the stairs as he walked toward the door to answer it. Truth be told, he was nervous as hell to open the door. When he'd picked up Nina the previous day, he'd been—for the first time—happy that it was Pete who'd been there instead of Tessa. Alex wasn't up for discussing his engagement.

He took a deep breath, ran his hands through his hair, and then opened the door. "Hey, Tess."

"Hi." Such a simple word, but said with enough coldness to freeze an Inuit.

"Uh, yeah. So, Nina's getting her stuff together. You want to come in?" Alex stepped back from the door so Tessa could enter.

"I'm good here."

Alex released an audible breath and moved forward slightly to resume his previous position in the doorway. *This is off to a good start.* "Okay." Alex dropped his eyes to the floor briefly, then quickly swept his gaze over everything *except* Tessa. He wondered when he'd subconsciously decided she was akin to Medusa and direct eye contact would immediately turn him to stone.

"While I have you alone for a second, maybe we can talk about the sudden change in your relationship status."

Alex's hand flexed as the impulse to scrub his face hit him, but he managed to catch the movement before his hand had more than twitched. He needed to be strong, assertive, or else Tessa wasn't going to buy that his engagement was as serious as it was. Or as he was supposed to pretend it was. *God, this is so fucking complicated.* "What about it?"

Tessa narrowed her eyes and jerked her head back. "Are you kidding me? You never even mentioned that you were dating someone, and now you're getting married?"

"Why would I tell you about who I was dating? It's none of your business."

"Who you bring around my daughter is absolutely my business."

Alex snorted. "Really? So when do I get to weigh in about Pete?"

Tessa's lips pressed into a thin line as she clearly struggled to keep her anger leashed. "Nina has never even mentioned this woman besides a fleeting comment here or there. Shouldn't your daughter be a little more familiar with someone you're planning on making her stepmother?"

"How well did Nina know Pete before you moved in with him?"

"God, will you stop answering my questions with questions? I'm not a criminal you're psychoanalyzing. I have a right to know these things."

Alex took a few steps over the threshold, forcing Tessa back so that he could pull the door behind him, leaving it only slightly ajar. "Why?" His voice was low and calm, but there was a sternness to it that he had perfected over his years with the FBI. He didn't want to fight with Tessa, but he was also reaching the end of his patience. He was a good man—an even better father—and Tessa damn well knew it. So her standing there questioning him like he was some deadbeat who couldn't be trusted to make good decisions was grating on his last nerve. Granted, he was lying to her—even he couldn't ignore that bit of irony—but Cass wasn't some back-alley hooker he'd picked up on a whim one night and decided to propose to. She would be a great role model for Nina, someone he was comfortable allowing his daughter to be around.

"Why what?" Tessa crossed her arms over her chest.

"Why do you have a right to know? You have never given me even an ounce of the same courtesy. I didn't know you were fucking your trainer behind my back until I called you out on it. I didn't know what type of man you were allowing near my daughter, other than him being someone who was evidently supremely comfortable breaking up a marriage. I wasn't even informed that sending Nina to Jersey for the summer was a possibility until it was already a done deal. So, why the hell do you think I need to run any of my decisions past you?"

Tessa clearly tried to maintain eye contact with Alex, but the watering of her eyes forced her to look away. She sniffled and took a moment before responding. Finally she released a heavy sigh and looked back at him. "I guess you don't."

Alex felt some of the tension that had coiled in his muscles drain as he looked at a chastised Tessa. For all the hell she'd put him through, he knew that she wasn't solely to blame for their problems. He was an FBI agent whose wife had been cheating on him for almost six months before he realized it, because he hadn't bothered to pay her enough attention to be suspicious. He knew that. They'd hurt each other enough. He thrust his hands in his pockets and willfully softened his expression. "Listen. You know me, Tessa. You know how much Nina means to me. I would never allow someone near her who wasn't a positive influence. So just . . . have a little faith, okay?"

It took a few seconds, but Tessa eventually nodded and uttered a quiet, "Okay."

"Good. I'll go check and see what's keeping Nina." As he turned and left Tessa standing in the doorway, he silently prayed his words to her didn't come back to haunt him. He was asking her to have faith in him while he hoped like hell that putting his faith in Cass wasn't the biggest mistake of his life.

Chapter 6

Launch

"We don't *need* to get you a ring, you know?" As they walked through the parking lot, Alex kept his eyes fixed on the jewelry store ahead of them. It was the third one they'd gone to that afternoon. "It's a waste of your money. We've been to two other stores, and neither of them had one that looked like Quinn's for a reasonable price. Besides, Nina and Tessa are the only ones who don't know we're not really engaged. One's too immature to care about your ring, and the other one is seven years old."

Cass laughed. "I think you're underestimating both of them. If I don't have a ring, none of this will be believable. We're planning a fake wedding; it has to seem realistic."

Rolling his eyes at the irony of her comment, Alex held the thick glass door open for Cass so she could step inside. "Do you ever say things silently to yourself before you say them aloud?"

Cass whipped her head back toward him and shot Alex a smart-ass grin. "Chances are, we wouldn't be here if the answer to that question was yes."

"Is there anything I can help you folks with?" Alex looked to his left to see a tall, thin, middle-aged man come out from behind the counter to approach them. "I'm Cameron," he said, extending his hand toward Alex.

"Alex Walker," he replied. "And this is my"—Alex clenched his teeth before speaking—"fiancée, Cassidy."

Cass reached out to shake hands with Cameron. "I actually prefer Cass."

"And I prefer Cassidy," Alex said. After two hours of unsuccessful jewelry shopping, he couldn't help but find something to entertain himself with. "It's much more . . . classy." Alex threw an arm around her. "Don't you think, honey?"

Cass plastered on a smile, which Alex was sure was as fake as their engagement. "Sure. Whatever you prefer. I aim to please."

"Oh, that you do." Then Alex turned to Cameron and chuckled, tapping his hand against the man's arm. "You know what I mean?"

Cass glared at Alex, putting a hand around his forearm. "Stop that, darling," she said sweetly, her grip beginning to tighten. "You're embarrassing me." Then she turned back toward Cameron, who had been looking nervously between the two of them. "We'd like to see some engagement rings."

"Of course. Right this way," Cameron said, as he led them past the cases full of watches.

"See, when Alex here proposed to me, he neglected to purchase a very important piece of jewelry first," she added, narrowing her eyes at Alex playfully.

Cameron stepped behind one of the cases and

gestured to the rings inside. "That's actually more common than people think. A lot of men don't know what type of ring to get, so they propose first and then bring their fiancées in to look at rings. That way the woman gets what she likes, and the proposal still stays a surprise."

Alex stole a quick glance at Cass, who was already focused on the jewelry. "Oh, it was a surprise, all right," Alex said.

Cameron smiled. "Oh yeah? I love hearing great proposal stories. What'd you do?"

Cass propped an elbow on the counter and rested her chin on her hand as she looked to Alex with rapt attention. "Yeah, Alex. Tell him what you did."

Alex swallowed hard, searching his brain for a creative idea. When he didn't come up with anything, he turned toward Cass, who was waiting for him to speak. "I think it's better coming from you, Cassidy. You're always such a great storyteller." Alex wrapped his arm around her and squeezed, placing a soft peck on her forehead. "Why don't you tell it?"

Cass blew out a sharp breath that resembled a laugh and smiled. "Gladly."

Cameron straightened, clearly expecting to be impressed. He probably heard about romantic proposals all the time. And now Cass would be forced to create one on the spot. Alex was going to enjoy watching her squirm as she tried to come up with a story worthy of Cameron's interest.

"Alex doesn't like to tell it himself because he doesn't like being the center of attention," she began. Cameron smiled genuinely. "The first time I met Alex was when he plowed into me from behind."

Alex nearly choked on a breath. *What the hell?*

The corner of Cass' mouth turned up into a small

grin. "I was sitting at a red light, waiting for it to turn green."

Oh, thank God she meant a car accident.

"Next thing you know, my face was smashing into the airbag," Cass continued. "And glass was everywhere—in my hair, on my arms and chest. I met Alex after both of us were taken to the hospital. It was love at first sight. And that's where he proposed to me three years later."

"It's true," Alex said, shrugging. Though the story made him seem like a complete dick, it could have been worse. He shook his head slowly and put a hand on Cass' as he tried to look remorseful.

"That's horrible," Cameron said. "You were both okay though, I guess?"

"I was perfectly fine," Cass said. "Just whiplash and a few cuts. But Alex had some pretty severe injuries. He thought his name was Samantha for a while."

Alex pursed his lips together before speaking. What the fuck should he say to that? "I thought my name was *Sam*. Not Samantha. My middle name's Samuel. I was just a little confused. It took a little while for my head to get back to its old self."

Cass turned around, eyeing the other customers around her. She lowered her voice as she spoke. "Thankfully it didn't take as long to get his *other* head back to its old self." Then Cass winked and tapped Cameron on the arm just as Alex had. "You know what I mean?"

Cameron's eyes widened and he let out a loud cough. "I'm sorry. What?" he asked as if he might not have heard her correctly.

Alex couldn't believe Cass would say something like that to someone she'd just met. This was a new low, even for her. "Cass," Alex said quickly, hoping his expression silently conveyed that the story had gone far enough.

Cass reached over to rub her palm on Alex's arm. "It's fine, sweetie. It's nothing to be embarrassed about. It's fully functional now. Contrary to popular belief, Cameron, you *can* break your penis."

I will murder her.

"Anyway," Cass added, directing her attention back to Cameron, who was still clearly in shock, "thankfully I was a surgeon at that hospital, so Alex—"

"You aren't a surgeon," Alex interrupted.

"I said *was*," she shot back. "Being on the surgical team just got too demanding, Cameron. Long hours," she said with a huff. "Traveling to conferences, all of that research and publication. It's just too much for someone who's ready to settle down and start a family. Don't you agree?"

Cameron nodded.

"So now I teach organic chemistry at Johns Hopkins a few nights a week. But as I was saying, Alex got the best treatment available at my hospital. They were able to fix any abnormalities. His . . . anatomy looks almost completely normal now."

Alex leaned his elbows against the glass case and collapsed his head into his hands. Thankfully, Cass seemed to be done talking for the time being, and Alex enjoyed the silence, no matter how awkward it was.

Finally Cameron spoke. "So, tell me about the proposal."

Alex had forgotten that was even the point of the story.

Cass thought for a few seconds. Clearly she'd forgotten too. "Oh yeah. Well, three years later we went out to dinner for our anniversary. I got food poisoning and ended up in the emergency room with dehydration a few days later. When Alex saw me hooked up to the IV and everything, I think it scared him. So he just popped the question right then and there."

Alex lifted his head enough to glare at her. Clearly the penis story was not only embarrassing, but it was also unnecessary. *Well done.*

"He proposed to me in the same ER where we first met. It was sweet." Cass shrugged and then pointed to a ring in the case. "Can I see that one?"

A part of Cass felt a bit bad about embarrassing Alex like she had. But a larger part couldn't help but enjoy tormenting him every chance she got. Especially when he was such a good sport about it. He'd quickly recovered from Cass' tale and had given his opinion on a few of the rings. Since Quinn's diamond was square with some small stones on either side, Cass had chosen several rings to try on that looked similar enough to Quinn's that Tessa hopefully wouldn't notice the difference.

Cass slid the first one on her ring finger, letting herself adjust to the feeling of it. She held out her hand, admiring how the diamond sparkled on her.

"I like it," Alex said as he leaned comfortably against the jewelry case to face her. "What do you think?"

"I actually think the band on this one's a little too thick. It feels"—she searched for the appropriate word—"intrusive."

"Well, how much are you really going to wear it? I mean, you don't plan to wear it to work or anything, right?"

Cameron furrowed his brow, obviously confused.

"Don't be silly," Cass replied. "I can wear it to work. It's not like I'm doing surgery anymore."

"No, you certainly aren't doing any surgery," Alex

replied. "Do you have a band that's a little thinner?" he asked Cameron.

Cameron handed two rings to Cass and placed the rest back in the case. "The others will be too big for your taste, I think. See how you like these."

"This one's pretty." Cass opened and closed her hand a few times. "And it feels comfortable. How much?"

"This particular setting is platinum, and the diamond is a little over a carat. The clarity is superb," Cameron said. "This one is forty-two hundred."

Cass winced at the price. "Do you have anything under two thousand? Maybe something that's less than a carat?" she asked. "And it doesn't even need to be platinum. Silver would be fine. No one will be able to tell the difference, right?"

Cameron's gaze snapped over to Alex and then back to Cass. "With all due respect, this a major purchase. It's a symbol of your love for each other. Most women don't want a silver engagement ring. We actually don't even carry any here."

"Well, I'm different from most women." Cass shrugged. "Material possessions aren't really that important to me. But I do recognize that a ring is a rite of passage. We're going to split the cost," Cass said, motioning between herself and Alex. "But that's a little out of our price range. Still trying to pay off those medical-school loans on a professor's salary," she added quickly. "Maybe you have a diamond that's a little more . . . cloudy?"

Cameron raised a brow. "I do have this setting in white gold. We could put a smaller . . . cloudier diamond in there. It would probably bring the cost down about fifteen hundred dollars or so." Cameron looked at them expectantly, probably wondering if he had

had to listen to a story about another man's penis only to have them leave the store empty-handed.

Cass stared at the ring, trying to decide if it was worth the money to her. Sure, she had a well-paying job and *could* buy it. But now, with such a major decision staring her right in the face, she couldn't decide if she should go through with it. Maybe Alex was right about not really needing a ring.

"We'll take it," Alex blurted out.

Or maybe he wasn't *right*.

"And put the whole thing on my card," he said, handing Cameron his American Express. "No future wife of mine is going to pay for her own engagement ring."

Chapter 7

Campaign

Alex wasn't sure that taking Cass with him to pick up Nina was a good idea, but that hadn't stopped him from suggesting it. He had been momentarily surprised she'd agreed so readily until he remembered who he was dealing with. Cass always seemed to excel in awkward situations—always cool and confident in her own skin. It was probably what made her so successful at her career. While Alex also had a job that required him to have an unflappable demeanor, his calmness was completely external—a superficial layer he coated himself in. But Cass' assuredness seemed to radiate from within, emanating from her core. It was who she was, rather than a role she played.

Even as they drove to Tessa's modest bungalow about twenty minutes from his house, Alex gripped the steering wheel to keep his nerves in check while Cass casually draped an arm out of the passenger's window, her hair blowing freely in the wind as she watched the scenery pass by, with a serene expression on her face. *Damn her.*

Alex pulled into Tessa's driveway with a perfunctory "This is it."

Cass nodded as she pushed open her door. "Nice place."

And it was nice. The lawn was well manicured, the blue shutters vibrant against the white house, the flower bed lush with colorful flowers. Alex tried to tamp down the sudden feeling of annoyance. Tessa had never cared for their home like she obviously cared for this one. Or maybe the gardening was Pete's thing. Either way, Alex and Tessa's place had never been as inviting as this one, and it made him wonder if what he was seeing was the difference between a house and a home. He shook his head to clear the unwanted thoughts, thoughts he'd never had before, and ones he hoped to never have again.

They walked up to the front door, and Alex looked over at Cass. "You ready for this?"

Cass pushed her sunglasses to the top of her head and shrugged. "Sure."

Alex cast a quick look down at Cass' hand to make sure the ring was in place. He didn't want to walk into this charade and expose their lie immediately because they'd forgotten the hardware that evidently sold this whole farce. After confirming that it was there, he rang the doorbell.

The door flew open and revealed an excited Nina. "Hi, Daddy." She wrapped her thin arms around his waist, and he hugged her tightly. When she pulled back, her eyes drifted to his right. "Cass! Hi." And then Nina was hugging Cass, and Cass beamed at the attention.

Alex felt a swift pang of regret. No matter how often Cass reassured him, he still worried about how Nina would take the inevitable breakup that loomed over them. Because even though he was doing this *for* Nina, it would hurt her too. And seeing how warmly she greeted Cass made him concerned for just how hard his little girl would take the news when the time came. But he didn't have time to dwell on it long, because Tessa joined them.

"Hi, guys. How's it going?" Tessa smiled as she spoke, but it didn't quite reach her eyes. It was the kind of smile that was more indulgent than sincere, almost patronizing in its fakeness. But at least she tried. He could give her credit for that.

"Not too bad. You?" Alex asked.

"Oh, you know. Same old, same old."

They both did that awkward nodding thing that people did when they'd run out of words to fill the silence.

"You have a beautiful home. I love all of the bright flowers," Cass said.

"I helped plant them," Nina chimed.

Cass' eyes widened. "You did? Well, you did a really good job. I thought a professional landscaper planted them."

Nina's smile brightened even more. "Nope. Me and Mommy did it."

"I'm very impressed."

Nina gasped, eyes wide. "Maybe I can use some of them for your wedding."

Alex couldn't keep the confusion off his face. "What do you need flowers for?"

"For me to throw down the aisle. I get to be the flower girl, right? My friend Jasmine got to be in her mom's wedding. She got a pretty dress. I get a pretty dress, right?"

Alex didn't know how to respond. He mentally scolded himself for not anticipating this question, especially since Nina had already asked about dress shopping several times. But now that she'd directly asked to be the flower girl, how could he tell her no? Especially in front of Tessa. He knew it would only make it harder on her when he had to break the news that the wedding was canceled, but he found himself agreeing anyway. "Of course."

"Yay!" Nina was bouncing with excitement.

Tessa was looking at Nina, her smile genuine. It remained firmly in place when she brought her gaze up to look at Cass and Alex. "Would you guys like to come in? Maybe we could sit and get to know each other a little."

Tessa seemed to be extending an olive branch, but Alex couldn't help but be wary. It felt a little like he and Cass were Hansel and Gretel, and Tessa was trying to lure them into her lair with promises of sweetness, while her true motive was to cook them alive. He spared a glance at Cass to gauge her feelings about the invitation.

She shot him a placating smile. "Sure. That'd be great."

Tessa pushed the door open wider as Nina bounced into the house. Cass and Alex lingered in the entryway as Tessa shut the door and turned to lead them through her home. They ended up in a cozy family room, Nina kneeling on the floor in front of the television, Pete sitting on the couch, thumbing through *Men's Health*.

How cliché.

Pete looked up as they walked farther into the

room, surprise clear on his face. He stood abruptly, dropped the magazine on the dark-finish coffee table, and extended his hand toward Alex. "Hey, Alex. Good to see ya." Though he smiled, his staccato words revealed his discomfort.

Not that Alex could blame him. Alex had never been in their home before, and his interactions with Pete had been limited in the years Pete had been living with Tessa. The longest conversation Alex had ever had with the man was when he'd cornered Pete in the parking lot of the gym he owned, and Alex had told him in no uncertain terms that if Pete ever hurt Nina, Alex would do things to him that would prevent Pete's family from having an open casket at his funeral. And after waving around a file that detailed every recordable aspect of Pete's life since birth, Alex interpreted Pete's blanched face as evidence that the message had been received. The meeting had left their interactions even more strained than they would've otherwise been. A scared Pete was a law-abiding Pete. Not that the guy had more than two speeding tickets and one trespassing charge from when he and his buddies had broken into their high school as a senior prank. But still, a little fear never hurt anybody.

"Good to see you too, Pete. This is my fiancée, Cass." Alex gestured toward Cass, who stepped forward to shake Pete's hand.

"Nice to meet you," she said.

"You too." Pete's gaze swiftly tracked over Cass' body.

It might have been a professional hazard—a customary assessment any personal trainer would make of an obviously fit person—but Alex didn't appreciate it. He wrapped a proprietary arm around Cass' shoulders and gave Pete a look that had him shrinking back slightly.

"Please sit. Can I get you anything to drink?" Tessa offered.

"No, thanks," Cass responded. "I'm fine."

"I'm fine too. Thanks."

They all sat: Pete and Tessa on the love seat and Alex and Cass on the three-seater. The only sound was the cartoon warble of the television.

Cass looked at Alex, the slight flaring of her eyes letting him know that she was feeling just as uncomfortable as he was. "So, Tessa," she started. "Alex told me you used to be a forensic accountant before helping Pete manage his business. That sounds really interesting."

"Yes, that's right. I mean, I think it's interesting, but I always have been a bit of a math nerd." Tessa let out a small laugh.

"Did you work for a firm or a government agency, or . . . " Cass let the sentence hang there so Tessa could fill in the correct reply.

"Both. I worked for the government briefly after graduating, but it wasn't for me. I preferred working for a private firm because I just wanted to crunch my numbers and go home without having to worry about bureaucratic red tape. Though working at the gym with Pete is by far the best job I've ever had. What do you do?"

Alex suddenly felt a little guilty. Obviously he'd talked to Cass about Tessa, but he hadn't even shared the most basic information about Cass with his ex-wife. Not that he had reason to—he rarely talked to Tessa about anything other than Nina—but it still didn't sit right with him.

Cass didn't miss a beat though. "I'm a public relations specialist."

Upon hearing Cass' answer, Pete sat up. "Oh wow. So you help people promote their businesses and stuff?"

"Basically. We help disseminate pertinent information between our clients and their target audience."

"I'd love to pick your brain sometime. I'm in the process of turning my gym into a chain, and I'd really like some insight."

Cass smiled. "I'll leave you my card."

Alex knew from the hard set of Tessa's jaw that Pete would never be calling Cass. A fact that made him relieved. All he needed was for Pete, the solid block of muscle, to worm his way into the life of another one of Alex's girls. *Wait . . . my girl?* Though technically Cass was his girl. At least in this parallel reality they'd created.

"So, when's the wedding?" Pete asked.

Alex whipped his head toward Cass, then schooled his features to hide his panic. *Why didn't we talk about any of this before coming over here?* Alex suddenly felt like the idiot he was. What had he expected? That he'd shove a ring on Cass' finger and that would magically answer every marital question they'd encounter? *Yup, pretty much.* "We're still working out the details," he finally answered.

"Oh." Tessa sounded confused. "Well, have you started looking at venues?"

"We've been doing a little online research," Cass offered.

"You two have been engaged for a few weeks, right? When we met you said Alex had just proposed to you the previous night."

"Yeah . . ." Cass looked at Alex as though she were

trying to telepathically communicate with him. "We've just been easing into the planning."

Tessa's eyes furrowed a bit. "Wow, most women can't wait to start planning. You have much more patience than I do—that's for sure. Are you going to hire a wedding planner or do most of the work yourself?"

"I'll probably do most of it myself. I'm kind of a control freak."

"I want to help," Nina called out. Alex had almost forgotten Nina was even in the room until she spoke.

"You do?" he asked.

"Yup." Nina smiled broadly, and Alex was again hit with a searing bolt of guilt. How could he let his daughter help plan a fraudulent wedding? What kind of father did that make him?

As though sensing his mental departure, Cass swooped in. "Maybe you can help us look up a few places on the computer when we get to your dad's."

"Awesome," Nina exclaimed, before turning back to her show.

Alex wasn't sure whether to thank Cass for interjecting or strangle her for involving his daughter in this sham even more than she already was.

"Well, I'm interested to hear which place you pick. Do you have a preference between a DJ and a band?" Tessa's words sounded like friendly curiosity, but Alex recognized that gleam in her eye. She was suspicious. Whether that suspicion was about the veracity of the engagement or about whether or not the relationship between Alex and Cass would last long enough to make it to the altar, Alex wasn't quite sure. All he did know was that he didn't like it. Because at this point, the only thing worse than telling the lie to begin with would be Tessa *finding out* that it was a lie.

"I'd prefer a band."

"Me too. We were definitely thinking band," Cass agreed.

"Pete has some contacts with local bands. Don't you, honey? Maybe you can give them some names."

"Uh, yeah. Sure. I have a bunch of contacts with local entertainment groups."

Alex would rather pour rubbing alcohol into his eyes than have Pete do him any favors. And if the self-satisfied smirk on Tessa's face was anything to go by, she knew it.

"Great. Maybe we can talk about it when Pete calls me for PR advice."

And with Cass' words, the smirk evaporated from Tessa's lips. Alex was tempted to add another diamond to Cass' ring for that.

"We'd better get going. Nina, you ready?"

"Yup." Nina rose and skipped toward the front door.

The adults exchanged good-byes as they followed Nina. Alex picked up Nina's backpack, which was sitting in the foyer, and opened the door.

"Thanks for inviting us in. It was nice getting to know you a little better," Cass said.

"Likewise. We'll have to do it again sometime," Tessa replied.

Not a chance in hell.

Soon, Cass and Alex were in the safety of his car, Nina buckled up in the backseat. They sat in silence for about ten minutes, listening to Nina quietly sing along with the radio as she played with some kind of hand-held device.

"She thinks something's off, doesn't she?" Cass asked quietly.

Alex sighed. It shouldn't have surprised him that Cass had picked up on Tessa's thoughts, but it did.

The only response he could come up with was the simple truth. "Yes."

Cass had left Tessa's Friday night feeling underprepared and uninformed—two things she detested. She'd hung out at Alex's a little afterward, surfing the Internet with him and Nina for venues. Together they'd made a list, but it still all felt surreal and abstract. Cass knew that Tessa had her doubts. She could tell by the way the woman reveled in stumping Cass, asking questions for which she guessed Cass had no reply. It would never happen again.

Which was why Cass had called Alex and told him to come over after Tessa had picked up Nina Sunday afternoon. He'd texted her about twenty minutes ago to say he was on his way, so he should be arriving at her place any minute. She grabbed a bottle of wine and two glasses. They were going to need it. She placed everything on the kitchen table when the buzzer signaled his arrival. She pressed the button to let him in and opened the door. "Hey," she said when she saw him come in.

"Hey." Alex followed her into the kitchen, and she watched him scan the mass of books, papers, and the laptop that littered her tabletop. "Whatcha doin'?"

"Planning a wedding. Wine?"

"You know it," he replied as he took a seat and eyed the mess on the table warily. "Looks like you've been busy."

Cass poured both of them a glass of Cabernet and sat. She watched Alex take a sip before she spoke. "If we're going to pull this off, we're going to have to go all in. Tessa isn't stupid. If we half-ass this, she'll know you're not really serious about marrying me, and we won't accomplish what we're hoping to."

Cass took a drink of wine to prevent herself from rambling. "The goal is to prove to Tessa that even when you get called away for work, that there will still be a responsible adult around to take care of Nina. She needs to be able to trust that I'm not some flighty head case, but someone who can actually care for a little girl. But when I can't even answer simple questions about my own wedding, I don't look very dependable."

"Okay." Alex drew out the word as if trying to come up with a solution in his head. "So we just pick a place and say that's where we're getting married. We do the same with the band and whatever else we'd need. Right?"

Cass shook her head. "The more lies we let build up, the easier it will be to get caught in them. We're going to need to keep this as honest as we can, which will probably be a challenge, considering it'll all be built on a lie. So we're going to need to book a real venue, hire a real band, order real flowers. We can pick a date that's a year and a half, two years down the road, so we'll have plenty of time to cancel and at least not lose everything. We'll still probably lose some though. It'll suck, and I know it's a lot of money but—"

"I'm not worried about the money. I'm worried about my daughter."

Alex sat there for a second, Cass guessed, so he could process everything. "Why?" he finally asked.

"Why what?"

Alex gestured to the books and wedding planners spread out across the table. "Why would you go through all of this? It's going to take up a lot of your time."

Cass let out a harsh laugh. "Because I got us into this whole thing. And because Tessa wanting to leave

Nina with her grandparents is bullshit. You're a good father. You deserve to see you daughter as often as you can. And besides, this is like a job to me now. Consider me your personal PR specialist."

"You may have set this whole debacle in motion, but you were just trying to help. You don't owe me anything. And maybe Tessa has a point. What will I do if I have to go into work when I have Nina? I have no family nearby. I'd be stuck." Alex scrubbed a hand over his face and then stared down at the table.

"Alex Walker, you look at me right now." When she had his attention, Cass continued. "First of all, you *do* have family nearby. Our little band of misfits—we're a family. And I already told you that I wasn't going to disappear on you. You can always count on me if you need someone to hang out with Nina for a little while. It's not like you get called into work every time you have her. It's normally a rare occurrence."

Alex sat quietly, seeming to try to work things out in his mind.

"Answer me this: in the past year, how many times have you had to call Tessa to pick up Nina because you had to go in to work?"

Alex thought for a few seconds before replying. "Maybe four. I usually know in advance if I'm going to have to work a weekend. It's only major breaks in big cases that call me away—and major breaks aren't as common as television would have you believe. It's just bad luck that it happened twice within the past month, but that's incredibly unusual."

"Okay, so you may need me in a pinch here or there?"

"Yeah. It probably wouldn't be a lot."

Cass extended her hand toward Alex.

"What are we shaking hands for?" Alex asked.

"I agree to some emergency babysitting stints, and you agree to help me plan a wedding. This handshake is as binding as a legal document."

Alex laughed as he continued to stare at her hand. "Handshakes don't mean shit anymore."

"Ours do," she replied, her gaze never wavering from his.

Alex hesitated for a second before grasping Cass' hand in his. "Okay, you got a deal."

Cass went to pull her hand away, but Alex continued to hold it. When she locked eyes with him, she saw earnestness there.

"Thanks."

She nodded. "My pleasure."

"Okay." Alex dropped her hand and rubbed his together. "Where do these books say to start?"

Chapter 8

Surveillance

"I still don't understand why we need to actually *visit* any venues," Cass said, gesturing up at the cathedral ceilings that made the large rustic space seem even more open. "I know we're trying to keep this as realistic as possible, but we could have just booked a place over the phone."

"Yeah, but we don't even know how much of a deposit they require. You know nice wedding venues won't give prices online or over the phone. And I didn't want to just pick some cheap place that I could reserve with a phone call. Tessa's smart enough to know I wouldn't have my wedding at some hole-in-the-wall."

"By 'smart,' you mean 'nosy as hell'?"

Despite Alex's scolding glare, Cass knew how Alex really felt about his ex. But she respected him for usually taking the high road, especially around Nina.

So many children of divorced parents had to contend with constant bitterness and biting words flowing around them. Not that Cass knew what any of that was like. Her upbringing had rivaled that of a 1960s sitcom—a working father, a stay-at-home mom, two older sisters who now had families of their own. Cass' childhood had been the epitome of traditional family life. It made her a little sad to think that so many children wouldn't know what it was like to have that.

Kevin, the gentleman who had been showing them around the grounds, stood about fifteen feet ahead of them, letting Alex and Cass take their time until they eventually reached him near the stone bar. "So, did you folks have any particular dates in mind?"

Cass looked to Alex, and when he didn't give any indication that he was going to answer, she spoke up. "You know, we really haven't talked about it much. We're probably pretty flexible. Maybe sometime next fall? What do you think, hon?"

Alex paused for a moment before answering, as if he were truly considering Cass' question. "I've always liked the fall. And this place is probably beautiful when the leaves start to change color." Alex leaned his shoulder against a nearby wall and gazed through the tall open window to the trees.

"It's gorgeous then," Kevin agreed. "And it's significantly cooler than the summer, as I'm sure you would've guessed. The stone walls help keep the temperature a bit lower in the summer, but with no air conditioning it can still get somewhat uncomfortable with the humidity and a roomful of people dancing." Kevin flipped open the iPad he'd been carrying and studied the calendar. "We have one Friday open this October and then several dates next fall if you'd rather have a Saturday wedding. Though Fridays are less expensive if cost is a concern."

"How much of a deposit do you require at booking for a Friday?" Alex asked.

"It's a thousand to hold the date, and the remainder is due a month prior to the wedding."

"Is the deposit refundable?" Cass added quickly. "You know, if something . . . happened and we didn't end up getting married?"

Alex furrowed a brow in what Cass knew to be feigned worry. "It'll be fine, sweetie. My mom likes you. She was just overreacting when she told you she'd never let her son marry a stripper."

"We prefer the term 'dancer,'" Cass said, pouting.

"Right. *I* know that." Alex moved from the window, strolling confidently over toward her. "And one day my mom will too. Anyway," Alex said, directing his attention toward Kevin, "there's no harm in answering the question. Is the deposit refundable? You know . . . just in case."

"As long as you let us know at least two months ahead of time and we're able to fill the date with another event. It's actually easier to fill Fridays, believe it or not, because schools and charities tend to book them because they're a bit less expensive. And they usually don't book them as far in advance," Kevin said. "By the way, how many guests were you thinking of having?"

"It would be small," Alex answered with surprising certainty. "Just close friends and family. What do you think, babe—probably no more than seventy people or so, right?"

Cass felt Alex's hand move gently across her shoulder blades and skim lightly down her back until it came to rest on her hip. She instinctively leaned into him, her head resting comfortably against the side of his chest. She gazed up at him, his dark brown eyes locked on hers as he waited patiently for her to respond. "Seventy's probably about right," she said.

"Well, this room can seat a hundred and twenty people comfortably with a dance floor." Kevin turned to look behind him and then back again, counting the tables quickly. "Right now it's set up for right around a hundred. But for your reception, the three tables in the center wouldn't be there, so we could actually expand the dance floor by about eighty square feet. What do you think?" Kevin looked at them expectantly.

"I think this October sounds perfect," Cass said.

Cass slid into the booth but stopped halfway, forcing her two sisters to take the bench across from her. She wanted to be able to see their faces for what she had in store for them. There was almost a perverse sense of pleasure thrumming through her body as she anticipated which of her sisters would blow a gasket first. Her money was on Rachel. She was the oldest, and therefore the least tolerant of what she often called "Cass' spoiled-baby-sister ways."

Other than quick hellos and hugs when they'd first arrived at the restaurant, they hadn't had a chance to say much else to each other. And just as Amy was opening her mouth to speak, the waiter appeared to get their drink orders.

He hadn't made it two steps away from their table before Rachel started in. "Okay, why did you invite us to lunch? I have to be back at work in an hour, so time's a-ticking."

Cass pressed her hand dramatically to her chest. "Can't I just miss my sisters and want to spend some time with them?"

Rachel and Amy looked at each other briefly. "No," they responded in unison.

"You wound me," Cass replied as she picked up the menu.

Rachel ripped it out of her hands. "I am going to wound you for real if you don't tell me what's up. I have three children, Cassidy. My patience is all used up."

Cass looked over at Amy. "When did she get so violent?"

"The womb," Amy replied, as the waiter returned with their drinks.

"You ladies all set to order?"

Rachel looked up at him and grinned politely. "We're going to need a few minutes."

He nodded and left, at which point Rachel dropped the smile and returned her attention to Cass.

"I thought you only had an hour. Shouldn't we order?" Cass asked.

"I'll get something to go. Spill."

Cass sighed heavily as she reached into her purse and withdrew two white envelopes. She slid them across the table, one to each of her sisters.

"What's this?" Amy asked.

Cass didn't reply; she was waiting for them to open them and see for themselves. She tried to mentally catalog the gamut of emotions that crossed their faces as they pulled out the cards: confusion, understanding, disbelief, a twinge of anger, and finally—

"What the fuck?" Rachel exclaimed.

Cass took a sip of her water. "Do you kiss your beautiful progenies with that mouth?"

"Is this for real?" Amy asked, concern clear on her face and in her voice.

"Yup." Cass let her mouth pop on the "p."

"But these are save-the-dates." Amy was trying really hard to understand.

Cass thought it was cute. "Yup," she repeated, thinking back to the previous week when they'd sat in Alex's kitchen making them.

"To a wedding."

Cass nodded.

"*Your* wedding." Amy's brain was clearly a bit slow on processing what her eyes were showing her.

"Very good, Columbo." Cass smiled around her straw as she took another sip of water.

"Who the hell is Alex, and why does this flimsy piece of cardstock say you're marrying him?" Rachel interjected.

"Now, that's not very nice. Those are of very high quality."

"Cassidy," Rachel warned.

"Rachel." Cass couldn't resist mocking her sister. "You should probably take out your phones and program October twenty-fourth in. I know how busy you soccer moms get. Wouldn't want you to miss my big day."

Amy dropped the save-the-date to the table and crossed her hands in front of her. "Cass, seriously. What's going on?" She spoke with the gravity of an interventionist. "Have Mom and Dad met him?"

"Of course not."

"Of course not! You're marrying a man your own parents have never met? Have you been huffing glue? What the hell is wrong with you?" Rachel was starting to get red, a sure sign that she was close to detonation.

"Have you spoken to them yet? What did they say about your save-the-date?" Amy asked.

"Nothing, because I'm not giving them one."

"You're not inviting Mom and Dad to your wedding?" Amy's eyes widened in alarm.

"I fully intend to invite them. If I'm ever crazy enough to get married." Cass smiled at her sisters, who looked at each other with bewilderment. "I'm not really marrying Alex," she explained. "It's sort of an elaborate scheme I cooked up on a whim to help him with a problem he's having with his ex-wife." Cass relayed the story from the beginning, stopping only briefly so that they could order lunch. When she finished, both Rachel and Amy looked a little dazed.

"So you're not even *dating* this guy?" Rachel asked.

"No. I mean, we bang every now and then, but we aren't a couple."

Both her sisters sighed heavily in what Cass guessed was probably relief. They were used to Cass' antics. And believing that she was *pretending* to get married was probably much easier than believing she actually *was*.

"Why the save-the-dates, then?" Amy asked. "Don't tell me you ordered them just to mess with us."

Cass laughed softly. "No. Well, not entirely for that reason. I figured since you two have known me all my life, if the save-the-dates were enough to convince you of my impending nuptials, then Tessa should have no problem believing it."

"You guys are inviting her to your pretend wedding?" Rachel seemed confused.

"Hell no. But we figured we'd send one to the house for Nina, so she'll see it then."

Amy and Rachel seemed to settle in to the idea of

Cass planning a fake wedding. Apparently Cass' explanation of the whole thing had sufficed, and her sisters had finally calmed down. "Just one more question," Amy said.

"Shoot."

"Who Photoshopped the picture of you that's on the card? Your tits look phenomenal."

Chapter 9

Community Relations

Cass hadn't been to the zoo in years. Despite having nieces and nephews, she'd managed to avoid the place. It wasn't that she didn't like animals. It was that her idea of a good time didn't necessarily involve hundreds of tiny humans running amok. But Cass realized that she needed to get to know Nina a little better, and this was what Nina and Alex had decided to do with their day.

Alex had expressed his reluctance—constantly—about Cass and Nina spending too much time together. But to Cass, little trips like this were necessary. And, ultimately, she was just tagging along on an excursion Alex had already planned. What could be the harm in that?

She arrived at Alex's at nine-thirty Saturday morning so that they could get to the zoo right as it opened. When Cass rang the doorbell, she heard a squeal through the door before it flew open.

"You're here! Now we can go." Nina ran down the hall, yelling for her dad.

Cass let herself in and closed the door behind her. She saw Alex walking down the hall toward her a minute later. "Hey, come on in. We're almost ready."

Cass smiled. "Seems like Nina's been ready to go for quite a while."

Alex shook his head, but his lips twitched into a smile. "She's been going crazy all morning. Let me just grab her bag and then we can hit the road."

Cass decided to wait by the door as Alex disappeared briefly. Minutes later, he and Nina were back. Nina grabbed Cass' hand and began pulling her out the door.

As they waited for Alex to lock the front door, Cass' phone rang. She looked down at it, the caller ID showing that it was her boss. "Good morning, Mr. Pritchett."

"Morning, Cass. I'm sorry to bother you on a Saturday, but we have a bit of a situation."

Cass rolled her eyes. Like her boss would be calling her for a friendly chat on a Saturday morning. "It's okay. What do you need?"

"Lydia was supposed to go to an event today that one of her clients is hosting. The client is known for putting her foot in her mouth, and they're expecting a lot of press. Lydia was supposed to make sure she didn't say anything damaging, but she had a death in the family and won't be able to attend. I was hoping you could fill in."

Cass hesitated for a second—not because she was contemplating what to do, but because she didn't want Nina to hate her for what she was about to say. "Sure. What time is the event?"

"It begins at noon. It's at Regalli's Catering on Broad Street. I'll forward you the pertinent information now, so you can review it before you go. Thanks, Cass. I can always count on you."

Her boss's words filled her with pride. She liked being his go-to person. As much as she didn't want to work on a Saturday, doing him this favor could go a long way in helping her advance in the firm. "My pleasure. Enjoy your weekend."

"You too."

Cass hung up and turned to Alex and Nina. "That was my boss. I need to go into work."

Nina looked like she was about to cry. "You mean we can't go to the zoo."

Cass didn't know what to say. Thankfully Alex stepped in and kept her from having to say anything. "No way, kiddo. You and I are still going."

Nina immediately brightened. "Oh, okay. Bye, Cass. Let's go, Daddy." She started running to the car.

Cass turned to Alex. "Sorry. Duty calls."

Alex looked at Nina for a few seconds before murmuring a "Yup." He turned back to Cass. "Well, I guess I'll talk to you later, then."

Cass couldn't help but feel like Alex was irritated with her, but she didn't understand why. It wasn't like the zoo trip hinged on her attendance. And Alex had a demanding job as well. He of all people should understand needing to go to work when your boss called. It was one of the reasons they were in this whole fake-wedding mess to begin with. "Yeah, I'm sure we'll talk this week."

"See ya," Alex said before he turned and walked to his car.

"Bye," Cass replied before doing the same.

* * *

Alex pulled out his black leather chair and sat down for the first time all day. He let out a long sigh. Though it was only Tuesday, he already felt spent. He'd worked the previous night, trying to wrap up some paperwork for one of his cases. And today, after spending two hours apprehending some motherfucker he was sure was guilty, he'd interrogated him for over an hour. But the asshole wouldn't give him anything.

Alex looked at the files spread across his desk, some opened, with the contents covering the majority of the glass surface. He rubbed a hand roughly on his forehead and took a sip of his coffee, hoping to relieve the headache he'd had for the past forty minutes. He'd get to the paperwork eventually, but right now he needed a break. He turned toward the window, letting the early-afternoon sun hit his face. But he enjoyed it for only a second before he was interrupted by the ding of his phone.

He unclipped it from his belt, happy to see that it was only an e-mail from Xavier and not something work related. He'd deal with his work in-box later on. Alex clicked on the e-mail—which was titled "NSFW"—and reclined back in his chair. He knew the warning had been meant for him and not Scott, who owned his own medical practice and could look at anything he wanted in the privacy of his own office with no repercussions. But Alex didn't have that same luxury. There was no way he would open any e-mail that Xavier sent on a work computer—with or without the NSFW disclaimer.

And the image staring back at him reminded him exactly why. He clicked on the video, lowering the sound since his door was open slightly, so he could watch some old woman gyrating on a dance floor until one of her boobs popped out. And "popped" might have been a generous term. It was more of a falling motion, and one that had Alex laughing, since the woman clearly noticed but did nothing to tuck it back in, even with a crowd standing around her.

But what really made Alex laugh was Xavier's caption. *Your grandmom's really got some moves, Scott. Maybe I'll take her as my date to your wedding.*

It was exactly what Alex needed to clear his mind. With a smile, he clicked out of the e-mail and went back to his in-box to check his mail before getting back to work.

Most of it was stuff he didn't need to look at now: coupons from a few children's clothing stores, a notification that the payment for his monthly gym membership had been processed, and a few others that he deleted immediately. Only one caught his attention: an e-mail from the venue he and Cass had chosen. Since he was insisting on paying for most of the "wedding," he'd provided his e-mail as the primary contact. He'd put a deposit on the place when they'd looked at it a little more than a week ago, but until now he hadn't seen the pricing specifics. He gave it a cursory glance and then forwarded it on to Cass so she could take a look. Then he set his phone on his desk and prepared himself for another long afternoon of paperwork.

Chapter 10

Interrogation

Cass put the beer bottle to her lips and took a slow sip as she relaxed on Alex's brown leather couch. "I don't understand men. This movie's awful, but every guy I know loves it and can recite it practically verbatim," she said, pointing at the TV.

Alex's head whipped to the right so he could get a clear view of her expression. *Yup, she's serious.* "*Billy Madison*'s a classic. If the guys were here, they'd agree with me." Alex knew Scott and Xavier loved the movie. Cass was right; what guy didn't? They'd watched it countless times in college when it was on TV. "It's probably the funniest movie Adam Sandler's ever done."

Cass shook her head. "No, it really isn't. You don't find it at all strange that a teacher is making out with a grown man who not only sounds like he's in second grade but *is*?"

"No." Alex stared at her as if the question was

ludicrous. "And that's his *third*-grade teacher. Haven't you been paying attention?

"You're just saying it's not weird because you probably think the teacher's hot, and it's, like, every guy's fantasy to bang his teacher."

"That's ridiculous." Alex let out a loud laugh. "That's only, like . . . seventy percent of the reason I'm okay with it. At most," he joked. "So, if you don't think this is one of his best movies, then which one do *you* like? And you'd better not say *Grown Ups* or something."

Cass put her beer down on the coaster and turned toward Alex, placing a hand on his. "I'm going to say something, and I need you to really hear me."

"I swear to God, if you say *Grown Ups 2*, I'm kicking you out," Alex said, pointing to the door. "Right now. You'll leave, and I don't think I can ever let you come back. I mean it. This friendship, it'll end right here."

"I wasn't going to say *Grown Ups 2*."

"Thank God, because the best part of that movie was Taylor Lautner. And I'm saying that in the straightest way possible."

Cass' expression lightened and she let out a soft laugh. "I'm not saying *Grown Ups 2* because I have no favorite Adam Sandler movie. They're all horrible. They actually make me wish I were blind. Or deaf. Or both, actually."

Alex inhaled sharply and put a hand to his chest, as if Cass had physically wounded him. Maybe she was crazier than he thought.

"For real, Alex. Those stupid voices he does—I can't even listen to them, let alone think they're funny. 'Back to school, back to school,'" she said, poorly imitating the famous line. "Please. That's so annoying."

"I think I have to break up with you," Alex said. "I mean it. The wedding's off. I can't pretend to marry someone who feels this way about Adam." He tried to keep a straight face, but he couldn't contain the smile that spread across it. And Cass returned it with one of her own. "So," Alex said, "if you don't think any of Adam Sandler's movies are funny, what movies do *you* like?"

Cass thought for a moment. "*Bridesmaids* was good. I'll watch that anytime it's on. When Melissa McCarthy leaves the bridal shower with the van full of puppies . . . that shit's hysterical." Cass folded her hands on her torso, looking relaxed. "What else? What else?" she said, running her tongue across her upper lip. "Oh, oh, and *Titanic*! I die laughing every time I see Billy Zane running around the ship with a gun, like some tuxedoed psycho. And then Kate doesn't even let Leo lie on the door . . . I love it."

"You know that's not a comedy, right?"

"Says who? The entire ship was flooded with seawater, and Billy's eyeliner never even smudged."

"Okay, okay," Alex said. "So favorite comedies are *Bridesmaids* and *Titanic*. What about TV? Last three shows you've watched full seasons of . . . Go."

"*Breaking Bad, Dexter, Shameless*. Your turn."

"The ending of *Dexter* was a cop-out. And I thought I was the one asking the questions here?"

Cass ran a hand through the top of her hair and let it fall to one side. "If you plan on asking a lot of questions, let's make this more interesting. Ever play Know It All?"

Alex shook his head. "What is it?"

"My roommates and I used to play it in college. One person asks a question to the other. If the person doesn't want to answer truthfully, they can lie or say 'pass.' But then they have to take a shot, and the question goes back to the person who asked it for them to answer."

Alex smiled before getting up. "I'm in," he said. "Tequila okay?"

"You have any limes?"

"I think I have lemons," Alex said, heading for the kitchen. There was something intriguing about this game. Though Alex and Cass had been seeing a lot of each other lately and he'd known her for more than a year and a half, he realized that he'd never really gotten to *know* her. At least not in the sense that he now felt he should.

"Lemons'll work," Cass called.

Alex chopped up the fruit and grabbed the bottle of liquor and two shot glasses from the cabinet. "You sure you want to do this? You know I interrogate people for a living, right?"

"I'll take my chances," Cass said, as Alex put the plate of lemons, the bottle, and the glasses down on the coffee table. Then he filled each glass.

"I'm assuming you're going first?" Cass asked.

Alex rubbed his hands together in excitement. *This is going to be fun.* "I'll start off easy," he said. "What was the first concert you ever went to?"

"No Doubt."

"No Doubt makes my skin crawl."

Cass laughed. "We actually have that in common then. I was never really a fan, but my sisters were going and they actually wanted to take me. I was eleven. There was no way I was passing up a night with my older sisters and no real adult supervision." Cass put a finger to her lips. "My turn," she said. "How many women have you slept with?"

"Oh, come on," Alex said. "I went easy on you."

Cass shrugged, a pleased smirk on her face.

"Four," Alex lied, before throwing back a shot and refilling it. "I feel like there's no right answer to that one. Question goes to you now."

"One," Cass answered simply.

Alex's eyes narrowed in confusion. "You've only slept with one person? You can't pass. You have to be honest."

"I was. I've slept with one woman."

A slow smile crept over Alex's mouth. "Fair enough. You go again?"

"Yeah, because you passed last time, so the one I just answered counted as your question." Cass toyed with the label of her beer bottle, peeling it and resticking it while she thought. "Okay, what pets did you have growing up?"

Alex was surprised by the question. Why would Cass want to know about his pets? But he didn't bother overanalyzing it; he was happy it was so innocuous. "I had two dogs: a chocolate Lab named Tootsie and a German shepherd named Mitchell."

"Mitchell?" Cass let out a laugh. "Who names their dog Mitchell?"

"Hey, Mitchell's a solid name. My sister named Tootsie after the candy. So when we got another dog a few years later, my parents said I could name him. I think Mitchell's a cool name. Strong, you know?"

"It reminds me of one of those guys from Best Buy who comes to your house to fix your computer so you don't have to bring it to the store." Cass squeezed the bridge of her nose. "Shit. What are those guys called?"

"The Geek Squad."

"Yes." Cass pointed at him. "Mitchell's part of the

Geek Squad. I mean, not your dog. You know what I mean."

Alex stared at Cass. "I named him after my grandfather, who died tragically the summer before we got the dog."

"Oh." Cass' face sobered. "I didn't mean . . ." Cass cleared her throat as she seemed to stumble for the right words. "You're right. Mitchell is a strong name—"

"Cass."

"Yeah?"

"I'm kidding."

Cass inhaled deeply and let her shoulders fall in relief. "I could really kill you sometimes."

"Well, don't kill me yet because it's my turn." Alex got up to go to the fridge to grab another beer for each of them. Cass had only a few sips left in hers, and though she'd been playing with the bottle and still taking a drink every so often, he knew it was probably warm. Alex took off the cap and handed the beer to her.

"Thanks."

"Okay, what's your best memory?"

"I don't know."

"So, are you passing?" Alex held up the shot class as an offering.

"Not passing. Just thinking," she said, taking a long drink from the new beer. "I guess I'd say it was a trip to Disney World when I was eight or so. We'd gone a few years before that because Rachel and Amy were older. But I was too young to remember. So when I was about six I started begging my parents to take me. I was obsessed with fairy tales. I wanted to be one of those princesses who lived in a castle, you know?"

Alex nodded, thinking that Nina was the same way. He was sure most little girls were.

"I remember getting to take pictures with all the characters: Snow White, Cinderella, Minnie. That was the last big vacation we took as a family. After that we just did smaller trips to the beach or whatever. I'm sure in a one-income household it was a financial stretch for my parents to take a family of five to Disney twice, so it meant a lot that we all got to go."

Cass smiled at the memory, a light in her eyes that Alex wasn't used to seeing. Not that she didn't usually look happy. She did. Cass was one of the most cheerful people he knew. But he'd never seen her look so . . . content. Peaceful, even. He let her stay that way, not wanting to interrupt her tranquillity.

After a few seconds of silence, Cass spoke. "What about you? What's your favorite memory?"

Alex was sure he must have looked similar to Cass as he thought back to seven years ago. It was always so strange to him how something that seemed so foggy could still be so clear. "The day Nina was born," he answered. He wasn't sure he wanted to elaborate, but Cass remained silent, her expression urging him to continue. "Tessa's water broke on a Tuesday night, and Nina wasn't born until almost ten p.m. the following night. I was up for, like, two days straight. I'm actually surprised I remember any of it at all."

"You didn't sleep while Tessa was in labor? My sister Amy was in labor for a long time with her first, but she got to rest a bit until the contractions really started getting bad."

Alex let out a short laugh through his nose. "Tessa slept a little, but I didn't. I was too nervous. I was worried about Tessa and about this life inside her that I hadn't even met yet. We didn't even know if we were having a boy or a girl." Alex ran a hand through the back of his hair, feeling some of the same anxiety he'd felt that night. "I didn't know how to be a father, and I was worried I wouldn't be a good one."

Cass put a hand around Alex's forearm and massaged his arm gently. "Nina loves you."

Alex knew that was true. But that didn't mean he was a good parent. Kids loved shitty parents all the time because they didn't know any better. In his line of work he'd seen it more times than he'd like to admit. "I know," he said, not wanting to get into the nuances of how love didn't always equate to good parenting. "Anyway, Tessa pushed for hours. They kept flipping her into all these different positions. She was yelling at me, at the nurses. It was pretty intense," he said on a laugh. "It looked like a scene from *The Exorcist* in there at one point."

"Stop." Cass gave him a playful shove.

"For real. I seriously don't know how women go through all that."

Cass smiled. "Me neither."

"After, like, the twenty-second hour, I was so dizzy and sick, but I didn't want to let Tessa know because she had to have been in worse shape than I was. I just kept telling her everything was going to be fine. They almost had to do a C-section, but they were able to get Nina out without one." He remembered how it felt to see his daughter for the first time, to feel like he had someone he needed to protect at all costs. "It's the craziest thing," he said with a goofy grin, "how one second you have no one you have to worry about other than yourself, and the next second you feel like you have everything."

Cass' eyes narrowed. "You had Tessa though. Before Nina. That was something."

Alex shook his head. "It's different. Even though we loved each other then, a love for anyone else is different from the love you have for your own child, you know?" Alex realized Cass probably didn't. Or maybe she did in theory. But no one could truly understand until they'd had children. "The best way I can explain it is this: no matter how much you love someone, deep down inside you know if you lost them, you'd be okay. It'd be hard, but you'd get through it." He felt his body tense just thinking about what he was about to say. "But not with your child. If something ever happened to Nina, the last thing I'd ever be again is okay." He inhaled deeply, realizing for probably the millionth time how much she meant to him. "When they put her tiny body onto Tessa and told me I had a daughter, a switch flipped in me that I'll never be able to shut off. And I don't want to."

"Wow," Cass said. "I've never heard anyone describe childbirth like that. When my sisters talk about it, they mostly just focus on epidurals and stitches."

Alex chuckled. "Guess I can't really relate to that part."

"Guess I can't either," Cass said.

"So, I've got to know. Why don't you ever want kids? You've never made that a secret, and there aren't many women who openly say that family life isn't for them. So what's the reason?"

"Is this part of the game, or you just asking?"

Alex shrugged. "I guess it's part of the game."

Cass didn't speak. She just sighed loudly, as if she weren't happy at the prospect of having to answer. Then she grabbed the shot off the table, put it to her lips, and drained it before squeezing a lemon into her mouth and sucking out all the juice. "Then I guess I pass," she said softly. "And since I can't ask you the same question, I think this is where our game ends." She stood, stretching her arms into the air as if the physical movement might make her feel more emotionally comfortable than she was. "Got any good snacks?" she asked suddenly as she headed for the kitchen.

Even by Cass' standards, that had been a poor transition. But after Alex's question, she knew she'd needed to change the subject. Though she'd never been embarrassed about not wanting a husband or children, hearing Alex talk about Nina had made her feel something inside herself that she didn't want to feel. And the scariest part was that she couldn't even identify it.

How could she justify not wanting children to someone whose life felt incomplete without his daughter? Alex would probably never understand, so she wouldn't even try to explain it. It was easier that way.

She pulled open both doors of Alex's refrigerator and moved some items around so she could look behind them. She'd been hoping to find some pudding or cake or something, but all he had that remotely resembled a dessert was fresh fruit. He was obviously in great shape, but didn't the man *ever* eat something unhealthy? "You have a seven-year-old," she yelled. "Tell me you have something with some sort of sugar in it. Cookies or ice cream or something?" she asked, heading to his pantry.

"I think there are Popsicles in the freezer," Alex called back.

Cass turned back around, pulled open the freezer, and spotted the treats immediately. "Jackpot! I don't think I've had a Popsicle in years. You want one?"

"No, thanks. I'm good," Alex said.

Cass plopped herself back on the couch, feeling better now that she had a distraction. Even if it was just an edible one.

"You okay?" he asked.

Clearly her sudden hunger hadn't been as believable an excuse as she'd hoped. Alex could tell there was another reason for her abrupt exit. "Yeah, I'm fine." She pulled apart the white plastic and slid it off the stick, tossing it onto the plate with her discarded lemon wedge. "I'll probably get going after I eat this, I guess," she said. *Is it awkward I'm just staying for a snack?*

"You don't have to."

Cass shrugged, pulling the red Popsicle out of her mouth so she could speak. "Well, I think I've had about as much of Adam Sandler as I can take for one night." She gestured toward the TV, where *Billy Madison* was still playing. Thankfully she'd tuned it out during their game.

Alex blew a low laugh out through his nose. "Well, have you had enough of *me*?"

His question threw her, but she wasn't sure if she was reading into it. Was he asking her if she was getting *sick* of him? They'd definitely been spending more time together lately, and a lot of it hadn't revolved around sex. "No, I'm not sick of *you*," she replied simply, still trying to figure out what he meant exactly.

Alex's movement toward her stopped her overanalysis of his question. "Good. Because if you keep sliding that Popsicle in and out of your mouth like that, I don't think that I'll be able to let you leave any-time soon."

Cass gave him a flirtatious smile. "You're going to hold me here against my will?" She ran her tongue seductively along the length of the frozen treat, know-ing the reaction it would stir in Alex.

"Oh, I'm pretty sure you'll be willing." Alex's mouth was now only inches away from hers, his lips wet from where he'd just licked them. She wanted them on hers.

She lowered her voice to a whisper. "Oh yeah? What makes you so confident?"

Alex brushed his fingers through her hair, tuck-ing it behind one ear. His hand massaged the back of her neck lightly before he pulled her more roughly toward him, so he could speak against her mouth. "Just a feeling."

The vibration of his deep voice sent a warmth down her body that only increased as Alex laid her back against the couch, spreading her thighs apart so he could settle between them. Cass let out an unsteady moan as she felt his cock press hard against her through their clothing. She wanted him to grind against her, give her the friction she was craving. But he didn't move his hips. Instead he kept her firmly pinned below him with his weight as he kissed his way from her lips down her neck and all the way along her arm, paying special attention to the spots that he knew drove her wild. Until Alex, she never knew how good being kissed on the inside of her elbow could feel.

"I'm going to be needing this," Alex said, holding one of her hands in place while he removed the red Popsicle from the other. He started first with her lips, running the ice along the outside of them until they instinctively parted so Alex could slide it into her mouth.

He groaned as Cass sucked on it, swirling her tongue around as if it were Alex's cock inside her mouth instead. Cass locked her legs around him, physically pleading with him to move.

And finally he did, his pelvis rubbing against her clit. "God, Cass, you know how hot you look with that in your mouth? I could come just watching you." After a few moments, Alex slid out the Popsicle and pressed his lips to hers, his warm tongue a welcome sensation in her cool mouth. "You taste sweet," he whispered against her as he yanked off her shirt and removed her bra. "But there are other parts of you I want my mouth on more."

Alex's words sent a rush of wetness to her already soaked panties. And when the contact with her ceased as he pulled away, she thought she might lose her mind. "Alex," she pleaded. "I need you inside me." She could hear how desperate she sounded, but she didn't care.

"Soon," was his only response, and Cass arched on the couch as she felt the cool ice hit her nipple, followed by Alex's lips. He wasn't as gentle as she was used to him being, his hand kneading her breast, pulling it roughly toward his mouth so he could suck harder. Then he did the same to the other, giving them equal attention as Cass' moans got louder. She was so ready.

Her eyes closed, Cass felt him drag the cool ice down her stomach toward the top of her jeans before popping the button and yanking down the zipper. "You're not going to fuck me with that, are you?" Cass asked, unsure.

Alex laughed softly. "Not with this. But I do plan to fuck you. Hard," he added, making Cass squirm as he tossed the Popsicle on the plate and slid her jeans down her legs. Alex took his time with her thong, dragging his fingertips lightly against the outsides of her thighs as he removed it.

When he was done, he settled between her legs, lifting one over his shoulder and kissing the inside delicately. Cass shivered as his lips deliberately avoided the place she wanted them most.

Finally, he pressed his mouth between her legs, sucking hungrily on her clit again and again. She bucked against him, his soft tongue swirling and flicking at varying speeds. When his fingers plunged deep inside her, she heard just how wet she was, a combination of her own desire and Alex's mouth on her.

He continued his erotic assault, his strong hands squeezing her ass, pulling her even harder against him. The tingling in her core increased with every smooth stroke of his fingers until she couldn't hold off any longer. "Alex," she huffed, "I'm going to . . ."

She couldn't even finish her sentence, her voice a mixture of pleasurable moans and soft curses. When Alex slowed his movements, he crawled up her body, kissing her skin softly with his wet lips.

She could feel the satisfied grin on her face, and Alex gave her one in return, clearly pleased with her reaction. She stroked the back of his hair and spoke against his lips. "Jesus, I don't even know what that was."

"Then let's say that was just the first of what's to come." He stood to remove his clothing slowly, giving Cass time to admire every flexing muscle as he removed his shirt and then his pants and boxers.

"Come on," he said, picking her up off the couch and throwing her over his shoulder. "I need more room for what I plan to do to you." Then he gave her a sharp slap on her ass and headed toward his bedroom, Cass giggling wildly in his arms. She wasn't sure exactly what Alex's plan involved, but whatever it was, she couldn't stop smiling about it.

Alex couldn't get her to the bedroom fast enough, and once he was there, he playfully tossed Cass onto the bed from a few feet away.

Cass laughed and shifted to lean on her elbows as Alex stalked slowly toward her. He took his time working his way up her body, lifting her leg to kiss from her ankle up to her thigh. But once there, Cass guided his face to hers. "I think it's your turn," she said simply.

Alex's cock twitched in excitement, stiffening even more at the thought of Cass' warm lips wrapped around it. "I think I'd like that," was his only reply as they flipped positions so Cass could maneuver herself on top of him. Alex let her hold his hands in place on either side of his head while she licked behind his ear and down his neck. Though she was straddling him, Alex could tell she was making every effort not to make contact with his erection. And it was killing him. He'd wanted to be inside of her since he'd tasted her earlier, and when she'd come, he'd nearly done the same. His cock jerked again, and he pushed his hips off the bed so he could feel Cass against him.

He settled back on the bed, willing his body to remain under control. At last she spread her legs a little wider, kissing down his body on her way toward her destination. It wouldn't be long before he'd be thrusting between those pink lips of hers.

She paused just below his belly button, placing light nibbles on his lower abs and his upper thigh. Her mouth grazed his balls for a moment, and he wondered if it had been intentional. He could feel how fucking full they were, how ready he was to explode with just the smallest touch. One hand had been pulling on Cass' hair, but he used the other to grip the base of his shaft. He hoped the pressure might help hold off his orgasm, but it had the opposite effect. He couldn't help but move his fingers over himself. Cass looked up at him, her eyes narrowing in the sexiest fucking way before she finally let her lips part just enough that Alex could slide himself between them. The feel of her warm mouth slipping over him, the sounds she made as she sucked him—it was enough to make him let go right now. But he'd promised he'd had plans for her. Though right now—with Cass' blond hair falling over his stomach as her mouth moved up and down his cock—he had no clear recollection of what those plans had even been.

"Slow down," he pleaded. Though he wanted her to continue exactly what she was doing, he knew he couldn't last much longer.

Cass swallowed, causing her tongue to press against his cock in the best way, but she hadn't slowed down. Alex tugged on her hair a bit, halfheartedly trying to guide her off him before he fucking lost it. But that only made Cass more aggressive. She pushed her mouth even farther over Alex's cock until the tip hit the back of her throat, causing Alex to release a low groan. "I'm serious . . . I can't . . . Oh God." And then Alex was coming, shooting warm bursts of semen into Cass' mouth. He watched her continue to move over him, her hand working the base of his dick while her lips slid up and down the rest.

When Alex had emptied himself fully and Cass had swallowed every drop of him, she crawled up his body. "How was that?"

Alex chuckled softly, resting an arm behind his head in satisfaction as he looked up at her. "How do you *think* it was?" he asked.

Cass smirked, looking quite pleased with herself. But she didn't reply. She just leaned down and gave Alex a slow kiss—one that let him know she'd enjoyed that *almost* as much as he had.

Chapter 11

Tactics

"So I was thinking," Cass said as soon as Alex answered the phone.

"That scares me."

"That's not very nice," Cass countered.

"You're right. It's not so bad when you're thinking. It's when you're *not* thinking that I end up planning a wedding."

Cass hesitated briefly before saying, "Touché."

"So what were you thinking about?"

"I want to take Nina out for ice cream."

"Okay," Alex said, drawing out the word. "Why?"

"Well, like I said, I was thinking, and us sending a fake save-the-date to your ex-wife's house isn't going to be enough to convince her to let you have Nina for those few months. She has to trust that *I* can be a good addition to Nina's life, and that she can trust me with her daughter when you're not around. So . . . ice cream. Then if Tessa asks Nina what she did this weekend, Nina will have a positive reason to mention me. Plus, I feel bad that I had to bail on our last excursion."

Alex sighed. It wasn't that it was a bad idea. It was a good idea, actually. Except . . . "I thought we were trying to avoid overly involving Nina in this fake wedding drama." He whispered the last words. Last he had checked, Nina was playing in her room, but kids were like ninjas. He didn't want her to overhear anything he wouldn't be able to explain.

"I'm not taking her to pick out china patterns. We're going for ice cream."

"I know." Alex rubbed a hand through his hair. "But if you guys start hanging out, she might get attached. It was one thing when the three of us were going to the zoo together. This would be just the two of you. More personal."

"Alex, we've been over this. You and I will still have a friendship when all of this is over. I'll still see Nina." Cass sounded exasperated, and he didn't blame her. They *had* been over this. But his worry never had diminished.

"It just feels like we're manipulating my seven-year-old. Like we're bribing her so she'll say good things about us to Tessa."

"So?"

Christ, why does she not get this? "So you're making Nina feel like you want to hang out with her, when you're really just doing it to win this mind game we've found ourselves playing with my ex-wife."

"No, I'm doing this because I like ice cream, I like Nina, and I usually like you, though I'm not such a fan right now. There's not a parent alive who hasn't tried to spoil their kids so they could be the fun parent once in a while. You're making too big of a deal out of this."

Alex thought for a second. "I do have some work I could get done while you guys are gone."

"Awesome. I'll be there in a half hour." And with that, Cass hung up.

He sat on the couch, staring blankly at his laptop for a few moments. He was going to have to get over his reservations. He'd agreed to move forward with Cass' plan, so forward he would have to go. Even if it didn't always make him feel very good.

He stood up from the couch and made his way up to Nina's room. He watched her from the doorway for a second as she played with her dollhouse.

She had a slew of dolls spread out in front of her, and she seemed to be carefully deliberating which dolls would serve her game best.

He went in and sat beside her. "Whatcha doing?"

"Playing."

He let out a small laugh. "I kind of figured that. What are you playing?"

"House."

The girl could give lessons to criminals on how to evade questions. "Can I play?"

"Sure." She quickly chose the rest of the dolls needed for whatever imaginary world she'd created and shoved a few at him.

"Who are these supposed to be?" he asked as he looked at the Ken, Barbie, and Skipper she'd given him.

"That's you, me, and Cass."

Alex's head shot up as his gaze raked over Nina's face. "Who are the ones you're holding?"

"Me, Mommy, and Pete."

"So there are two of you?"

"Yup."

"Why?" Alex wasn't sure he wanted the answer, but he couldn't resist asking anyway.

"Because sometimes I wish there were two of me so I could spend every day with you *and* Mommy instead of going back and forth."

Alex felt like his heart had been ripped out of his chest. "Is it so bad? Going back and forth?"

Nina looked up at him and seemed to think hard about her answer. "No, because otherwise there'd be no Pete and Cass."

"Do you like Cass?" It was a question he realized that a normal father in a normal situation would've asked his daughter *before* he proposed to someone. But that wasn't something he could fix now. He'd just bank it away for the future, in case he ever got engaged for real.

"Sure. She's fun and pretty and nice."

Alex felt a warmth spread through him that caught him off guard. He logically knew that it was important for Nina to like Cass, but the emotional response it stirred surprised him. He was glad Nina liked Cass, and not just because it would help them sell a lie, but because *he* liked Cass. She was a good friend to him. She was trustworthy and caring and warm—everything a father could want in a role model for his little girl. "Cass is coming over soon to take you out for ice cream."

Nina's eyes lit up. "Yay! I love ice cream." The dolls were immediately forgotten as Nina rushed around, shoving her feet into shoes and taking off down the hall.

Alex sat and stared after her, smiling at her exuberance. Then his eyes dropped to the three dolls he still held in his hands. Without even thinking about what he was doing, Alex propped them in the tiny house.

* * *

Cass and Nina spent an hour getting ice cream, and they even brought some back for him. Cass didn't hang out long. Alex assumed she had better ways to spend her Saturday night. *Maybe she has a date.* That thought irritated him for some reason. But he chalked it up to hurting his chances of selling their engagement if Cass was seen hanging around with other guys.

He'd settled Nina into bed about an hour ago, and he then decided to go back to poring over case notes at his kitchen table. Alex both loved and loathed his job. He'd always had an innate desire to help people, to right wrongs. He also was a bit of a risk taker, which was considered a positive attribute in his line of work. Alex was routinely required to confront danger when most people would run away from it. His primary focus was apprehending some of the country's most violent offenders—when a chance to take them down arose, he couldn't hesitate to act, no matter what personal peril could await him.

But working at the National Center for the Analysis of Violent Crimes also meant he saw things he would never be able to unsee. The things people did to each other—the absolute torture they could inflict—was nauseating on the best of days. It was downright terror inducing on the worst.

Alex wasn't a trained psychiatrist. He'd been a criminal justice major in college, knowing that his passion was in law enforcement. But his superiors had quickly observed that he had a knack for connecting dots, a way of seeing the evidence that others often missed. And he loved it. He loved reading between the lines, trying to see beyond the crime to uncover the motivation behind it, all of which could lead to the apprehension of some of humanity's worst creations. So when he'd been asked if he'd like to help hunt down serial killers, he'd jumped at the chance without giving a whole lot of thought to the toll it would take on his family. There were times when new evidence popped up, a lead needed to be chased down, or a suspect was taken into custody, and Alex would drop what he was doing and head into work. The thing he really regretted was that, a lot of the time, he hadn't *needed* to drop everything. He'd *chosen* to. He'd put the needs of the public over those of his family because, at the end of the day, he couldn't let the job go. He *was* the job. It wasn't until after Tessa had left, married Pete, and started her own suburban bliss with Nina that it had hit him. Specifically it was the day he'd had to practically drag a screaming five-year-old away from her mother so he could spend time with her. Nina hadn't wanted to go with him for their weekend together. She'd clung to Tessa as though a stranger were trying to take her. It had been embarrassing and eye-opening.

Alex had always told himself he'd do everything he could for Nina, that he loved her more than anything. And the words were true. But the actions weren't there to support those words. Because the truth that was screeching at him on Tessa's front lawn was that his daughter didn't like him very much and didn't want to spend time with him. It was just the wake-up call he'd needed.

His job was still demanding, and there were times when he'd had to drop Nina off early so he could go in to work, but those instances were much rarer than they'd been in the past and were reserved for true emergencies. Over time, he'd built a solid relationship with his daughter. They enjoyed being together, and Alex wanted to ensure that they never drifted apart again.

Which was why it was so important to him that he get to spend the eight weeks with Nina over the summer. He didn't want Nina to look back on it and think that her dad hadn't wanted, or hadn't been able, to take care of her. That she'd needed to go with her grandparents because he wasn't up to the task. So he'd gone along with Cass' lie, and he was perpetuating it at the risk of hurting his daughter's feelings, because ultimately he thought it would strengthen the bond between them. Maybe it was selfish. Maybe it was delusional. Maybe it would backfire. But maybe it would also give him a great two months with his daughter. Two months where he could step up and show her how important she was to him.

With that thought in mind, he gathered the notes in front of him and shoveled the papers back into the folder. Work could wait. If they got up early enough, he and Nina could hit the diner she loved before the morning rush. He scooped up his cell phone, turned off lights, and shot a text to Cass, inviting her to breakfast, on his way to his bedroom.

Mondays were always a special kind of hell in Cass' office. It never failed that one of her firm's clients did something epically stupid and everyone had to scramble to minimize the damage. There must have been a full moon the previous two days because Cass was looking at an e-mail from her boss, alerting her that two of her clients had gotten in trouble. One had been caught urinating in public and evading arrest when he'd decided to play an elaborate game of hide-and-seek in order to avoid being ticketed. The other had been photographed in one of D.C.'s prominent gay clubs, grinding with a half-naked dancer. The photo was all over social media, but Cass still probably could have worked with it if the man had hired her firm for almost any reason other than wanting help in attracting members for a nondenominational church he was opening . . . with his wife. It was only ten a.m., and she already needed a drink.

Her Outlook pinged with another incoming e-mail. *Please don't let today get any worse.* Thankfully it was just an e-mail from Alex. He wanted to let her know that the venue they'd chosen was having a food tasting in a couple of weeks, and to ask if she wanted to go. Far be it from Cass to turn down food. She replied that she was in. She also thanked him again for inviting her to breakfast the previous morning. His offer had been considerate as well as tempting, but Cass had promised her sister that she'd watch the kids for some brunch Amy and Ben needed to go to. So she'd had to sacrifice a delicious breakfast for Play-Doh and cartoons.

The day wore on slowly. Cass had made the public pisser promise to donate some of his time to a local shelter in exchange for the city's dropping the evading-arrest charge. And, luckily, since prosecuting the case would have been more hassle than it was worth, the ADA had quickly agreed. The man paid his fine and went on his way without his name being released to the public.

The fine pastor was a different story. He wanted to deny it was him, since the picture circulating was slightly obscured, due to his having his tongue down another man's throat. However, Cass convinced him that lying would only exacerbate the problem. There were tons of witnesses that could place him in the club. Ultimately, he had two choices: refuse to address it and hope it went away, or admit to the infidelity and, with his wife by his side, agree to seek counseling for his marital transgression. Either way, Cass thought he was screwed, but she still had a job to do, and she'd try to do it to the best of her ability.

The only reprieve from the sucky day were the sporadic e-mails she exchanged with Alex. Most of them weren't about anything of importance—just the usual banter that existed between them. Cass was glad that the added stress of fake-wedding planning hadn't interfered with their friendship. The last thing she wanted to do was cause a rift between them. Wanting to make sure they hung out and did things that didn't involve the wedding, she told him about a band Simone had asked the girls to go see this coming Friday night. She was happy when he replied that he'd talk to the guys and was most likely in. She closed his e-mail, content with the fact that nothing had changed between them. They'd get through the upcoming months just fine.

Chapter 12

Disorderly Conduct

Alex took a long sip of his Corona and tried to appreciate the band that was playing on stage. The girls had been raving about this band for weeks. "What is it you like about this band exactly?"

The girls all did a slow pan toward him. It was creepy as fuck.

"Um, have you seen the lead singer?" Simone asked, as if Alex were incredibly stupid.

Alex looked back toward the stage and took in the longhaired, possibly homeless man gyrating his crotch against the mic stand. "Yeah."

Simone widened her eyes as though simply gazing upon the specimen before him should be explanation enough. She huffed out a breath. "He's gorgeous."

Alex let his eyes dart back to the waif screeching into the microphone. He squinted as if altering his vision would somehow alter what he was seeing. "You have really bad taste."

Simone jerked back. "I'm an artist. I have better taste than anyone here."

Alex smiled. "Let me guess. You specialize in abstracts."

Simone looked like she was trying to fight the grin threatening to spread across her face. "Asshole."

Alex looked to Cass. "You think he's hot?" He was more interested in her response than he thought he should be. Why should he care who Cass found attractive? But the truth was that he did care, so he watched her closely as she studied the creature on stage.

Cass shrugged before turning back to Alex. "He's hot in a Jared Leto kind of way."

Alex didn't know what the hell that meant. The guy on stage was the very antithesis of Alex—skinny to Alex's stocky, lithe versus Alex's heavy musculature, smooth to his rugged. *Is that what Cass likes?* "He's the opposite of every guy sitting at this table. If he's the type you girls like, you're keeping the wrong kind of company."

Everyone laughed, which was good, because their taking his words as a joke hid his own insecurity. Especially since he wasn't even sure why he felt that way. Alex could bench-press the guy on the stage. He could incapacitate him in seconds without so much as breaking a sweat. What the hell did he have to feel jealous about? *Wait. . . .Jealous? Is that how I feel?*

Lauren's voice broke him out of his meandering thoughts. "It's just the hot-rocker thing, really. He's like a fantasy, an ideal. Not someone any of us would actually go for in reality."

"Speak for yourself," Simone muttered.

"But we're here to listen, not watch. He sounds like a drowning walrus," Alex said.

Cass looked at him curiously. "Can walruses drown?"

Alex looked at her like she'd lost her mind.

She must have taken that as a cue to continue. "They live in water. Can animals that live in water drown?"

"They're mammals, so it'd make sense that they could drown if they were forced to stay underwater for too long," Quinn answered.

"If a walrus is drowning, can it make a sound at all?" Lauren asked.

The seriousness of the unfolding conversation flabbergasted him. He looked at his male counterparts around the table, all of whom looked equally confused.

"Are you girls seriously discussing walruses?" Scott asked.

"I'm not," Simone stated. "I'm imagining the lead singer naked."

"That's . . . way worse," Alex said.

"Are you just not a band kind of guy?" Cass asked.

It took Alex a second to process her question, since it was such a departure from where the conversation had just been. "I like bands. Just not this one."

"Oh. I thought maybe you were more of a DJ kind of guy."

"DJs are okay too. I guess it just depends on what I'm in the mood for."

Cass smiled. "Since this is the third time we're having this discussion, maybe we should settle it."

Ugh, not this shit right now. It had been a while since they'd all been able to get together, and he had hoped they could do it without mentioning his impending non-nuptials.

"We're having that debate too," Lauren added.

"Scott wants some Motown band, but I think we're better off with a DJ who will be able to play something for everyone."

"Everyone loves a good band. Any loser with an iPod can DJ nowadays. Bands are timeless," Scott said.

"Except this one," Xavier said as he gestured toward the stage. "I think their fifteen minutes is just about up."

Simone turned to glare at him before returning her attention back to the stage.

"Since Cass said you already discussed this, what were you guys thinking of doing?" Scott asked, his eyes darting back and forth between Cass and Alex.

Alex felt his brow furrow. "We were thinking of not actually getting married."

Scott rolled his eyes. "Well, I know. But you guys are still planning a wedding, right? So which way were you leaning?"

"Dude, are you seriously trying to compare wedding-planning notes with me?"

"I was just asking." Scott sounded oddly defensive.

"How is it planning a wedding you're not actually going to have? Isn't that . . . a waste of energy?" Quinn asked.

"And money?" Tim tacked on.

"We need to be able to sell it. How are we supposed to do that if we don't plan out some of the details?" Cass explained.

Quinn's eyes widened in excitement. "You should turn it into a party. That way it wouldn't all be for nothing."

"It's not for nothing. It's for Nina and Alex." Cass' voice was quiet but sharp. Her words touched Alex, and he sent her a small smile.

Quinn looked abashed. "I didn't mean it like that.

Of course it's not for nothing. I just meant that you're doing all the planning anyway, so you'd may as well celebrate the fruits of your labor."

Alex thought about it for a second before looking at Cass. "It's not a bad idea."

"Really?" Cass looked surprised.

Alex nodded. "We should do it."

She smiled a bright smile that made his dick harden. "Okay. So, band or DJ?"

The group spent the rest of the night bickering amicably, laughing, and having an all-around good time like they always did. Sometimes it surprised Alex how well they all jelled. They each brought a strong personality to the table, but it improved the dynamic instead of disrupting it. When the band ended their set, the friends all remained for one more round, then settled up the tab and made their way out into the cool spring evening. Everyone said good-bye and headed toward wherever they'd parked their cars.

Cass turned to Alex, seemingly about to say good-bye, but Alex interrupted her. "I'll walk you to your car."

She smiled softly and nodded. Threading her arm through his, she led him in the direction of her car. When they reached her red Acura, she turned and opened her mouth to speak.

But Alex stopped her again. The dim streetlight gave them relative privacy, and he couldn't resist moving toward her. He used his body to push her gently against the car so her back was flush with it, settled his thigh between her legs, cupped her jaw with one hand, and kissed the ever-loving hell out of her. All night he'd felt it—a quiet, steady thrum of desire. It crackled through him, made his blood boil. He couldn't take it anymore. The need to act on it— to take what he craved—was too overwhelming to be ignored.

When he finally pulled back, Cass didn't open her eyes right away. She seemed to be savoring the same feelings he was. Finally she looked at him. "That was a helluva good-night."

Alex kept his body pressed against hers, maintaining the proximity that his dick was clearly appreciative of as it hardened in his jeans. "Maybe it wasn't good-night." His eyes searched hers.

They crinkled with her smile. "You're much better at planning a seduction than a wedding."

"Is that a compliment or an insult?" he asked as his gaze dropped to her lips.

"Whatever makes you want to fuck me more."

He buried his head in her neck to suck on the skin there. "Hmm, that's a tough one. I do love when you berate me."

She slapped his shoulder playfully before wrapping her arms around his neck. "My place is closer," she whispered in his ear.

Alex let his hands drift down her back until they cupped her ass. "Your car is even closer."

Cass gasped at his caress. "We couldn't leave it parked here though. This street is too busy." She looked around for a moment. "Follow me."

At that point, Alex was so hard he'd follow her anywhere.

Cass made her way into a narrow alleyway between two large brick buildings. She walked in just enough for the streetlights to cast a pale glow on them, and then turned toward one of the walls, resting her arms against the brick. She pitched forward slightly, arching her back and sticking out her ass. "Fuck me, Alex."

It took him a second to get over the thrill of her words, but he recovered quickly, stepping up behind her and rubbing his cock against her ass. Even through two layers of denim, the feeling was amazing. "You're really going to give it up to me on the street? You are a dirty, dirty girl, Cass. I fucking love it."

Alex's hands were everywhere, roaming over her body, completely unsure of where they wanted to settle. Finally they stopped to pop the button on her jeans and lower the zipper. He pushed her pants and thong down roughly, lowering them just enough to give him the access he needed. He let his fingers drift over her clit and through her wetness. He'd never been so turned on, and it felt like she was right there with him. Undoing his own jeans, he pulled the material down enough to free his straining erection. He dragged it through her crease, pushing his cock back and forth between her thighs.

"Stop teasing," Cass scolded breathlessly.

Alex fished a condom out of his wallet and sheathed himself before pushing immediately inside of her. There was no place for slow and romantic. They both needed hard and carnal. This was the most erotic fuck of Alex's entire life, and it propelled him to take her—to pound into her wildly. "Fucking amazing," was all he could grit out.

"So good, Alex. I'm already close."

He was close too. His fingers dug even more deeply into her hips, trying to hold her as steady as possible as he drilled into her. She was bent at nearly ninety degrees, fully extending her arms so she didn't go careening into the wall. The slap of skin against skin reverberated through his ears, dragging him closer to release. Quickly losing his control, Alex slid one hand around her hip and down to her clit so he could work her toward climax.

"Fuck," she mewled. Then he felt her body tense before she shuddered with the intensity of her orgasm. He rode her through it, watching her body buck and shiver with pleasure.

He managed about four more thrusts before he was emptying his release into the condom. Shallowly rocking into her, he let her milk all of the cum from him. Alex dropped his head between her shoulders, allowing it to rest there as they both came down from the high they'd just experienced. But he didn't linger long, the sounds of the street reminding him of where they were. He pulled out, tied off the condom, and walked farther into the alley to dispose of it in a trash can. By the time he returned to Cass, he'd tucked himself back into his pants and Cass had straightened out her clothing as well.

He stepped right into her space and slid his arms around her waist, dropping a soft kiss on her lips. The action was in contrast to the raw encounter they'd just shared, but as great as that had felt, this felt right too.

Cass slid her arms around his neck and nestled into him. "That was the single hottest moment of my life," she murmured against his neck.

He snuggled her closer. "Glad I could be of service."

She huffed a soft laugh but didn't move to pull away. They stood there for a few minutes, and Alex felt as though they were reconnecting in a way— sloughing off the hardened edges of what they'd just shared and allowing the genuine affection they'd begun to feel for one another to soften the entire experience. Cass shivered slightly in his arms, causing him to pull back to look at her.

"Cold?" he asked.

"I think you had me so hot and bothered, the cool air is starting to shock my system."

Alex smiled. "Let's get you to your car, then." He didn't let himself think about the action before he laced his fingers in hers and walked her back to her car.

Chapter 13

Public Opinion

"Jake, just sit down and I'll get it." Cass watched her sister Rachel try to placate her oldest son, who was insisting on fixing his own plate.

"I can do it myself," the boy declared with a stomp of his foot for emphasis.

The truth was, Cass thought, Jake probably could do it. He was eight, after all, a year older than Nina, and in all the time she had spent with Alex's little girl recently, Cass had never felt the need to plop food on a plate and cut it up for her. Not to mention that the entire ordeal looked exhausting. Rachel would still have to repeat this complicated plating ritual two more times for her five-year-old son, Jonas, and three-year-old Jessica. Cass looked at Rachel's husband, John, the progenitor of the "J" tribe, as he hacked at the turkey Cass' mom had made for dinner.

Normally her dad, Tom, carved—it could actually be considered carving when he did it—but he'd recently hurt his wrist when he'd fallen off a ladder in the garage. Her mom had said he was lucky he didn't break his neck, to which he'd replied with a swat of his uninjured arm. In his thirty-plus years in this house, Cass' father had managed to escape no fewer than ten potentially fatal catastrophes. "Klutzy" didn't even begin to describe the man. Even more amazing was that he'd never seriously injured himself, which was a blessing, because Cass' mom, Gloria, practically had to tranquilize him to get him to the doctor.

"White or dark meat, Cass?" John asked as he swiped his arm across his brow to soak up the moisture there.

"Whatever's easiest," she replied with a smile as she passed her plate to him so he could put some turkey on it.

Cass' head turned as she heard a thump to her left. Amy's toddler, Asher, had dropped his sippy cup. Again.

"Ben, can you grab that?" Amy asked her husband.

"Why? He's just going to chuck it down there again."

Cass had always liked Ben. He was sarcastic, loud, and unapologetically honest—almost like a Cass in male form. He was a good balance for the sweet and witty Amy. And their kids were adorable . . . and total ballbusters. It was clear that Asher, even at two, was already adept at fucking with his parents. His sister, Zoey, was more subtle in her torture, but no less effective. Cass often thought that the beautiful four-year-old would either grow up to cure cancer or become a criminal mastermind. Cass watched as Zoey asked her mom to get her potatoes. But it was all a diversion so the little girl could transfer the broccoli from her plate to her mother's. *Genius.*

Cass' plate was handed back to her, and once it seemed as though everyone else had everything they needed, the Mullen clan dug in. About three minutes of silence passed as everyone enjoyed the first bites of the meal. But quiet never lasted long with this crew. They normally congregated for dinner at her parents' house twice a month, and it was always chaotic and noisy. Cass loved it. It made her think about the calm meals she'd shared with Alex and Nina. The three of them never lacked for conversation, but it was relaxed, tranquil. She realized that she loved that equally as much. Cass wondered what Alex and Nina would make of the zoo that currently surrounded her. There were at least five conversations going on, each trying to be heard over the others. The funny thing was, Cass could picture Alex and Nina here, fighting to get a word in edgewise. Because despite their laid-back personalities, they both had a confidence about them that commanded attention. She'd been spending time with them for only about two months, but she'd learned a lot about them in that time. However, it had never really occurred to Cass how similar Alex and Nina were until now. She wondered if Alex knew that his strong, intelligent, thoughtful little girl was exactly like him.

"What are you smiling about?" Rachel's voice jerked Cass out of her musings.

"Huh?"

"You were smiling. What were you thinking about?"

Of course the table had fallen silent to hear Cass' explanation. She hadn't even been aware she was smiling. *Friggin' Rachel.* "I don't know. I'm just happy, I guess."

"Lame," Ben muttered beside her.

Cass turned to him. "Did you just call me lame?"

"No, your excuse was lame. Take a minute and regroup. I'm sure you can do better."

Cass looked at Amy. "Can't you, like, forbid him from talking?"

Amy sighed. "If only."

Ben chortled before shoveling more food in his mouth.

"What has you so happy? Something, or *someone*, you want to tell us about?" Gloria said with a raise of her eyebrows.

Cass felt herself grimace.

"Yeah, Cass. Anyone you want to tell us about?" Rachel said. Cass could see her sister smirk behind her water glass as she took a sip.

Cass tried to telepathically convey her hope that Rachel would drop dead. "No. I just like spending time with all of you. Is something wrong with that?"

"Of course not. I'm happiest when we're all together too," Gloria replied.

And Cass knew that was the truth. Her mom was one of the greatest people Cass had ever met, and that wasn't just bias speaking. Gloria Mullen had the patience of a saint mixed with a deep commitment to her family. Her mom always put her husband and daughters before herself. Always. She had been at every sporting event, chaperoned every class trip, participated in every PTA function, kissed every boo-boo, and chased away every monster lurking under their beds for the duration of their childhoods. And Gloria's first two daughters had inherited that same love of motherhood, that same dedication to their families, though with more of a twenty-first-century twist. Both of her sisters worked, while Gloria had been a stay-at-home mom. But Cass could see it in the way Amy absently pushed her hand through Zoey's hair, or the way Rachel listened attentively to her kids' nonsensical stories as though they were spouting Shakespeare. The absolute devotion and self-sacrificing love was evident.

Cass was not built that way. Maybe because she was the baby, or because she'd always been more of a daddy's girl. Whatever the reason, Cass had never been able to identify a single maternal bone in her body. Sure, she loved her nieces and nephews. But Cass wasn't the type to sacrifice the success she'd worked so hard to achieve. As far as she was concerned, there was no balancing work and family life like her sisters did so effortlessly. When Cass did something, she did it a hundred percent. And she just couldn't give all of herself to a family. That probably made her a little selfish, but Cass was okay with that. It was a trait she recognized in herself and never made excuses for. She liked the praise that working hard brought her. She liked spending all of her time doing what made her happy. She liked having to be accountable only to and for herself. Her mother's entire identity was wrapped up in her family. Cass couldn't live that way. Gloria had given up her goals to raise her children. Not that she knew what her mother's goals were, but Cass was sure she'd had at least a few that didn't involve shuttling ungrateful teenagers around like a taxi service and making them home-cooked meals they never appreciated.

Cass was a kind and decent person who had no interest in ever having a family. She wasn't ashamed of it. Being able to admit the truth actually made her proud—like she could see her own shortcomings and accept them. But now, as she glanced around at her family, who'd all gone back to their conversations, she found herself feeling slightly . . . bereft. For the first time in her life, it bothered her that she wasn't more like the people surrounding her. *Alex is.* The thought popped into her head out of nowhere, but it was true. She often caught Alex running his hands through Nina's hair as they relaxed on the couch, or listening to her with rapt attention as she recounted every minor detail of her day. Yes, Alex would fit in nicely with her family. And for the first time in a long time, Cass wished she fit in too.

Alex's phone rang, the ringtone telling him who it was without him needing to glance at the caller ID. "Hey, Chris," he said as he flopped down on the sofa. He hadn't talked to his sister in a while—an occurrence that always made him feel guilty, even though he never did anything about it. Despite the fact that they loved and supported each other, they'd never been particularly close.

"Hey, stranger. How ya been?" Christina asked.

"Not too bad. You? How are the boys?" Alex hadn't told Christina about the drama with Tessa or his crazy plan for dealing with it, and he didn't intend to. Their conversations were always like this—superficial and brief. It wasn't that they didn't care about each other's lives. They did. But the Walkers were a stoic and self-reliant bunch. Their problems were just that: theirs. He and Christina had gotten a little closer when their mom had died when Alex was in college, bonded together a little tighter by the knowledge that they had only each other. But there was still an impenetrable distance between them. Their father had died of a heart attack when Alex was fourteen, and his mom had gone six years later, after a long and painful battle with breast cancer. Even though his mother had fought the illness for almost two years, Alex actually knew very little about her battle. She'd kept it largely to herself, suffering in silence because ... well, because that had been the way she was. The way they *all* were. That is, until they lost her, and Alex and Christina came to an unspoken agreement that they wanted more of a relationship than what they'd previously had. It wasn't much more, but it was something.

"They're good. Baseball season is starting, which is the busiest time of year for us. Between the school team and their traveling teams, it's a logistical nightmare." Christina sighed before pressing on. "But they love it, and I guess that's all that matters. How's Nina? We have to get together soon. I haven't seen her in months. She's probably getting so big."

Alex couldn't help the smile that drifted to his face, as often happened when he thought about Nina. She was the first person in his life that had really opened him up. Even with Tessa, despite the fact that he'd loved her, he'd never put himself fully out there for her. But he didn't hold himself back with Nina, at least not anymore. Wanting to be a better dad for her had woken him up, made him realize that he couldn't compartmentalize his entire world. Loving Nina had made him better in every aspect of his life. "She's growing like a weed. I swear, she's going to be six feet tall if she keeps going at her current rate."

Christina laughed. "It's amazing how time flies. It seems like just yesterday the boys were knee high. Now Caleb is taller than I am, and Price isn't far behind."

"We definitely have to get them all together. Maybe once summer hits we can arrange something." They lived only about forty-five minutes apart, but actually finding time to see each other was always like trying to arrange a meeting between foreign dignitaries.

They chatted for a few more minutes before Christina had to rush off to pick up one of the boys. And even though they'd made a promise to get together soon, Alex knew they probably wouldn't. It saddened him how okay with that he was.

Alex had a lot of acquaintances, but he wasn't particularly close to very many people. He had Scott and Xavier, who had somehow become staples in his life without him even realizing it. It often seemed like one day he hadn't even known who they were, and then the next the three of them were inseparable. He'd never had friends like that before those two—people who just barged into his life and staked a place there. Then there'd been Tessa, even though that had gone south fairly quickly. And, of course, Nina. Beyond that, Alex was a fairly private person.

But after hanging up with Christina, Alex felt . . . lonely. It was a feeling he wasn't used to. He normally found solace in being his own company. He looked around his empty apartment, and then down at the phone in his hand. He quickly typed out a text. What are you up to?

Cass' reply came almost immediately. Watching my nieces and nephews systematically break down their parents' sanity.

Alex laughed, thinking how preferable all of that sounded to what *he* was currently doing. He relaxed into the couch again and replied, hoping Cass wouldn't misinterpret his honesty for sarcasm. Sounds like fun.

Chapter 14

Emotional Intelligence

"Finally," Alex said, "a step in the wedding planning I can actually enjoy." He sliced into his prime rib, dipped it in horseradish and some mashed potatoes, and put it in his mouth. "How's the marsala?" he asked.

Cass finished chewing the piece of chicken that was in her mouth before speaking. She had to agree with Alex; going to a food tasting was fun. The venue was set up similarly to how they'd seen it when they'd visited before, with large round tables decorated with crisp black and white linens. Though the tables could hold up to ten people, there was only one other couple at theirs. Around the room's perimeter were several food stations, including options that were available at an extra cost. She'd already been up to the fondue station twice, loading a plate with white chocolate–covered strawberries for her and Alex to share. How could someone not love complimentary food and alcohol? "The sauce is fantastic," she said. "Do you want to try some?" She picked up a piece of chicken with her fork, dipped it in the brown sauce, making sure to get a mushroom too, and held it out for Alex to try. She thought he was going to take the fork from her, but instead he leaned in and opened his mouth so she could feed it to him.

"I like that too. And we both thought the blackened salmon was good. It's such a hard decision."

"I know, right? We're stuck too. The food is amazing here," a male voice across from her said, interrupting their conversation. They'd made small talk with Joe and Val when they'd arrived, but since then all four of them hadn't said much to one another; they had been too focused on the food to chat.

"Yeah, but we need to offer some healthy options as well," Val said.

"That's what the vegetarian option's for."

"Yeah, but that's pasta. Just because there are vegetables in it doesn't mean it's healthy."

"Can you just forget about your caloric intake for one day? It's our wedding." Joe let out an awkward laugh, probably just remembering that Cass and Alex were there.

Val rolled her eyes, but there was a playfulness to it. "Healthy eating is a way of life for me. You know that."

"This is true. She's constantly posting Facebook updates about her workouts and meals," Joe replied.

Val returned his comment with an elbow to the side, but her smile never broke.

He tossed an arm around her shoulders and placed a light peck on her cheek. "And somehow I love you despite that."

Though at first glance they appeared to be bickering, they seemed like they were actually in love. It made Cass suddenly self-conscious of her relationship with Alex. Could people tell that they weren't really a couple? If strangers could, then surely Tessa would be able to. Cass felt her expression fall at the thought. She knew how important this was for Alex.

Val gestured between them. "So, how did you two meet?" she asked between bites of tilapia.

Cass opened her mouth to answer, but Alex spoke before she had a chance to. "I'll tell it," he said, placing a hand gently on top of hers on the table.

She shot him a glance that she hoped conveyed how much she did *not* want him to get her back for the little tale she told while they were shopping for rings. She would have just told Val and Joe that they met through friends. This didn't seem like the time or place to discuss broken penises. *Of course, neither is a jewelry store.*

"It's really not that interesting of a story. We have mutual friends who were dating at the time," Alex began. Then he looked to Cass. "I guess 'dating' might not be an accurate term."

"They were definitely dating. They just didn't want to admit it."

"That's probably true," Alex agreed. "Anyway, because Lauren and Scott wanted to prove to everyone how *non*committed they were, they had us all meet at a club. The guys got there first, and we were grilling my buddy Scott about Lauren's friends, because he was the only one who'd met them."

"You grilled him about me?" Cass tried to act surprised, but truthfully she wasn't. It would have been more shocking if Alex hadn't asked any questions. He did it for a living.

"Well, not about you specifically. And it was actually Xavier. He just asked how hot all of you were." Alex shrugged as if it were no big deal.

Now Cass was interested. "And what did Scott say about me?"

Alex hesitated, and Cass was unsure if it was because he really couldn't remember or if he just didn't want to tell her. "He told us you were blond and compared you to a praying mantis," Alex said.

"A praying mantis? Why?"

"Because you were fun to look at, but if we got too close, you might bite our heads off."

This time Cass didn't have to feign her shock. But it wasn't because she was insulted. She just couldn't believe Scott had figured her out so easily after meeting her only once. "And what did you think when you saw me?"

Alex's expression softened at her question. He'd been laughing a bit at the memory, but his smile faded slightly until just one corner of his mouth was raised. She didn't even notice he'd slid his arm around to her back until his fingers began stroking her hair lightly. "That you were the most beautiful woman I'd ever seen."

Cass inhaled a shaky breath as she stared back into Alex's deep brown eyes. They were the kind that were so dark, she felt like if she gazed into them long enough, she might lose herself completely. And in that moment she did.

"That I had to have you," Alex continued. "You were all I thought about for weeks."

Cass swallowed the lump in her throat, unable to respond.

"Aww, that's so sweet," Val said. "So did you ask her out that night?"

Cass had almost forgotten that there were other people in the room, or, more specifically, at their table. As far as she was concerned, it was just her and Alex.

He broke eye contact with Cass so he could look across the table. "No. I just kind of let things progress naturally. I guess I hoped that she'd eventually feel the same way about me as I did about her."

Val's face lit up. "Well, obviously she does," she said, dragging out the last word. "Or she wouldn't be here with you now."

"Yeah, well I am pretty hard to resist." He shot Cass a wink.

Cass wasn't sure how to interpret the gesture. Was he winking because his last comment was a joke, or because his entire explanation was the joke and he couldn't believe Val and Joe had fallen for it? Cass knew that she was reading too much into it either way, but she found that she felt kind of let down. The emotions Alex's story stirred in her quickly fizzled into a sense of disappointment Cass couldn't explain.

"What club was it?" Joe asked, and Cass was thankful for the shift in the conversation.

"Nothing Gold. You ever been there?" Alex asked.

"Plenty of times. My cousin bartends there, actually," Joe said. "We'll probably all go there after the bachelor and bachelorette parties."

Cass' face lit up at the idea of a bachelorette party. How had she neglected to think about such an obvious part of wedding tradition? This might be her only chance to have a bachelorette party of her own, and she certainly wasn't going to miss it. "That's a good idea," she said, her eyes shifting to Alex to gauge his reaction. "We should do that when we have ours. You can go out with the guys, and I'll go out with the girls, and then we'll all meet up afterward."

Alex took a sip of his drink and gave her a genuine smile. It held a sweetness to it that she'd just realized she'd become accustomed to seeing lately. "Yeah, that'd be fun." He took his napkin off his lap and stood, placing it on the chair and holding his hand out for Cass to take it. "Now let's go get some cake."

They spent the next half hour or so stuffing their faces with red velvet, chocolate chip with cream cheese icing, and lemon pound cake. Then they grabbed two cups of coffee and headed outside.

"This place really *would* be beautiful for a wedding. I always thought it'd be nice to have an outdoor ceremony," Cass said, though she was speaking hypothetically, of course. She ran her hand along the smooth wooden deck railing and looked over the expansive grounds. The springtime grass was perfectly green, and the woods surrounding the venue gave the lawn an intimate privacy.

"Yeah, I wanted a place like this when Tessa and I got married—something outdoorsy, more rustic."

Cass turned her head toward him, her forearms resting comfortably on the railing. "Where'd you get married?"

Alex shook his head, but laughed loudly. "The Hilton."

"I'm guessing that was Tessa's choice?" she asked, though she knew the answer.

"You guessed right. The wedding's kind of the woman's thing. The guy's just along for the ride. You know?"

Cass understood what Alex was saying, but she didn't necessarily agree with it. "Yeah, but I never really got the whole bridezilla thing—why women get so worked up over one day when it's the rest of the marriage that's important." Cass pushed back off the railing and walked down the steps toward the grass.

"I found that out the hard way."

Cass couldn't contain her curiosity. She knew the ultimate end to Alex's marriage was Tessa's infidelity, but she didn't know the whole story. "What actually happened?" she asked, but she quickly realized Alex might not want to discuss it. "You don't have to answer if you don't want to, and this time I won't even make you take a shot of tequila."

Alex gave her a small smile, one that let her know she hadn't crossed the line. He shrugged but hung his head. "It's okay. It's pretty simple, really; I was married to my career instead of my wife. For a long time I blamed Tessa because she was the one who cheated. But truthfully, I left the marriage long before she did. It doesn't really matter that I didn't leave it for another person."

Cass knew this wasn't something Alex shared with just anyone. He was a private person when it came to his family. And she was thankful he included her in that small circle of those who knew the circumstances of their split. "You asked me why I never wanted to get married and have a family, but I never answered you," she said.

Alex nodded.

"Well, you basically just summed it up for me. I'm pretty career-minded, if you haven't noticed."

"I have."

Cass laughed quietly. "I just know I don't have the time for everything. I see all these moms like my sisters running around to work and their kids' practices. They cook dinner and help with homework, and somehow manage to still look presentable." Cass directed her line of vision toward the ground and dug at a divot in the dirt with the toe of her shoe. "It's just not me, you know? I can't do all of it, and something would have to get sacrificed." She raised her head again, her hazel eyes piercing into Alex's dark brown ones. "My fear is that I'll sacrifice the wrong thing."

She knew Alex couldn't tell her she wouldn't. He'd made the same mistake she was scared to make. So as she'd expected, he didn't say anything. He just put his arms around her and pulled her close. And somehow that was exactly what she needed.

Chapter 15

Arson

Cass stuffed the chicken into a plastic grocery bag, tied it up, and then plopped it into Alex's kitchen trash can. "The mashed potatoes are still okay," she said with a shrug. "Not quite sure what happened to the main course."

Alex waved the remainder of the smoke toward the window he'd opened. "I'm pretty sure you burned it."

"*We* burned it," she joked. "It's your kitchen, so I refuse to take sole responsibility." Though, truthfully, she should have. When she'd offered to make dinner for Alex and Nina, she'd said that she had a great recipe for baked chicken. And it wasn't a lie. The *recipe* was great. It was the execution that left something to be desired. Her mother had even talked her through it on the phone the day before, reminding her to take off the aluminum foil fifteen minutes before she removed it from the oven, so the skin would get a little bit crispy. But it didn't matter. By the time the three of them had come inside from drawing sidewalk-chalk murals, it was too late. "My mom said to let it cook for forty-five minutes. I don't know what happened."

Alex looked at the display on the oven. "On four fifty?"

Shit. Cass bit her bottom lip. "I think I might have been about a hundred degrees off."

Alex laughed, flashing a bright smile that comforted Cass as he handed her a menu out of his junk drawer. Then he called to Nina, who was in the powder room, washing her hands. "Do you want chicken fingers or a cheeseburger, Nina?"

"Chicken fingers," she yelled back. "With honey mustard."

"This is my treat," Cass insisted. "I promised you dinner. Takeout I can do. Cooking, not so much. I'm not sure how my mom managed to make a home-made meal almost every night for five people. That right there," she said, pointing toward the trash, "is the stuff nightmares are made of."

"I'm not letting you buy us dinner," Alex said. "You already paid for the chicken. And Nina's *my* daughter," he added.

Cass lowered her voice. "If I can't *cook* dinner for my pretend future husband and stepdaughter, then at least let me buy it." She looked up from the menu, her eyes pleading with him in a way she knew would make him cave.

"All right," Alex said, dragging out the second word. "But they don't deliver, so at least let me go pick it up." Then he added, "As long as you don't mind hanging with Nina for a half hour or so."

Cass wasn't going to argue with that. Though she hadn't spent a ton of solo time with Alex's daughter, the time they had spent together had been fun. Nina was fairly mature for her age. Combine that with Cass' immaturity, and the two of them averaged somewhere around fourteen years old. "Sure," Cass said, glancing toward Nina as she entered the kitchen. "Your dad's gonna go pick up the food. You want to hang out with me for a little while?"

Nina's eyes lit up with what looked to be excitement. "Yeah, okay," Nina said. "Can you paint my toenails like yours?"

Cass looked down at her light turquoise polish. Since the weather had finally started to warm up a bit, she'd just gotten a pedicure a few days before. "Um, well I don't have this color here."

"That's okay," Nina said. "I have purple. I brought it from home, but Daddy doesn't know how to paint nails right."

Alex folded his arms across his chest. He'd been watching them silently until that moment. "Is that supposed to be an insult?" Alex asked. "Because I feel like it would be more embarrassing if I did."

The fact that Nina referred to her mom's house as "home" made Cass' heart break a little for Alex. But if he noticed Nina's word choice, Alex didn't let on. Maybe he'd just become so desensitized to it that he didn't even hear it anymore. Or maybe he'd just come to accept a hard truth: that Tessa's house *was* home to Nina. It's where she spent the majority of her time and where Nina probably felt a sense of family. And that's when Cass' heart broke for Nina too. She wished Nina had that at her father's house too. "I've got the nail thing covered," she said with a wink. "You just worry about dinner." Then Nina grabbed Cass' hand and began to pull her down the hall toward the foyer. "I'll take the blackened chicken alfredo," Cass called from the bottom of the stairs before she let Nina guide her up to her room.

Alex had waited at the restaurant longer than he'd expected to. He'd chosen that one because he knew it was one that Cass loved. Despite the fact that it was the only spot in town that had authentic Cajun cuisine, their service was usually pretty quick. But he'd had to wait a half hour when he'd arrived, and he hoped Cass wasn't having to deal with a hungry and irritable Nina. It was already going on eight thirty, and he hadn't even given his daughter dinner yet. Maybe there was some validity to Tessa's argument that he'd have a difficult time being a full-time father.

He shot Cass a quick text when he left the restaurant to say he was on his way, but by the time he pulled in his garage fifteen minutes later, he still hadn't gotten a response. *I hope Cass survived.*

He pushed open the door and walked through the foyer to the family room. His fears were assuaged when he saw the girls on the couch, so engrossed in whatever movie they were watching, neither of them even turned around to acknowledge his presence. He walked quietly to the kitchen, gently setting the bag of food on the counter. Though it was getting late, part of him didn't want to interrupt them. He felt as if he were observing a natural phenomenon that shouldn't be disturbed. He leaned back against the counter, taking them both in. Cass rested comfortably on the couch, her body leaning against the plush armrest. She must have thrown her thick blond hair up into a loose bun sometime after he'd left. Nina sat next to her, noticeably closer to Cass than she needed to be. Her dark brown hair was now in two long braids, and Alex had no doubt that Cass must have done it; they were too perfect to have been Nina's work. He heard a chime and Cass picked up her phone. She looked at it quickly before setting it back to sleep and putting it back down next to her.

Finally he pushed off the counter and approached them slowly as he moved toward the love seat. "Food's here," he said. Their heads snapped in his direction, no doubt in his mind that they'd just noticed he'd gotten home. "Sorry it took so long."

Cass sat upright, stretching her arms in the air. "No problem. We had girl time. Hair, pedicures," she said, pointing to Nina's freshly polished toes. "I let her eat a little snack though. Hope you don't mind. It was getting kind of late and she was hungry."

Alex shook his head and gave her a small smile. "Thanks."

"I'll still eat the chicken fingers though," Nina said. "I only had an apple."

As they rose from the couches and headed into the kitchen, Cass' phone chimed again. "This stupid thing." Cass pushed a few buttons and then slid it into her back pocket.

"You need to get that?" Alex asked.

"Nah, it's just my boss sending me some info he wants me to review. It can wait."

Alex nodded. The three of them moved through the room silently, getting out plates and silverware, pouring drinks, and setting napkins on the table, as if they'd done it countless times before. And as they sat down to eat and Alex let his eyes drift over to Cass and Nina, a part of him wished this seemingly rehearsed dance would continue.

Chapter 16

Noise Complaint

Alex dipped a fry into some cheese and popped it into his mouth. "Too bad the music's not as good as the food," he said. "And their food isn't really all that good." His expression remained serious, but Cass recognized the hint of humor in his voice.

"Would you stop being a grump and give it a chance? This is just the opening band anyway." Cass took a sip of her Corona Light and put it down on the cardboard coaster. Though she was quick to defend the music, part of her was slightly worried. Alex was right. These guys sounded like a high school garage band.

"Do you think they take requests?" Alex asked, pointing toward the stage.

"Probably. What did you want to request?"

Alex set his drink down. "Silence," he said without cracking a smile. "I hope the band we're here to see is better."

"You're an ass," Cass joked. "And Simone swore they were good. She went to college with the drummer. She's heard them play a thousand times."

Alex looked unconvinced. "After the last band Simone dragged us to, I'm not sure I trust her taste in music. How come you've never seen them before?"

Good question. Cass shrugged. "Not sure. But Cockfeather plays weddings all the time. I'm sure they'll will be fine for a party."

Alex nearly spit out his drink. "Cockfeather?"

Guess I forgot to tell him the name.

"There's no way we're hiring a band named Cockfeather. Even for a party to celebrate a fake wedding." Alex laughed. "We have to maintain *some* standards."

"What's wrong with their name?" Cass asked, like she didn't know why Alex had an issue.

He rolled his eyes. "Come on, Cass. You're not going to sit there and try to convince me that they named themselves after a rooster's plumage or something, are you?"

Cass stared back at Alex, trying her best to keep a straight face. "Doesn't that seem more plausible than it referring to the other meaning? Out of all the penises I've seen, I have yet to come across one with feathers on it."

Alex looked slightly disgusted. But he didn't argue. Obviously he knew she had a point.

"Besides," she said, "don't judge a book by its cover. The lead singer won a bronze medal in archery at the Olympics years ago. A cock feather is one of those colored feathers on an arrow. They just combined the words because they thought a one-word name looked better on T-shirts."

"Stop," Alex said. "You're making that up. No way there's something called a cock feather."

Cass took out her phone and immediately began Googling. "One of these days you'll learn never to doubt me." She thrust the phone at Alex, and then leaned back against the booth as he read silently. His eyes widened. "I had the same reaction you did when Simone told me about them. I was actually disappointed that their name came from something so innocuous."

"No shit?" Alex said, his eyes still fixed on the screen.

"Go ahead. Read it out loud." Cass loved being right almost as much as she loved hearing Alex say the word "cock."

"'Cock feather,'" he began, and Cass had to hold in a laugh. "'The colored feathers on the shaft of an arrow at right angles to the nock. Also called a shaft feather.'" Alex burst out laughing, and Cass joined him. "I feel like 'shaft feather' sounds even worse."

"It definitely does." Cass took one more bite of her burger before deciding she was done. She had to admit, Alex was right about one thing; the food wasn't that good.

The current band played one more song before Cock-feather came out to the small stage located in the corner of the bar. Alex eyed the band, an eclectic mix of humans. He did his best to shut off his tendency to analyze people, but it was part of his nature—and his job—to do so. Cockfeather had four members, and it shouldn't have surprised him that the person with the shortest hair was also the only woman. She had the physique he was beginning to associate with all lead singers: an emaciated look that he guessed served two purposes: one, it allowed her to survive off ramen noodles and flaxseed while she lived out of her van; and two, it gave some credence to the whole starving-artist thing.

Two of the guys had longer hair; one had his pulled back in a ponytail, and the other wore it down in front of his shoulders. But the third guy was the deal breaker. No way Alex's buddies would ever let him live it down if he hired a band that included a member who thought a pink Mohawk and a shirt that said CLOUDY WITH A CHANCE OF TITTIES was a solid fashion statement.

But despite Alex's initial judgement, he had to admit that the band knew how to play. Much of the previously disinterested crowd had now gotten on to the small dance floor in front of the stage. Cockfeather played a mix of covers, from "Boys of Summer" to "Tainted Love" and their own spin on Taylor Swift's "Bad Blood." He could definitely see their appeal. Cass had been subtly dancing in her seat for at least ten minutes, and even Alex found himself nodding to the beat. And it wasn't long before his whole body wanted to move. "You want to dance?" Alex asked, gesturing toward the crowd.

Cass put a hand to her chest and rose from the booth, smiling. "I thought you'd never ask."

Alex stood, leading her by the hand through the maze of tables toward the stage, until he found a place on the dance floor where they had some space. He wasn't much of a dancer, at least not before a few drinks. But something about being near Cass, her body swaying to the beat, made him *want* to dance. Or maybe it was just that he wanted to dance with *her*.

The two moved in time to the rhythm, or at least Cass did. Alex wasn't so sure about himself. But for some reason it didn't bother him. "So, the lead singer really went to the Olympics for archery?" he yelled over the music.

"Yeah, that's what Simone said. I may be creative, but the truth is definitely better than fiction this time."

"That's impressive. And I'm sure this makes me sound sexist, but I pictured a man when you told me that," Alex said, glancing up at the frail woman whose mouth was pressed so close to the microphone, he was sure she'd probably licked it a few times.

"Me too," Cass replied. "Then I found out her name was Slim and all I could picture was Jennifer Lopez from that movie *Enough.*" Alex's expression must have revealed his confusion, so Cass continued. "She plays this woman who's a victim of domestic violence. She runs away with her daughter to escape her ex. But when she realizes he won't stop coming after her until she's dead, she takes a self-defense class and comes up with an elaborate plan to kill him before he gets to her and her little girl."

"Wait, I'm still confused. So Jennifer Lopez's name is Slim in the movie?"

"Oh yeah," Cass said on a laugh. "Sorry. Guess I never said that. She's a complete badass in that movie. We should watch it."

The song came to an end, and Slim said something into the microphone about CDs being for sale after the show.

"I mean, it's no *Billy Madison,*" Cass joked, "but I think you'll like it."

And Alex had no doubt that was true. He enjoyed spending time with Cass, no matter what they were doing. Her carefree nature was a good balance to Alex's serious side—which had been making an appearance less often lately. But when he heard the first few chords to "Simple Man," one of his all-time favorite songs, he felt that part of himself emerging again. "I love this song," he said, pulling Cass in close to him. Her chest pressed against his, and his body responded immediately. But his reaction was more visceral than sexual. He could feel her breathing change. The rapid breaths she'd been taking as they danced to the faster songs had slowed considerably to match the song's rhythm. He looked down at her, Cass' eyes meeting his as he moved some stray hairs from her face and tucked them behind her ear. "My mom used to sing it to me when I was a kid."

Cass gave him a small smile, one that made him feel a sense of comfort he hadn't felt in a long time. "Tell me about her," she said.

Cass took another bite of ice cream and brought both her legs onto the couch, crossing them so she could face Alex fully. When she'd asked about his mother, the comment had just kind of left her mouth before she'd had a chance to fully think about what she was saying.

He could have said no to sharing something so personal with her. But instead he'd just said he'd rather have the conversation in a more private location. And it had been Cass' idea to pick up the ice cream on the way to Alex's house. No emotional purge would be complete without it.

So now here they were, sitting in Alex's family room with a half-gallon of mint chocolate chip and two spoons between them. He'd told her about his mom—how she used to bake peanut butter cookies every Christmas, and she'd always let Alex put the Hershey's Kisses on the top. And how she could never stay angry with him for more than fifteen minutes. How she always stood up for her children—defended them—even if they weren't always deserving of her defense. "She could do anything." Alex smiled. "Or at least it seemed that way when I was a kid. We always had the best jack-o'-lantern in the neighborhood because she had one of those books that showed how to do carvings of famous people. She'd do most of the work, but she'd let me and Christina take the credit for it."

Cass could see why Alex was so good with Nina. He'd had a good teacher. "She sounds sweet."

"She was," Alex said. Then he let out a soft laugh. "Most of the time. But she had a way of keeping us in line that even my dad didn't have. It was weird. I was a little afraid to get in trouble with my dad, but I just didn't want to disappoint my mom. She never gave long lectures or yelled or anything like that. Christina and I just kind of knew her thoughts without her having to say them."

Cass knew exactly what Alex meant. "My dad was the one who was like that with us. I remember one time in eighth grade . . . the first time I tried smoking." Cass chuckled at the memory. "I guess it was also the *last* time I tried it. My friends and I were hanging out in front of a convenience store a few blocks away from our middle school, and this girl Joanna had gotten some guy to buy cigarettes for us. Joanna smoked already, and I'd said I'd try it. She gave me a lit cigarette, but even though I only took a small drag from it, I started coughing immediately." Cass realized that she'd accidentally shifted the conversation from Alex to herself, but he didn't seem to mind. He was looking at her with rapt attention as he put a bite of ice cream in his mouth. So she continued.

"Joanna and Lauren—the Lauren you know—told me to try it again and inhale this time. So I put the cigarette up to my mouth and tried again. Then I heard Laur yell, 'Cass, your dad!' The phrase had its intended effect because I breathed in quickly and then let the smoke out easily. It was a trick that people in my school used to do to get their friends to inhale, so I didn't think anything of it. I just smiled proudly until I heard my dad say, 'Get in the car, Cassidy.' I looked over my shoulder, and he was in the parking lot."

"Oh man. Seriously?"

Cass raised her eyebrows. "Seriously."

"What did he do?"

"Nothing. It's what he didn't do that had the biggest effect on me. The ride home was silent. He didn't yell, he didn't talk to me, he didn't even look at me. He just drove me home, turned off the ignition, and sighed before going inside."

"He didn't punish you?"

"He didn't ground me if that's what you mean. But I got my punishment. Letting him down was enough. Smoking was the one thing that I knew my dad would never tolerate. His father died of lung cancer when my dad was a teenager." Cass bit her bottom lip. "He wasn't mad; he was hurt, and the guilt I felt was worse than any punishment he could've given me." Cass shook her head. "Sorry. This wasn't supposed to be about me."

Alex gave her a warm smile and reached out to rub her knee. "Don't be sorry," he said. "I like hearing stuff like that. I just need it in small doses, because the father in me wants to put Nina in some sort of cocoon and freeze her there indefinitely. I don't know how any man raises three girls."

"Well, if it helps, I think you have a while before Nina starts packing a miniskirt in her backpack so you don't see her leave the house in it."

Alex's eyes widened in what Cass identified as horror. "Do girls really do that?"

Cass swallowed. "Would it help if I said not *all* girls do it?"

Alex stared at her, his expression blank as he shook his head slowly.

"So tell me about the song," Cass said, hoping to bring the subject back to the reason for their conversation. "'Simple Man.' Did she sing it to you as a baby?"

Alex remained quiet for a moment. "She sang it to me for as long as I can remember, but I'm not sure when it actually began," he said. "I just know when it ended." Alex dropped his gaze to the spoon in his hand and began moving it over the ice cream in the carton without picking any up. "My entire life I heard how all she wanted was for me to grow up to be happy and have a family of my own. But she died before she got to see either of those things. And the worst part is, I wasn't even there for her." Cass narrowed her eyes in confusion, and Alex continued. "I was up at school when she relapsed." Now Alex fixed his stare on Cass while he spoke. "I could've come home, taken the semester off. She'd been in remission. I knew the cancer might come back, but I chose to enroll in a school hours away from home."

Cass' heart went out to him when she realized the guilt he must have felt—the guilt he must *still* be feeling. "You were a kid."

Alex let out a humorless laugh and shook his head. "I hadn't been a kid since my dad passed away when I was fourteen. It wasn't long after that when my mom was diagnosed with breast cancer for the first time. And when that happened, any trace of innocence I had left disappeared."

Cass wanted to reach out and touch his hand, put her arms around him. But there was nothing she could do to make anything better. So she chose just to listen.

"Looking back on it, I probably went to Brown because I needed the space—almost like the physical distance might disconnect me from the situation altogether. But it had the opposite effect. Since I had no idea how she was, I probably worried about her more at school than I would have if I'd been home." Alex paused for a moment and propped his head on his hand, resting his elbow on the top of the couch. "She promised me she was okay and that she'd get through it, and part of me believed her. She told me to stay at school and try not to worry because Christina was there. She had an apartment nearby with friends, and she'd moved back in when my mom got sick again. But *I* should've been there too. I mean, I know I couldn't have done anything to change the outcome. That always would've been the same. But I could've been there. So much of life is just showing up." Alex let the words out in a rush, like he'd been holding them in for so long that once he'd started speaking, he couldn't make himself stop until he'd said all he'd needed to say.

Cass didn't know how to respond. So she decided not to say anything. Instead, she reached out to take his hand, running her thumb over the top. Gradually her hand worked its way softly up his arm to his shoulder and around the back of his neck. She ran her fingers through the rough hair on the back of his head, and Alex let out a low growl as he closed his eyes. Cass took that as the invitation she'd been hoping for. Not that she ever needed one. She'd made the first move plenty of times.

But tonight felt different. Alex had just opened himself up to her—shared something incredibly personal to him, and she wasn't sure how he'd felt about it. She didn't want to take the moment to a place he didn't want it to go. But the current physical contact wasn't enough for her. She needed to be closer, needed to feel Alex's hard body pressed against her— his weight on her as the scruff on his face brushed roughly against her skin. Just the thought sent a chill through her whole body.

"You okay?" Alex asked, in an obvious response to her sudden shiver.

"Yeah," Cass answered softly as she leaned into him and placed a gentle kiss on his lips. They parted slightly, just enough for their tongues to touch and for Alex to tug on her bottom lip with his teeth. Gradually their movements increased their speed, their hands tugging at each other's clothes until both sets lay in a pile next to the couch.

Alex hovered above her, placing light kisses on her forehead and down her neck to her chest. She watched how he explored her, his fingers trailing up and down her sides and over her breasts. She sucked in a sharp breath as his teeth grazed over one of her nipples before his mouth was on it completely. She was certain that the wet warmth of it matched what she felt between her thighs.

Her entire body ached for the man. But she didn't want to be the sole recipient of this pleasure. She suddenly had the urge to run her tongue over his whole body, like he'd done to her countless times. So she pressed her hands against his chest, guiding him back to a sitting position on the couch and straddling him so that his erection pressed against her in just the right way.

Alex let out a groan as she slid against him. "God, you're so fucking sexy," he rasped as his hands roughly massaged her breasts. His eyes locked with hers, and he bit his lip as his hips moved in perfect circles below her. "You're gonna make me come if you keep doing this."

She thought about telling him no, that she wanted him inside her. But what they were already doing felt so good, so raw. She dropped her gaze to watch the tip of his cock pressing against his stomach as she slipped along his long shaft. Cass could come like this too—admiring his slippery erection beneath her, the way his head fell back against the top of the couch cushion.

"Cass," Alex let out through a breath as his hands gripped her hips to slow her motion.

She knew her name was a warning. But she didn't heed it. "I want to watch you," she whispered, and the admission seemed to surprise Alex as much as it did her.

His eyes widened as he let out a deep moan. Now he did nothing to hinder Cass' movements. Both of them were frantic, racing toward an end they both knew was near. Cass could feel her body begin to tense, her smooth strokes over Alex's cock becoming sharper and more erratic. Alex's eyes were barely open, his eyelids fluttering in pleasure. The tip of his cock was nearly purple and beaded with moisture.

"I'm so close, Alex."

He choked out a few unsteady breaths in response and squeezed her ass with both his hands.

The feeling caused her to grind against him even harder, and she felt her orgasm nearing to the point that she wouldn't be able to hold it off much longer. Not that she wanted to. "Oh God," she huffed. It took only a few more strokes of her body over his before his cock was spurting onto his stomach in quick bursts. And that was all Cass needed to push her over the edge. Her insides clenched as she slid over his length, milking every drop from him as she rode out her own climax.

The release was different from anything she'd ever experienced before. It was sweet. It was consuming. And it was fucking dirty as hell. She looked at the remnants of their encounter between them and then gave Alex a soft kiss on his lips before standing to take both his hands in hers. "How about a shower?" she asked.

Chapter 17

Press Release

Alex wasn't sure who had suggested that they spend their evening at the trendy new club, Haven, but he was banking on Simone. *We really need to demote that girl from being our group's social planner.* The place was all hazy air and flashing lights. And if Alex saw one more gym rat who'd managed to squeeze himself into a kids' medium white shirt, he was going to lose his shit. It didn't help that the girls were all bouncing around on the dance floor, attracting the attention of every guy in the place. They'd done a fairly good job of closing ranks around one another, keeping the *Jersey Shore* look-alikes at bay, but Alex didn't think they'd be deterred for too long. Beside him, Scott was getting antsy. He was tasked with not only making sure Lauren didn't get the police called on her, but also with making sure no one got handsy with Quinn.

Alex also had initially declined the invitation to channel his inner fist pumper. He had been feeling a little . . . conflicted lately. He wasn't sure if he and Cass were getting too into the wedding planning or if it was a by-product of all the time they'd been spending together, but things were shifting between them. The fact that he'd told her about his mom's cancer battle—a topic he normally avoided at all costs—was a big enough sign that they were venturing into dangerous territory. They hadn't spoken about what was going on between them, so he had no idea if Cass felt the same, which only made him more uncomfortable. He didn't want their fake relationship to screw with their real one. It was easy to play the role of happy fiancé, but he needed it to remain just that: a role. Letting himself get too caught up in the ruse could have disastrous consequences. So despite thinking that they'd both benefit from a night out without the other around, he'd caved. It was Tessa's weekend with Nina, and Alex's best friends were going to Haven. It wasn't that he didn't have other friends he could call and hang out with, but his best friends were here. He wouldn't have been as happy anywhere else.

But as he watched Cass flitter off toward the bar—with the leers and smirks that followed her—he realized he wasn't too happy here either.

"I feel like I should have bathed in self-tanner before coming in here," Xavier remarked.

Alex and Scott laughed. "I'm actually surprised they didn't ask to see proof of a gym membership when they carded us at the door," Alex added.

"The girls are enjoying themselves." Scott's tone made it clear that he wasn't pleased by that fact.

Alex's eyes drifted back to the bar. He felt his body tense as he saw Cass still waiting for her drink. She wasn't alone. Alex felt himself slip into investigator mode. The guy who'd moved to stand next to her wasn't like the majority of the male patrons he'd been making fun of for most of the night. He was actually fairly normal-looking: dark hair, medium build, maybe a little shorter than Alex's six-foot-one frame, and dressed in clothes that didn't look like they came from Baby Gap. Alex instantly hated him.

Cass seemed engaged in the conversation, which only irritated Alex further. Suddenly, he wished that Cass had worn the ring he'd given her. Because even though his view of them was partially obscured by other patrons and by the distance between him and the bar, he still recognized interest when he saw it. And he saw it in both of them. In a few months, when this sham was over, Alex wouldn't care at all if Cass flirted with another guy. But for now, he couldn't risk a friend of Tessa's recognizing him and reporting back that his so-called fiancée was eye-fucking strangers at the bar. Or exchanging . . . *Wait, is he giving her his number?*

Alex all but slammed his still-half-full beer on the tabletop. "I need a drink." He stalked off before his friends could reply. Striding up to the bar, he didn't let himself think about what he was going to do or say when he arrived. If he had, maybe he would've come up with something less cavemanish than wrapping an arm around Cass as he pulled her closer to him and said, "Hey, babe. Who's your friend?"

Cass wasn't sure what she was more surprised by: Connor's—*That's his name, right?*—persistence or Alex's possessiveness. She'd been trying to politely disengage from Connor since he'd approached, but the bar was jammed, so she'd gotten stuck talking to him. Not that there was a solid reason she didn't *want* to talk to him. He was polite and good-looking. So she'd been smiling and nodding for the past five or so minutes, all the while hoping like hell the bartender hurried up.

She wasn't even sure why she was so disinterested. Maybe it was because she was here to hang out with her friends, not score a date. Or maybe because she was here with Alex, though that didn't make sense to her. It wasn't like she was on bride-to-be duty. If she wanted to talk to a guy whom she wasn't pretending to marry, then she could. But she didn't *want* to. And that realization nearly short-circuited her brain. Cass wasn't some kind of bar slut, but she liked to keep her options open. She enjoyed playing the field a little—it was a decided benefit of her insistence to remain single. But talking to this guy felt wrong in every way, and yet in no way she could identify. She'd accepted his number when he'd written it on a bar napkin, and even tried not to judge him for the old-school move. None of it mattered. "Disinterested" didn't even begin to encompass the depth of her feelings. Which was why she'd been so happy to see Alex. Until he'd basically yanked her into him and practically pissed on her leg. That shit was *so* not going to fly.

"This is Connor. Connor, this is my friend Alex." She made sure to enunciate "friend," more to piss off Alex than to clarify anything to Connor.

Connor extended his hand. "Nice to meet you."

Cass felt bad for him. Connor looked legitimately confused, and she couldn't blame him. She was pretty confused herself.

Alex grasped Connor's hand after he'd sufficiently eyeballed the poor guy for a few seconds. "Nice to meet you too." Alex shifted his body so he was fully

facing Cass, a silent *Fuck off* to Connor. "You still waiting on your drink?"

Cass eyed him warily, wondering what the hell his
deal was. "Uh, yeah?" She wasn't sure why it came out
like a question, but she could attribute it only to her
confusion over what was happening.

"Let me see if I can flag him down." Alex stepped
up to the bar, forcing his body between Cass and
Connor. He raised a hand at the bartender.

Connor looked around Alex's back. "It was nice
meeting you, Cass."

Even though Cass had wanted Connor to go away
since he'd approached her, she felt bad about the
way Alex had basically forced him away from her.
Connor didn't deserve to be pulled into whatever dick-
measuring contest Alex had challenged him to. She
actually gave him credit for not stooping to Alex's
level. "You too, Connor."

Connor left, and Alex turned and leaned against
the bar. "This place is nuts."

"Yeah, almost as nuts as you are."

Alex's brow furrowed. "What do you mean?"

"What the hell was that?"

"What was what?"

"Don't play dumb." Cass felt herself getting more
and more riled. She was angry at Alex's brutish display, and his feigned innocence wasn't helping.

Alex shrugged. "I thought he was bothering you, so
I came to help out."

"And why would you assume he was bothering me?"

"He just didn't seem like your normal type. I figured you needed an exit strategy, so I thought I'd
give you one. I was just trying to protect you."

"You were just trying to protect me? How? By making some poor guy feel like an asshole for trying to talk to me?" Then Cass remembered the first part of what Alex had said. "And how the hell do you know what my type is?"

Alex's jaw flexed as though he were gnashing his teeth. He was getting pissed. *Good.* "Guess I don't."

"No. No, you really don't. And just for the record, I can protect myself."

Alex took a breath and let it out in a long huff. "Sorry. I didn't mean it like that. I know you don't need someone taking care of you. It's just . . . I wasn't sure if . . ." Alex left his thought unfinished, but he didn't stop talking. "What if one of Tessa's friends had seen you? We're supposed to be engaged, you and me." He motioned between them. "You can't just talk to other guys in public like that."

Cass glared at Alex as she tried to quell the anger rising inside her. "Don't tell me what I can and can't do." And with that, Cass whirled around and walked back to their table. Quinn and Simone were there with Xavier. "Where are Lauren and Scott?"

Quinn nodded toward the dance floor. "Out there practicing for their wedding night."

The last thing Cass wanted to hear was the word "wedding." She grabbed the gin and tonic Quinn had been nursing for the past hour and took a swig. "Should we join them?"

Quinn and Simone exchanged a look before Quinn said, "Uh, sure."

Cass threw herself into the music, letting her body bump and grind on anyone in her vicinity. She knew she was punishing Alex for his over-the-top display. She also knew that what he'd done didn't warrant the anger she was feeling. The urge to punish him was beyond her comprehension, but she suspected that it had to do with Alex thinking he could claim her just because they were in a pretend relationship. The arm around the shoulder, the "babe," the hostility toward Connor—all of it was part of the illusion they were creating. Okay, so maybe it wasn't that far beyond her comprehension after all. Because the more she thought about it, the more she recognized that the anger was covering up a much scarier emotion: hurt.

She leaned into Simone so she could be heard over the blaring techno. "I think I'm going to take off. I'm not feeling too great all of a sudden."

Simone appraised her for a second before yelling back, "I'll walk you out."

Cass shook her head. "I'll ask Xavier to walk me. Have fun." Cass threw her a smile before walking off the dance floor. She started toward their table, but stopped when her eyes locked with Alex's. Instead of continuing toward him, she changed her trajectory and made her way toward the exit.

"I'll be back," Alex said to Xavier before following Cass out of the bar. He'd been a dick earlier, and Cass was obviously royally pissed at him. In all honesty, he wasn't sure that what he'd done had been deserving of the level of ire she'd exhibited, but he hated knowing that he'd made her mad at him. She'd been so good to him over the past couple of months—helped him above and beyond what could reasonably be expected from a friend—so if he needed to beg for forgiveness, he would.

Once outside, he jogged to catch up to her. "Cass, hold up a sec." He was actually surprised when she stopped. "I'm sorry about before. I really didn't mean to piss you off."

Cass turned toward him and took a deep breath before meeting his eyes. "I know. But you did."

Alex pushed his hands into his pockets. "I just . . . I didn't . . . God, I don't know . . ." He sighed deeply and tried to figure out what he wanted to say. "I guess it's just harder than I thought it would be. To turn the relationship thing off and on. I mean, I obviously know that the relationship isn't real, but it's weird to go from picking out wedding food and bands to watching another guy flirt with you. It fucked up my head, and I wasn't thinking clearly."

Cass seemed to think his words over for a second before one corner of her mouth tilted up in a slight smirk. "So you're saying you were jealous?"

Alex pushed one hand through his hair, thankful that the mood seemed to be lightening. "I think your fiancé was jealous more than I was."

Cass laughed. "What? Do you have multiple personalities now?"

Alex chuckled but sobered quickly. "Don't we both?"

"Yeah. I guess we do," she replied, her tone now more serious.

"This may be totally unreasonable for me to ask, but do you think that, for the sake of us trying to navigate all this confusing stuff we have going on, that we could keep other people out of the equation?"

Cass sighed. "I wasn't trying to factor anyone else *into* the equation. I was just talking to him. Not making plans to slip off to the nearest bathroom stall."

Alex winced at her words. *Is that what she believes I thought?* "I didn't think that's what was happening. I'm sorry if I came across that way. It's probably just my own insecurities coming out. My real wife cheated on me, so watching a guy be interested in my pretend future wife pushed all the wrong buttons. It doesn't excuse how I reacted, but it's the only explanation I have."

She shifted slightly. "No, that makes a lot of sense, actually," she said, hesitating as if deciding what to say. Despite the fact that they were hashing things out, there remained a certain level of emotional distance between them. "So, you wanna, like, go steady, huh?" Cass laughed, and Alex immediately felt some more of the tension melt away.

Alex smiled. "I know it's a little backward—getting engaged before declaring monogamy—but it suits us, I think." Alex let the smile slip off his face. "What I'm asking isn't really fair to you. I know that. You don't stand to gain anything from this arrangement, and now here I am, asking you to put your life on hold and not see other people until this is over. But I . . . I'd really appreciate if you'd agree to do it anyway."

Cass stepped closer to him. "You're about all I can handle right now anyway." She slipped her arms around his neck. "Besides, who says I'm not gaining anything? You can repay me in sexual favors."

And right before she pressed her lips to his, all Alex could think about was how he was still coming out ahead.

Chapter 18

Lawyer Up

Nina was bouncing up and down as much as she could with her seat belt buckled as she sat in Cass' backseat. "Can I get any dress I want?"

Cass glanced in the rearview mirror and shrugged. "Sure. I guess." Nina had been bugging Alex for weeks about her dress, so Cass had offered to take her. But she hadn't actually discussed anything about the dress with Alex. He'd just given her his credit card so she could pay for the dress and Nina could take it home with her when Cass dropped her off at Tessa's afterward. "Do you know what color you want to get?"

Nina put a finger to her lips like she was thinking hard. "White. I want it to match yours."

Cass diverted her eyes from Nina and focused back on the road ahead of her. There wouldn't be any matching Cass' dress because there wouldn't be a dress at all. Unfortunately, Nina would never get to wear hers either.

Cass was thankful for a chance to change the subject when she pulled into the parking lot. "Here we are. There's Lauren," Cass said, pointing to her best friend, who was already standing in front of the store, waiting for them.

Nina couldn't get out of the car fast enough, but Cass grabbed her hand before she ran across the parking lot toward the store.

"Hey, Nina," Lauren said. "You excited to try on some dresses with me?"

Nina nodded enthusiastically as they entered the store.

Lauren had asked to come along so she could try on a few dresses herself, and Cass was thankful to have her there. It would give Cass something to focus on besides looking at flower-girl dresses for a little girl who wouldn't actually get to *be* a flower girl. A wave of guilt washed over her. It was the first time Cass had really second-guessed this whole thing.

But she didn't have time to harp on her decision for too long, because Nina was already moving around the store at rapid speed. "Come on, Cass. I can't find them," she called from the side of the store.

Cass put a finger up for Nina to wait a minute.

As expected at a bridal shop, one of the consultants welcomed them immediately. "Good morning. I'm Diane. Can I help you ladies find something today?" she asked with a smile.

While Cass' eyes stayed glued to Nina, who was across the store, rifling through the racks, she let Lauren introduce the three of them. "I'd like to try on some wedding dresses, and we need to find a flower-girl dress for the little girl over there," she said, pointing to Nina.

"Wonderful," Diane replied. "When's your wedding?"

"We haven't actually set a date yet," Lauren answered. "Probably next April."

"Perfect. So you have time then. Did you have a particular style in mind?" Diane asked as she led them closer to Nina. "All of our wedding dresses are on this side of the store, and bridesmaids' dresses are all over there," she said, pointing to the opposite side.

"This is actually the first time I'm looking in person, so I have no idea what will look good on me. I definitely don't want anything too poofy." Lauren gestured widely with her arms out to the side. "Just something simple that kind of flows naturally." Lauren flipped through a nearby rack. "Something similar to this would be nice," she said, holding a dress against herself.

"That one just arrived a few weeks ago actually. It's a French designer. Hand stitched," Diane said.

Lauren took a look at the price tag. "Yup, definitely hand stitched."

Diane smiled politely. "Why don't you take a look around and pull a few that you like. Once I get a sense of your taste, I'll grab some as well, and we'll set you up with a dressing room. What about your flower girl?" Diane asked. "Did you want to share a fitting room with her and both try them on at the same time?"

Lauren looked to Cass and then back to Diane. "Oh, Nina's actually Cass' flower girl, not mine. Sorry. We should've explained that."

Diane looked surprised. "Oh, congratulations to you as well. When's your wedding?"

Never. "October twenty-fourth."

"Oh, that's less than five months away. I'm guessing you already have your dress. So that means we can just focus on the little one. "

Cass adjusted her purse on her shoulder, feeling the need to fidget with something. "Yeah, I've actually—"

"She's been waiting until I was ready so we could try them on together," Lauren interrupted.

Cass turned her head slowly in Lauren's direction. She felt her jaw go rigid as she stared at Lauren's profile. Cass wished she were Cyclops from *X-Men* just so she could burn the flesh right off Lauren's face with her eyes.

Diane clasped her hands together, and her eyes lit up like she'd just won the lottery. Two brides *and* a flower girl—Cass could practically see the dollar signs in Diane's eyes. "Oh, fantastic," Diane said. "I'll get you ladies each started with a dressing room then."

Once Diane turned away from them, Lauren made an attempt to move toward another rack. But Cass' solid grip around Lauren's forearm stopped her. "Oh no you don't." She lowered her voice. "I'm not trying on any wedding dresses."

Lauren spun around to face her, and Cass let go of her arm. "Oh, come on. It'll be more fun if we do it together. Pleeease," Lauren begged. "You're just trying them on. You're not buying one. It'll be like when we were in high school and we used to try stuff on in stores that we knew we couldn't afford just to see what we'd look like in it."

Cass rolled her eyes, but she could already feel the beginning of a smile starting to betray her. "Fine," she agreed. "I'll try on three. And I'll even let you pick them out." Mainly because Cass didn't want to, though she chose not to think about why. "But that's all. I'm not staying here all day." Cass saw Nina coming toward them with no fewer than six dresses in her hands. "I'm here to get a flower-girl dress for Nina, not play dress-up."

The smile that had been slowly creeping up Lauren's face now seemed to cover it entirely. "Yes!" she nearly yelled before turning to the racks to pick out what Cass was sure would be three of the most ridiculous dresses she had ever laid eyes on.

Nina bounded toward her, nearly tripping over the dresses she was carrying. "I found some! Can I try these on?"

"I think the woman's getting us a dressing room. What did you pick out?" Cass asked, taking the dresses from Nina's outstretched hand. "I bet you'll look like a princess." And it was the truth. From what Cass could see of them, most looked like they were better suited for a Disney movie than a wedding. She couldn't believe people actually let their daughters wear these things. "Where did you get them?"

Nina pointed across the store, already pulling Cass in the direction she'd just come from. "Over here."

When they got to the section with the flower-girl dresses, Cass flipped through the rack herself, pulling out two more she thought would look pretty on Nina. Both were white, like Nina wanted. "What do you think of these?" Cass asked. Though Nina wasn't actually going to be a flower girl, Cass didn't want Tessa thinking she was throwing a tacky wedding. She was going to have to enforce *some* fashion standards.

Nina studied them for a moment, feeling the material. "I like this one," she said, running her fingers along the satin. "It feels smooth. And I like the blue bow," she added, referring to the sash tied around the waist.

Cass knelt down and made space on a low rack. "Okay, we'll try this one on, then," she said, keeping the white satin dress off the rack as she hung up the rest. "Why don't you pick two more you like best from the ones you chose so you have three to try on."

Nina didn't look sold on putting any back but agreed anyway. She examined each dress closely—and some more than once—before finally choosing two. "I think I'll pick these," she said, taking them off the rack and handing them to Cass.

Cass put the rest of the dresses back where Nina had found them, and then the two headed toward the dressing rooms where Diane was standing with Lauren.

"I started a fitting room for you both right in here," Diane said, holding the dressing room door open for Cass and Nina.

"Your dresses are already in there," Lauren said to Cass.

"You're trying dresses on too?" Nina asked, obviously excited.

This is what I was trying to avoid. Cass' head snapped over in Lauren's direction, and Lauren's expression softened as she seemed to finally understand the implications of what she'd done. "Yeah," Cass replied. "I can't wait."

Sorry, Lauren mouthed silently.

Cass shook her head but gave her a small smile. *It's fine,* she mouthed back. Though Nina was obviously excited to see Cass in a wedding dress, Lauren was probably right. Cass wasn't purchasing one, so there was really no harm done. Well, no harm done that wouldn't be done anyway. Cass hung Nina's dresses on the hook in the fitting room without looking at the dresses Lauren had chosen for her. She'd decided that those gems could wait until later. "Why don't you try yours on first," Cass said, stepping out of the dressing room so Nina could enter.

Nina's only answer was her entrance into the dressing room. A few minutes later she came out in her first dress, an off-white one with a lace overlay. "What do you think?" she asked, lifting her hair so Cass could help zip the dress the rest of the way. Nina stepped up onto the small platform so she could look at herself in the angled mirrors.

Though the dress was a bit big, Cass thought Nina looked adorable. "You look pretty." I like the pink," she said, referring to the small embroidered flowers.

"'Kay. Next one," Nina said, hopping off the platform and turning away from Cass so she could unhook the dress and pull the zipper down a bit. Nina came out of the dressing room quickly the next time, but she didn't seem nearly as excited. "I don't like the sleeves on this one." She pulled at one of the capped sleeves and let it snap back into place.

"Okay, that one's out then," Cass said simply. She was glad that the first one had looked nice, in case they didn't like the last.

But there was no need to worry. Nina nearly squealed with delight when she emerged from the dressing room a third time. "Can I get this one, Cass? Please?"

Cass smiled. "Hang on. Can I at least see you in it first?" she asked, zipping Nina up again and then watching her spin around on the platform while she admired herself in the mirrors. Cass took a step back so she could get a better look at her. The dress fit Nina almost perfectly. She was in a floor-length white dress made of satin. A light blue sash was tied around her waist, and the bow with flowing tails came almost to the floor when she spun around. "You look beautiful," Cass said.

Lauren and Diane both agreed.

Nina beamed.

"Guess we'll take this one," Cass said.

While Diane went to bring Nina's dress to the register, Lauren and Cass made their way into the dressing rooms. "Stay right there, Nina," Cass called.

"Okay."

Cass turned toward the hook where Lauren's dress choices hung. "Uh-uh. There's no way I'm trying this on, Laur." But Cass knew her friend wouldn't let her off the hook that easily, so she began undressing.

She heard Lauren laugh. "It's your fault for letting me pick them."

"This looks like an ivory version of my mom's prom dress." Behind her back she pinched the excess fabric between her fingers as she reluctantly exited the fitting room.

Lauren was already waiting for her in the gown she'd tried on—one that someone would actually want to be seen in. She burst out laughing when she saw Cass. "That's better than I pictured." The entire dress was lace and had long sleeves that extended down past Cass' hands. "You look like Morticia Addams."

"Who?" Nina asked, making the girls laugh even louder.

"Just a woman on TV," Cass answered. Then she rolled her eyes and headed into the dressing room again, thankful to see that at least one of the gowns Lauren had chosen was appropriate for this century. It was a simple sleeveless dress with a V neck and lace detailing that got sparser toward the bottom. She was definitely trying this one on next. The white Cinderella knockoff behind it would have to wait until later.

She put the dress on as well as she could, but had to let Diane help her with the buttons that ran the length of her spine over the sheer back. Cass stepped up onto the platform this time, after Diane had pinched the excess fabric with a clip, and from the front it looked like it fit her perfectly. The floral lace hugged the curves of her breasts, torso, and hips before flowing down naturally toward the floor.

"It's gorgeous," Lauren said. "*You're* gorgeous."

Cass had never seen herself like this before. Sure, she'd gotten dressed up plenty of times. And she'd been in other people's weddings. She lived by the old adage "Always a bridesmaid, never a bride." Or at least she used to. But now, as she stared at her reflection—her blond hair falling delicately over her shoulders, her eyes staring back at her—she couldn't see herself any other way. She looked like a bride. And more shocking was that she *felt* like one.

The stinging that developed in the corner of her eye as she blinked back a tear told her all she needed to know. That this would've been *the* dress. *Her* dress. She wondered if this was what all brides felt when they found the perfect gown to wear down the aisle to marry the perfect man.

Because she was pretty sure she'd found both.

The ride to Tessa's house was mostly silent. Nina had probably tired herself out with all the excitement, and Cass was glad, because she didn't feel much like talking anyway. She wasn't sure what to make of the feelings she'd experienced at the bridal shop. She hadn't expected herself to feel so . . . connected, maybe? She'd thought she could try on the dresses and it would all just be a joke—one that she and Laur could laugh about when they told everyone about it later.

But nothing about putting that dress on had seemed funny to her. Especially not with Nina telling her how pretty she was going to look walking down the aisle. She wondered if Lauren recognized the emotion in Cass' eyes. When she'd looked at herself in the mirror at the bridal shop, it was like she was staring into a future she'd never imagined but wanted anyway. Though wanting something didn't make it good for you. She clenched the steering wheel, wishing Nina weren't there so she could scream. What the hell was happening to her?

She was thankful when they pulled up outside of Tessa's, if only for the chance to get some space. The car ride had seemed exceptionally confining, and she needed to move around. She opened her door and then Nina's, grabbing her bag out of the trunk before heading up the driveway to the house.

Tessa must have been waiting for them because she opened the door before they even got to it. Nina sprinted up the path when she saw her. "Mommy, I want to show you my dress!" she yelled, holding up the bag from the bridal shop.

"Okay, honey. Pete's in the kitchen. Why don't you show it to him first and then I'll be right in. I just need to talk to Cass for a minute."

Pete waved hello from down the hall, and Cass waved back to him. Nina gave him a hug and then immediately began pulling the plastic off the dress.

"Guess the shopping trip was a success?" Tessa asked with a genuine smile.

"Yeah, we had a fun girls' day."

"Well, thanks for taking her. I think it's important that she gets to spend some time with just the two of you." Tessa put her hands into her pockets. "It was a little weird for me at first, I guess. But you seem to really care about her, and I can't let myself feel anything but thankful for that."

Cass swallowed the lump in her throat. She was sure her voice would come out shaky, but somehow she was able to steady it. "I do care about her," Cass said. "And I'm sure I don't need to tell you how much Alex cares about her too." Tessa opened her mouth to speak, but Cass continued before Tessa had the chance to say anything. "He's really trying, you know." Cass thought she could see a bit of empathy in Tessa's eyes. "You should see them together. They're quite a pair." Cass shifted from one foot to the other. "They'd both really benefit from spending those eight weeks together. I know the decision is yours, and that I shouldn't even be interfering. But . . . just think about it?"

Tessa nodded. "I will."

"Thank you. Say good-bye to Nina for me?"

Tessa smiled slightly. "Of course."

And with that, Cass nodded farewell and headed for her car, hoping like hell all of this wasn't for nothing.

Chapter 19

Sentiment

Fear wasn't something Cass handled well. It made her quieter, more reticent. Her family had definitely noticed, if their inquiring glances throughout dinner had been any indication. But they hadn't asked, probably knowing her well enough to understand that she wouldn't share until she was ready.

She watched her sisters run around their parents' backyard, playing with their families. There were varying sizes of balls, bubble makers, dolls, and action figures littering the green grass. There were also giggling children running from their smiling parents. *Nina and Alex would fit right in here.* As much as she was trying to avoid thoughts of her pseudo-family-to-be, since they were the cause of her racing mind, she couldn't stop herself from picturing both of them here. Alex would get along great with her brothers-in-law, and Nina would have a blast playing with all of the kids. She'd thought the same thing last time she was here—how well Alex and Nina would fit in. But this was the first time she'd ever wished she could have brought someone—or in this case, two someones—to dinner at her parents'. And the wish was stifling. As much as Cass loved her sisters and their families, watching them was making her feel like she was drowning. So she got up and wandered into the house.

She should've known she'd end up in the kitchen. It was where her mom was. Despite feeling like she couldn't be more different from the woman who'd brought her into this world, Cass had always been drawn to her when she'd had a problem or just a general feeling of unease about life. Gloria Mullen had never failed to right Cass' world when it'd been flipped upside down over the years, and she'd often been able to do it without uttering a single word. Just her presence—and her love—was enough.

Her mom was standing over the sink, cleaning the dinner dishes. She often forced her family out of her kitchen, declaring that cleaning soothed her, when all the rest of them did was mess up her perfectly ordered cabinets.

Cass slid onto a stool at the kitchen island and watched her mom for a second. "Doesn't doing all of this get exhausting?"

Her mom started slightly, clearly not realizing Cass had come in. She turned just her head as her hands kept working. "All of what?"

Cass gestured around at the dishes, pots, pans, silverware, and leftover food that surrounded them. "All of this. Doesn't it get old, having all of us over? Cooking for us and cleaning up afterward? You should let Rachel or Amy host the family dinner once in a while. Their houses are big enough, and I know they've offered."

"I like doing it." Her mom answered like it was the only logical explanation.

But it wasn't. Not to Cass. "But why?" Cass wasn't trying to question her mom's priorities. She genuinely needed to know.

Her mom seemed to sense it. She dried her hands on a dish towel and sat down on a stool across from Cass, giving her daughter her full attention. "Because I like taking care of my family. It makes me feel good. I know it doesn't seem like it, but my motives are more selfish than they appear. I like to feel needed. To know I can still take care of you sometimes, even if you can take care of yourselves."

Cass let out a sigh and looked down at her clasped hands.

"Let me help, Cass. Tell me what's going on."

Cass loved how her mom was able to read between her lines—to know when one of her daughters needed her help. But Cass still wasn't sure how to answer. Part of her wanted to stew with her own thoughts for a while—try to sort through what she was feeling. But another part of her knew that her mom could help her navigate the murky waters that were submerging her mind. Understanding her mom would be the first step in understanding why she felt like her entire life was crumbling. Or maybe it was just changing. Cass decided to just come out with it. "Do you feel like you missed out on anything by having a family?" Cass glanced up at her mom to gauge her reaction.

Gloria didn't look offended or confused by the question, but rather contemplative. She seemed to mull over the question for a few seconds before answering. "Yes."

Cass' head jerked back slightly. She definitely hadn't been expecting *that* reply. Even though Cass had wanted an honest answer, she had also thought she *knew* what the answer would be.

Gloria smiled. "Of course I missed out on things, Cass. Every choice we make causes us to miss out on the things that we would've experienced had we chosen a different path. When your father and I were raising you girls, we didn't have any weekend getaways or late nights closing down the bars. I didn't go on girls' weekends or go on shopping sprees for things I didn't need. So yes, I missed out on things. But if you're asking if I *regret* anything about the choice I made, then my answer is no. If my choices had been different, I would've missed out on a lot more." Gloria reached across the island and laid her hand over Cass'. "Why don't you tell me why you're asking?"

Cass sighed. She hadn't told her mom about Alex or the wedding, and she didn't really want to now. That wasn't the conversation she needed to have. So she decided to keep that whole story for another time. "I've been . . . reevaluating."

When Cass didn't continue, her mom asked, "Reevaluating what?"

Cass looked at her mom again and shrugged. "Everything."

Concern etched itself on her mom's face. "What's going on, Cass?"

"That's just it. I don't really know. It's just . . . I've spent my life having a very clear picture of who I wanted to be: successful, independent, career driven. And I *am* that person. I'm who I always told myself I wanted to be, but . . . now . . . I don't know." Cass plopped her head down on her hands in frustration.

"Cass, do you think I'm not those things that you mentioned?" Gloria's voice wasn't angry, but full of genuine curiosity.

How do I answer that? Cass didn't want to hurt her mom's feelings, but the truth was, no, she didn't think her mom was those things.

Thankfully her mom saved her from having to answer. "I have raised three beautiful, intelligent, and happy daughters. I've been married to the man of my dreams for almost thirty-six years. We have a beautiful house that I turned into a home. What about that doesn't scream success? And I did most of those things on my own. Your father worked six days a week for a lot of your childhood to support us financially, but I supported all of you emotionally. I managed this house, handled things in the way I saw fit. I've never been dependent on anyone to make those things happen. And while I didn't leave the house every day to go to work, my job was still important. You girls were my career, Cass. That was the life I chose for myself. And I was always driven to succeed at being your mom."

Cass felt her eyes burn. She'd never thought of her mom's life that way. That she didn't get saddled with a family; she'd *chosen* one. Cass swiped at a falling tear. "I feel like an asshole."

Gloria laughed. "Why?"

"Because I never gave you enough credit. I always thought you were just coping with the hand you were dealt, when really you were the one dealing all the cards."

"You and I have lived very different lives on the surface. You wanted the high-profile job, wanted to make your own money and blaze your own path through life. But ultimately, the dedication to achieve our goals has been the same. You and me? We're not as different as you might think, honey."

Cass took a shuddering breath. "But you're happy with your life? You look back on it, and what you see makes you happy?"

Gloria smiled. "Being a stay-at-home mom definitely came with days where I wasn't the happiest. You girls were rough teenagers." Both of them chuckled. "But yes. I look back on my life and I'm happy with what I've built. I wouldn't have had it any other way." Gloria patted Cass' hand. "I thought you liked your job."

"I do. I love it. I'm good at it, and it makes me feel important. But . . ."

"But what?"

Cass looked into her mother's eyes—eyes she'd never before realized were much like her own. "But I don't know if it's enough anymore. I think I could be happier."

"The only thing I've ever wanted for all of my girls was for you all to be the happiest you could be. So if there's more you need to do to make that happen, then do it." Her mom stood and came around the island to hug her daughter. "It doesn't need to be all or nothing, Cass. You can be successful at work *and* have a successful personal life too. If anyone can balance the two, it's you."

Cass smiled at the incredible, brave, strong woman who'd raised her. "I think I can too."

Alex turned on his computer and opened Skype. Tessa had texted him earlier that Nina had something she wanted to show him, and would he be available to visit with her via the Internet when he got home from work? He couldn't wait to see what had Nina so excited, so he texted Tessa as soon as he'd walked in the door and set up the call. He put in Tessa's name, and the call connected quickly. "Hi, Tess. What's going on?"

"Hey. She wanted to do a big reveal, so she asked me to answer the call. You ready to see her?" Tessa was smiling and her eyes kept darting off the screen, presumably to where Nina was waiting.

"I'm ready."

"Then let me introduce you to your flower girl." Tessa moved out of the shot, and she was instantly replaced by a very excited Nina. "Back up so he can see you," Tessa instructed.

Nina moved back, and Alex took in the sight before him: she had put on her flower girl dress and was spinning so he could see all of it.

Alex was momentarily speechless. She looked like an angel. He cleared his throat, hoping to unlock the words that were stuck there.

Meanwhile, Nina had stopped spinning and was grinning widely at the webcam. "Do you like it, Daddy?"

"Yeah, baby." Alex was thankful his voice was working, though he sounded raspier than normal. "You look beautiful. I've never seen a prettier flower girl." Alex was torn between the happiness of seeing his little girl so excited and the despair that he would eventually have to destroy that excitement. *I should've said we weren't having a flower girl.*

Nina hopped with joy. "Wait until you see Cass. She's going to be the prettiest bride ever."

Alex smiled, but he knew it didn't fully reach his eyes. "I'm sure she will be. So I'm guessing you had a good time dress shopping with the girls?"

"The best time ever." Nina continued to relay the day to him, and Alex did his best to listen intently, though his thoughts were all over the place.

"Doesn't she look adorable?" Tessa's voice filled the room as Nina bounded off to change. "I'm going to have to hide that dress so she doesn't try to wear it every day."

"She looks gorgeous in it," was all Alex could reply.

Tessa smiled. "While I have you on here, I wanted to talk to you about a couple of things."

Oh God. Alex's brain was still all reeling from seeing Nina in her flower-girl dress, from picturing what Cass would look like in a wedding gown, and from trying to understand why he was so disappointed by the fact that he'd never actually get to see either of them wear their dresses in person. He wasn't in a place to have a serious conversation with Tessa, but what could he say? "Sure. Shoot."

"When Cass dropped Nina off after they went dress shopping . . . I haven't seen Nina that elated in a long time. I mean, she's usually a pretty happy kid, but there was an added spark in her that day. Cass brings that out in her, I think. They seem to really enjoy spending time together."

Alex wasn't sure if Tessa thought that was a good or a bad thing. "Yeah, they get along really well."

"I'm glad. I'm not saying it's not hard sometimes. No mother wants another woman to play such a big role in their child's life, but Cass seems good about not overstepping and trying not to undermine my place as Nina's mother. I really appreciate that." Tessa bit her lip, and Alex could see her arms move as though she were fiddling with her hands. "It made me think that maybe I wasn't always as fair to you as you and Cass have been to me."

Alex sat back in his chair. This wasn't where he thought this conversation was going to go.

"I introduced Pete as a father figure almost immediately after you and I split. And I did that while also fighting to limit your time with Nina. I . . . I want to apologize to you for that. It was wrong and could have really hurt your relationship with Nina. I was so consumed by my own anger at you, at how I felt neglected for the years leading up to the divorce, that I used Nina to hurt you." Tessa shut her eyes and released a deep breath. "That was wrong, Alex. On so many levels. You're a great dad, but I made being one difficult for you. And now you have Cass and you're settling down, and Nina is over-the-moon in love with you. I don't want to punish you anymore. I called my parents this morning and told them that you'd take Nina while Pete and I are away. Assuming, of course, you still want that. I guess I should've asked you first. But I figured you did, so—"

"Tess," Alex interrupted. "You're rambling." They both laughed. "I'd love to have Nina. And thank you . . . for everything else you said. I think . . ." Alex rubbed a hand over his face. "I think we both did things to one another that we wish we could take back. But we're in a good place now, and for Nina and for ourselves, I'd really like to let the past go and move forward from here."

"I'd like that too."

Alex smiled broadly. "Good. And I mean it—thanks for letting me have the time with Nina. It means the world to me."

Tessa nodded, looking a little emotional. "Well,

I'll let you get on with your evening. I'll let you tell Nina about the change of plans."

"Perfect. Talk to you soon."

"Bye, Alex."

The call disconnected, and Alex collapsed against the backrest of his chair. *Did that really just happen?* Tessa had apologized. She was going to let him have Nina for the eight weeks. Cass' plan had actually fucking worked.

But that last thought brought him up short. There had been a niggling flicker of guilt that had resided within Alex since this whole thing began. Guilt that he was lying to Nina, that he was letting her get attached to a woman who was never going to be what he'd promised, that he was convincing Tessa to give him the time by lying to her. As he sat there and examined it, he realized there was now another layer to the guilt.

The past couple of months had all been part of a *plan*. He'd been in a contrived relationship that had an expiration date. Cass was only in it because she was a good friend who wanted to help him. But what he'd done to her was unforgivable. For the girl who was dedicated to her career, who never wanted a husband or a family, he felt guilt too. Because he was fucking falling for her. And he wasn't sure he'd be able to let her go when this was all over.

Chapter 20

Objective

Alex put a hand on Nina's shoulder and pulled open the door so she could enter the restaurant. He felt the peanut shells crunch beneath his shoes as he approached the hostess. "Two, please." He was happy to see that Nina's favorite place to eat wasn't as crowded as it usually was. But he wasn't all that surprised. It was a Tuesday night, and they'd gone on Saturdays before. Not to mention it was only five-thirty. He wanted to make sure that he got Nina back to Tessa's at a reasonable hour, since she had school the next day.

The hostess glanced down at the iPad in front of her and then back up at Alex. "Right this way," she said. "Do you need a kids' menu?"

Alex looked at Nina. "I think two adult ones will be fine."

Nina smiled, clearly pleased with Alex's request.

The hostess seated them, and a few minutes later

a waiter came by to bring them some rolls and take their drink orders. Alex ordered an iced tea for himself and a Shirley Temple for Nina, which he knew she loved and got only on special occasions.

"I get to have soda at night?" Nina said, obviously excited.

"Just this once," Alex replied. "But make sure you go to bed whenever your mom tells you to, okay?"

Nina pulled a roll apart and began buttering it. "Okay."

For a minute Alex was silent, just wanting to take in the moment: his daughter happy, here with him on a night that wasn't "his." But the truth was, though he'd been excited to tell Nina that she would be staying with him for the summer, a part of him was worried that she wouldn't share his same enthusiasm. Though Nina knew that her mom and Pete were leaving for the summer, she already thought she'd be staying with her grandparents, whom she loved and didn't get to see very often because they lived a few hours away. It had just now occurred to him that though this was supposed to be a celebratory dinner, it might have a very different tone for Nina. "What are you getting to eat?" he asked, not wanting to share the news just yet.

"Can I get ribs?" she asked, peeking over the top of her menu.

Alex raised his eyebrows. "You know they have bones in them, right? And they're messy?"

Nina gave him a quick nod. "I know. Pete makes them sometimes."

Alex felt himself wince a bit at the mention of Pete, but he gave her a small smile in an attempt to cover it. "Just making sure you knew. You can get whatever you want."

A minute or two later, the waiter returned with their drinks and took their orders. Nina sipped on her Shirley Temple and twisted the straw wrapper around her finger. "You ever play that game with these?"

"The one that makes them look like worms?" Alex scrunched up his own wrapper and put a few droplets of water on it until it wiggled and appeared to grow.

Nina laughed. "No, silly. The one where you find out if someone's thinking about you."

Alex was genuinely confused.

"You tie the wrapper in a knot, and if the knot stays together and the paper doesn't rip, it means the person you love is thinking about you right that second."

Alex shook his head. "I've never heard of that one."

Nina's eyes brightened. "Let's play then."

"Okay. You want to see if Mommy's thinking about you?" He handed the other wrapper to Nina, but she didn't take it.

"It's not for me. It's for you to do with Cass," she replied simply.

Nina's mention of Cass caused Alex's breathing to falter and his heart to beat a little faster. Alex followed Nina's instructions. But it wasn't until the wrapper broke in half and the knot came apart that he realized how much he'd been wanting it to stay intact.

Nina's smile fell a little, and Alex felt his do the same. Though he wasn't really sure why. It was just a kids' game.

"So what are you gonna get for dessert?" Alex asked, grabbing the small menu of treats from the end of the table so he could change the subject.

"A sundae!" Nina nearly shouted. But a few seconds later, she gave him a curious look. "Wait—soda *and* dessert? How come you're letting me have all this stuff?"

Alex shrugged, surprised at how quickly Nina had caught on that something was up. Though he really shouldn't have been. The girl had clearly inherited his keen observation skills. "Can't I just let my daughter have a fun night out?"

Nina looked unconvinced.

Damn, she's smart. "Okay, okay," Alex said, moving closer to the table and folding his hands on it. "You caught me. I have exciting news." He immediately regretted his word choice. If Nina didn't think it was exciting, then he didn't want her to feel obligated to act that way. "I mean, *I'm* excited about it. I'm not sure how you'll feel though, so you'll have to tell me."

Nina edged closer to him in anticipation. "What is it?"

Alex took a deep breath. "Well, you know how your mom and Pete are going away this summer for work, and she said that you were going to stay with your grandparents in New Jersey?"

Nina nodded and sat up a little taller. "Yeah, they said I could ride a horse."

Shit. "Well your mom changed her mind, and she said that you could stay with *me* this summer." Alex tried to gauge Nina's reaction, but since she didn't immediately reply, it was tough to tell what she was thinking. "What would you think about going horseback riding with me instead?" he added, hoping to soften the blow.

"With you?"

"Yeah, with me. Why do you say it like that? You don't believe I can ride a horse?" he joked.

Nina's expression told him that's exactly what she believed. "Can Cass come?"

"What? I'm not entertaining enough on my own?" Alex held out his arms and grinned widely.

Nina smiled back, a few teeth still missing, which made her cuter than she already was. "No, you're fun, Dad. But I like it when it's all three of us."

Alex knew the feeling. He reached across the table, grabbed both of Nina's hands in one of his, and gave them a squeeze. "Yeah, baby," he answered. "Cass can go."

The two spent the next few minutes talking about what type of horse Nina wanted to ride. Alex told her he didn't know if a white pony with round brown spots would be available, but said he'd do his best to find one. By the time their meals arrived, the conversation had gotten considerably lighter than it had originally felt. Nina was excited that she wouldn't have to leave her friends and that she'd get to go to camp each day. And the more they discussed the summer, the more excited Alex felt about the time they'd have together. It would be a chance to take her to some of the places he never felt like he could squeeze into their weekends.

Nina finished her ribs, and Alex helped her wipe the last of the sauce off her face and hands before her sundae arrived.

"That looks pretty good. Can I have a bite?" Alex asked after the waiter had set the ice cream down in front of her.

Nina's eyes widened at the enormous dessert, and Alex could tell she was contemplating trying to eat the whole thing. "Fine, I guess you can have a bite. Just one though."

Alex laughed, a spoon already in his hand.

As their time together came to a close, Alex appreciated even more how nice it was going to be to have Nina full-time, to feel like he had a real family again. Not that their little "family" of three was *real* in the traditional sense. But sometimes it couldn't help but feel that way.

Telling Nina about the summer had been a success, and they were both looking forward to their two months together. But as Nina had pointed out, they were a unit—incomplete when one of them wasn't involved. That was what prompted him to call Cass after he dropped off Nina.

"Hey, you," Cass answered.

The way she said it brought a smile to Alex's face instantaneously. "Hey. I just dropped Nina off."

"Sooo? How did it go? I've been thinking about you."

Alex laughed.

"What?"

"It's nothing. Just this game Nina and was playing. Dinner was good. She seemed excited."

Cass sighed as if she were as relieved as he'd been. Maybe she was. "That's so great. I'm so happy for you guys."

"Me too." Alex caught a glimpse of himself in the rearview mirror. His eyes shone with a light he hadn't seen in them in years. And he had a feeling it had to do with more than just his dinner with Nina. Almost by habit, he made a left at the end of the street and then a quick right. "What are you up to?" he asked.

Cass laughed. "You're not gonna believe this, but I'm watching *Happy Gilmore*."

Alex felt his smile grow even wider. "You're right. I don't believe it. I thought you hated Adam Sandler."

"Yeah, I kind of still do." He heard Cass blow out

a soft laugh through her nose. "But I guess I've just had the urge to give things a chance lately."

Cass pulled at the soft cotton of her oversized T-shirt, thinking about how she was already ready for bed and it was only eight thirty. She wasn't sure when she'd stopped catching up on extra work at night or when she'd stopped feeling the need to fill her social calendar. She just knew she liked it.

"Well, there is *one* thing that makes an Adam Sandler movie better every time," Alex said.

"Oh yeah? What's that?"

Alex was silent for a moment before he answered her. "Company."

Cass felt her lip turn up into a half smile. "That would definitely make it better. How far away are you?"

"Uh . . . this probably sounds creepy, especially coming from someone who locks up weirdos for a living." Alex hesitated. "But I'm standing outside your apartment building."

Cass pulled the phone away from her ear and hung up. She hadn't even thought to buzz him in. Her desire to see him had her throwing down the phone and making her way downstairs.

She could see Alex through the glass door, still holding the phone. He put it into his pocket when he saw her. For a moment as she approached him, she caught a glimpse of her reflection. Though it was only in glass and not sharp enough to make out the details, she saw herself just as clearly as she'd seen herself in the bridal shop. It didn't matter that she wasn't in a fancy gown. The woman she saw staring back at her was the same. And standing right next to her—more clearly than she'd ever seen him—was Alex.

Cass pushed open the door so Alex could enter. And when he did, his proximity alone caused a warmth to rush through her body.

They didn't speak on the way up the stairs. They didn't need to. Once inside Cass' apartment, the two went to the couch. Alex sat first, gently gripping her arm and prompting her to rest her head on his lap so he could stroke her hair. "You're right," she said after about ten minutes. "This movie *is* better with company."

"Told you," he said.

And that's how they stayed until the movie ended—Cass lying on Alex like she belonged there.

She was pretty sure she did.

Once she finally felt like moving, Cass stood up and began walking to the kitchen. "I'm gonna get a drink. Do you want anything?" she asked, already pulling a bottle of water from the fridge and taking a few gulps. She put the bottle on the counter and was turning around to ask Alex again, since he hadn't answered. But as she spun, she realized Alex was right behind her. She jumped, startled, but recovered quickly.

Alex rubbed his hands along her biceps and pulled her close. "Sorry. I didn't mean to scare you."

Cass didn't answer with words, letting her body respond for her instead. She leaned into Alex, pressing her breasts against his solid chest, her nipples hardening under her shirt. Already she felt so ready. She wanted this man. And it didn't feel only sexual. The way he wrapped his arms around her, breathed softly against her neck, made Cass melt into him.

Alex's hands roamed her body as if they were exploring her for the first time, his fingers tracing delicate paths up and down her sides that made her flesh tingle. She let out a low moan and pulled him harder against her. Cass' back arched over the countertop as Alex held her in place with his body. She could feel his erection pressing into her, and she wanted to move against him.

He groaned into her mouth as he kissed her, his tongue a perfect combination of sensual and wild. Her mind blurred with desire as she ground shamelessly against him. And as if he sensed her need, he asked, "What do you want?"

It was a simple question. But one that sent the synapses of Cass' brain firing in all directions. For years she thought she knew what she wanted. But she'd been wrong. What she'd accomplished made her feel proud. But what it didn't make her feel was fulfilled.

But this right here—this made her feel all those things and more. "You," she answered. "This. I want all of it."

With that, Alex pulled her away from the counter, spinning her so he could walk her backward toward her bedroom without letting her go. His mouth disconnected from hers just long enough for him to mutter a soft, "Me too," before he picked her up and carried her to her bed.

The moment her back hit the mattress, Alex was removing clothing from the two of them until they were both naked, exposed in the soft streetlight streaming in through Cass' partially open curtains. He lay beside her, suddenly in no rush. Propping up his elbow on the bed, he supported his head with his hand and used the other to skate lightly over Cass' skin.

Her breath hitched at his touch as his fingertips grazed over the soft flesh of her neck and then down to her nipples, which were peaked with desire. Cass wanted his fingers lower, rubbing over her throbbing clit and deep inside her.

But she also wanted this moment. Alex's muscles flexed as his hands explored every inch of her, discovered places on her that she didn't know could make the ache between her thighs grow stronger. She wanted to touch him back, feel the soft hair on his muscular chest, his sculpted abs, how stiff his cock was. She'd touched him so many times before, and it had always been so easy, so . . . comfortable. And though this time was both those things, it also felt different somehow. Less rushed, maybe. More special.

Cass looked over to Alex, searching his face for a sign that he was thinking the same thing. She wished she could tell him her thoughts, but she didn't even completely know what she was thinking herself. So instead, she closed her eyes, surrendering herself to the man next to her as he moved to climb on top of her, his hard cock teasing her deliciously as it slid against her.

"So sexy," he rasped. "Look at me, Cass."

She breathed deeply, opening her eyes to gaze up at him. His hair was slightly messy from her hands running through it, and his dark eyes were hooded, heavy in the dim light as he looked down at her. She brought a hand to his cheek, brushed her thumb over it gently, and then brought it around to the back of his neck so she could pull him against her lips.

And with that, the delicate moment disappeared, and they were all carnal need—their lips sucking on each other's greedily like neither could get enough. Alex's mouth was everywhere in a matter of seconds, kissing from her ankle up to between her thighs where she was slick with her hunger for him.

"Don't," he said, when he could tell she was ready to come. His tongue slowed its movements, but they didn't cease completely. "I want to be right there with you."

And she wanted him to be too. So she pulled his face up toward her own, a silent command for him to stop what he was doing before it was too late. He complied, allowing his face to meet hers again. Cass' legs wrapped around him tightly, and she could feel him at her entrance. "I want you, Alex," she pleaded, grabbing the flesh of his muscular ass and urging him inside her.

Just as she thought he would, he resisted. At least his body did. She was sure his mind had other plans. "Cass, I need—"

"No, you don't," she said. She'd been on the pill for years, and Alex knew that. They'd always chosen to use a condom anyway. But this time she couldn't bear the thought of having anything between them. Even a thin layer of latex was too much. She wanted skin on skin, wanted to feel every inch of him.

Alex seemed to understand her intended message and thrust himself inside with one long drive. He stayed there, unmoving, for a moment, his fingers tangling in her hair as he pressed light kisses to her forehead and the bridge of her nose. Then he began to move slowly, and the feeling lit her up: the push of soft skin over hard steel as it slid inside of her. She'd already been so close to coming with Alex's mouth on her, and now as his rhythm increased, she didn't know how long she could hold off.

Alex groaned into her neck, and the sound vibrating against her was nearly enough to make her lose it. She felt herself on the edge, seconds away from plummeting over it. And she wanted Alex there with her. "Please, Alex," she begged through an exhalation. "Come with me."

He gave her a few sharp thrusts, his body rubbing over her clit as the tip of his cock hit a spot inside her that made her unravel around him. Then she could feel him let go too, his cock twitching inside her as he filled her with every drop he had. Gradually, their movements slowed until they stopped completely and Alex rolled off her, resting his arm across her stomach.

She knew she should go to the bathroom and clean up, but she couldn't bring herself to move. "That was . . ." She let her voice trail off, unsure of how to finish her sentence.

Then Alex spoke, his voice no more than a whisper. "I know."

Chapter 21

Arrest

The setting was familiar but the plot wasn't. Cass didn't normally welcome overnight company. It had always seemed more intimate than she'd been willing to get with any of the men she'd dated in the past. But feeling Alex's naked, solid body behind her, the weight of his arm draped over her, the steady rise and fall of his chiseled chest, she had to admit—she was suddenly a fan. She snuggled closer, allowing the unmistakable press of Alex's morning erection to nestle between her ass cheeks. *Yeah, I can definitely get used to this.*

A quick swat to her backside startled her. "Stop molesting me in my sleep," Alex murmured as he pressed his face into her hair and placed a soft kiss at her nape.

She ground her ass harder against him. "Are you really complaining?"

Alex tightened his hold on her and growled. "Hell no. Do that again."

Cass reached back and tangled her hands in Alex's hair as she rocked into him, his cock sliding up and down the crease of her ass.

"Fuck, that feels so good." Alex slipped his hand down her bare stomach and in between her legs. He began rubbing her clit slowly as Cass sped up her movements. Neither of them tried to turn it into more; what it was was already *so* good. This coupling was all about the chase for release, so different from the sweet melding of bodies they'd experienced the night before.

Cass came first, her body shaking from the unbelievable torrent of sensations running through her. Alex exploded on her back a minute or so later. It was raunchy and carnal and hot as hell.

Alex pushed her gently onto her stomach. "Stay put. I'll get something to clean up with." He dropped a kiss on her shoulder before getting up. He returned quickly with a warm washcloth and wiped her back before snuggling back down beside her. "Have anything to eat around here?"

Cass scoffed in mock horror. "You expect me to feed you too?"

She felt Alex's chuckle reverberate through her body. "You wore me out. The least you can do is replenish my energy."

"No, the *least* I can do is point you toward the nearest coffee shop. What time is it anyway?"

"Six thirty."

Cass groaned. "My alarm isn't set to go off for another half an hour. Let's go back to sleep."

"For thirty minutes? What's the point in that?"

"The point is that sleep is awesome," Cass replied,

her eyes already closed and her breathing starting to even out. She was startled back to alertness by Alex's fingers digging into her ribs.

"You are not seriously going back to sleep."

Cass bucked and slapped at Alex's hands. "Stop assaulting me. I'm tired."

Alex rolled over onto all fours and began bouncing on the bed. "Get up, Cassidy. I'm more persistent than any alarm clock."

"'Annoying' is a more accurate term." She rolled onto her back so she was looking up at him. *God, he's gorgeous.* It wasn't that she'd never noticed how attractive Alex was, but there was really nothing that compared to sleep-rumpled Alex, with his hair sticking up in all directions, a sexy stubble spread across his chiseled jaw. Cass lifted her hand to rub over the roughness on his face. "You're pretty," she said with a sincere smile.

He returned her smile as he bent down to place a closed-mouth kiss on her lips. "You're not so bad yourself."

They stared at each other for a moment, Cass' hand gently grazing over Alex's skin. There seemed to be more said in those few minutes of silence than had been spoken in the nearly two years they'd known each other. Of course, Cass could project her own thoughts only through her eyes—that their relationship was shifting, that they both wanted more, that this was the beginning of something equally terrifying and exhilarating. Finally Cass dropped her hand. "I guess I can whip something up."

Alex dipped again and nipped at her shoulder. "Don't say the word 'whip' when you're naked under me." He pulled back, reluctantly it seemed, and let her roll out of bed. After pulling on his boxers while she put on a camisole and underwear, he followed Cass out of the bedroom.

Cass opened the refrigerator, and Alex pressed up against her so he could peer inside as well. "Omelet?" she asked.

"Sure. What do you want in it?"

They chose cheese and a few vegetables she had. Moving around each other seamlessly, they made breakfast and settled down to eat together at Cass' small kitchen table. Alex had retrieved both of their phones, and they ate quietly as they scrolled through their favorite news sites. Despite the fact that they weren't saying much, Cass was overcome with a sense of how *right* it all felt.

"Why are there so many people here?" Cass asked as she looked around the arena at the plethora of fans.

Alex turned to her, his brows knitted. "What do you mean? Why wouldn't there be people here?"

Cass shrugged. "I guess I didn't know this was such a big thing. I've never even heard of any of these guys."

"Just because you haven't seen them on TMZ doesn't mean they're not talented."

Cass decided to ignore his TMZ comment. "They're clearly not *that* talented. Otherwise they'd be playing real football."

Spreading his hands before him to gesture to the field, Alex said, "This is real football. What the hell are you talking about?"

"This is *not* real football. This is arena football. Which you, for God only knows what reason, dragged me two hours away to watch. Seriously, with the price of gas, I'd think you'd be less wasteful."

Alex stared at her for a second. "I'm really not sure what I see in you."

Smirking, Cass replied, "I'm great in bed."

"Yeah, that must be it."

"We could be in a bed right now. Instead we're watching a bunch of guys getting all sweaty together." Cass snapped her fingers. "I get it. This is like a kink for you. I can get into it. Just give me a second."

"I'm seriously considering leaving you here."

"You used to be more fun. Wedding planning has changed you."

Alex let loose a laugh that he'd clearly tried to hold in. "You're the one who's not fun. This place is packed with people who enjoy these games."

Cass looked around. "Very true. Too bad they're all ten."

"Totally untrue. Their parents are here too."

Cass burst out laughing, which caused Alex to smile. Damn, how she loved that smile. It was white and perfect, and she wanted to trace it with her tongue.

Alex slung an arm around her shoulders and pulled her close. "Stop fucking with me, and watch the game," he whispered in her ear.

She curled into him, resting her hand on his chest. "But I love fucking you."

Alex's face lit up with that damn smile again. "Stop flirting with me when we're surrounded by ten-year-olds," he said, throwing her wiseass remark back at her.

"Flirting with you? You just accused me of fucking with you. Which is it?"

"You have an odd ability to do both things simultaneously." He pointed to the field in front of them. "Watch."

Cass sat back in her seat and watched the game for a few minutes. Her gaze drifted from the field to the adoring crowd cheering for the Richmond team as they plowed down the turf and scored. She had to admit, it was kind of fun. "This is my first arena-football game."

"You're kidding," Alex deadpanned.

She bumped his shoulder with hers. "Shut up. I just mean I never would've thought to come to one of these. But I have to admit, it's not so bad."

"What a ringing endorsement. You should e-mail your thoughts to the team. I bet they'll want to add your opinion to their Web site to attract new fans."

"I hate you."

Alex smirked at her, making it clear that he knew she far from hated him.

He still had his arm around her, and she continued to lean into his hard body. It was amazing how much had changed between them in such a short time. For starters, they were almost always touching now. Simple gestures like a hand to the small of her back as they went out to grab dinner together, or her legs draped over his as they sat on the couch and argued about who liked shittier television, or the way they'd get lost in looking at one another at random points during their time together. They had been close for a long time, but there was an intimacy between them now that Cass was sure they both felt even though they'd never discussed it.

If she were being honest with herself, it was a bit overwhelming for her. Cass had always been one to like her space, but Alex had infiltrated every aspect of her life. And she liked him there. *Isn't that some crazy shit?* What she liked even more was waking up next to him, which had been happening with more frequency lately. She told herself that they were just banging each other's brains out before Alex had Nina full-time. Because soon Nina would be around constantly. And while she was happy that Alex was getting to spend the time with his little girl, Cass was definitely going to miss being able to fuck him on any available surface anytime she wanted to.

"Come on! Stop him!" Alex yelled, effectively ending Cass' internal musings.

"Why are you yelling? They can't hear you."

Alex glared at her, causing her to laugh again. She couldn't deny it—she loved winding Alex up. She had a true talent for it, and Cass was a firm believer in exploiting her strengths.

It didn't take more than a quarter for Cass to get caught up in the game and begin yelling alongside Alex. Despite her earlier ribbing, she had always liked football. The aggression spoke to her on a cellular level.

By the time the game ended, they'd each consumed three beers and an obscene amount of junk food, and Cass had conned Alex into buying her a giant foam finger, which she was sure he instantly regretted since she'd used it as though it were her real hand for the rest of the game. She couldn't help it if she was a hand-talker—or at least she was when she had an awesome foam finger. Too bad Alex snatched it from her and gave it to a young kid near them during the fourth quarter.

They left the arena with their hands clasped, fingers interlaced like it was the most natural thing in the world. And it truly felt like it was. But the naturalness threw Cass even more. While part of her liked it, part of her feared it too. So once they settled in the car and began the long drive home, Cass decided to get them back on more comfortable ground.

Casually leaning on the center console, she let her hand rest just above Alex's knee. "How often do you go to those games?"

Alex shifted a little in his seat. "Not that often. I wish I had time to go more."

"We should take Nina," Cass said as she shifted her hand up higher on his thigh.

"That'd be fun."

She drifted her hand over the denim so that it was halfway up his thigh. "You know me. I'm all about fun."

"Are you now?"

"Mmm-hmm." Cass' hand migrated up to the crease where his leg met his hip.

"You may need to prove that to me," Alex said as his breathing picked up.

"Well," she started as she cupped him through his jeans, "you know how I love to prove myself." Her ministrations over his cock were slow, but if the hitch of his breath was any indication, her hand was having the desired effect. "Am I proving how much fun I am, or do you need more evidence?"

Alex's eyes were on the road but his head was pushed back into the headrest, his strong hands gripping the wheel. "I'd hate for you to not give a hundred-dred percent effort."

"Very good point." Her hands moved to unfasten his belt, unbutton his jeans, and drag down the zipper. She reached into his boxers to wrap around his cock and pull it through the opening. Cass couldn't deny that the sight of Alex's cock always turned her on. "Hmm, my hand's getting tired."

"Oh yeah?" Alex's words were coming in pants, his arousal as evident in his voice as in the hardness in her hand.

"Yeah. Maybe I should rest it." And with that, Cass

bent over the console and sucked Alex into her mouth. She kept one hand wrapped around the base as she took as much of him in her mouth as she could. She bobbed over him with fervor, not interested in teasing or dragging this out. Giving a sexy-as-hell FBI agent road head was hitting all the right buttons, and she couldn't have slowed her pace if she'd wanted to.

She dragged her tongue up the vein under his cock before licking the head, paying specific attention to his slit. She lapped at the precum leaking from him like he was a melting Popsicle, making him moan and slap his hand against the steering wheel.

"Cass . . . fuck."

She pulled off with a pop. "That's going to be difficult to maneuver while you're driving," she teased. Then she sank her head over him again, taking him deep over and over.

"Shit, fuck, I'm going to come."

She hummed around his cock, knowing that the vibration would increase his pleasure. His groan was all the affirmation she needed. She hummed again and that was all it took.

Alex released a guttural sound as his orgasm tore through him.

Cass swallowed his cum, sucking him dry as if he were the best lollipop she'd ever had. Once she had licked him clean, she let him fall from her lips. She took her time tucking him back in and closing up his jeans as best she could. Then Cass straightened in her seat and glanced over at Alex. He looked like he had just finished a marathon. "You okay there, champ?"

"Never better," was his slightly breathless reply.

Cass couldn't help but feel proud of herself as she watched this supercop lose his composure. She sat quietly, looking out the window as Alex recovered.

But her head whipped to look out of the windshield and then over at Alex as the car quickly jerked off the highway and onto the shoulder. "What's wrong?"

Alex thrust the gearshift into park and unclipped his seat belt. "I need you to drive." Then he opened his car door and got out, slamming it behind him.

What the hell? She watched him discreetly adjust his jeans as he rounded the front of the car. Cass didn't have time to react before Alex was ripping open her door.

"You need to drive," he repeated.

Cass' eyes widened as she got out of the car. "So you said." *Why is he acting like such a nutjob?* She walked around the car and climbed into the driver's side, immediately adjusting the seat to accommodate her shorter stature.

"Don't forget your seat belt," Alex warned.

She shot him a look of disbelief before buckling herself in. "Any other requests, Your Majesty?"

"Nope. That should do it."

She sighed before merging carefully back into traffic. Once she got up to cruising speed, her mind started to ponder why Alex had suddenly gotten all weird on her. *Did I suck his manners out through his dick?* Her thoughts came to an abrupt halt when she felt Alex's hand above her knee.

"Maybe we could take Nina to a baseball game instead. Then we wouldn't have to drive as far," he said.

Cass furrowed her brow at yet another sudden shift in Alex's demeanor. "Okay."

"When was the last time you went to a game?" he asked as his hand ghosted up her thigh.

Ah, so that's the game he wants to play. "Last season. We had a corporate event in one of the club boxes."

"Did you have"—he hesitated as his hand brushed against her clit through her jeans—"fun?"

"I already told you. I'm all about fun."

Alex's fingers continued rubbing her through her pants. The rough fabric and firm inseam felt phenomenal against her. "I'm starting to come around to your way of thinking. I've had more fun over the past few months than I've had in years." His voice was low and seductive and a total fucking turn-on.

"Guess I'm a great influence."

"Guess so." Alex unbuttoned her jeans and pulled down the zipper before pushing his hand inside her pants and thong. "I'm not as skilled as you are, but maybe practice will make perfect."

Cass moaned as his fingers caressed her clit. "That's definitely a winning attitude."

"You're all about fun, and I'm all about winning. Sounds like a killer combination."

Alex was definitely killing her all right. "That feels so good." Cass shifted down in her seat a little to give him better access.

Alex toyed with her clit before pushing his finger back a little farther and thrusting it inside of her.

"Oh my God."

"Keep your eyes on the road, Cass. God won't do the driving for you." He kept up his assault, her wetness allowing his finger to slide fully in and out of her. He worked her like a man who knew her body as well as his own. Because he did.

She wanted to hold out. Wanted to bask in the pleasure for a while longer. But she had already been so aroused from blowing him that she was operating with a hair trigger. When he leaned over and sucked on her neck as he finger-fucked her, she completely lost it, crying out her orgasm as the evidence of it coated his nimble fingers. "Jesus Christ," she said on a sigh as she came down from the high.

"You're invoking a lot of holiness tonight."

"Don't talk. You'll ruin my orgasm."

Alex barked out a laugh as he relaxed in his seat. "If you want me to drive, you can pull over."

"No way. Because if I get back in that seat, I'll be tempted to initiate another round of road-head chicken."

Alex laughed again. "As you wish."

And what Cass really wished, she was quickly coming to realize, was to have more nights like this one. Many more.

A few nights later, Alex pulled open the door to Duffy's Tavern, the place he'd agreed to meet Cass for dinner and drinks. Tessa would be dropping off Nina tomorrow for her eight-week stay, and even though Cass and Alex were both excited that things had worked out the way they had, they'd also wanted to get together for a night out before their twosome became a constant party of three.

He spotted Cass sitting at a high-top against one of the windows. He walked over, placed a hand on her back, and gave her a quick kiss. "Hey. Been waiting long?" he asked as he slid onto the stool across from her. He was momentarily taken aback by how instinctual it was to lean into Cass' space and kiss her hello. It was very . . . relationshipesque. *Are we in a relationship?* They hadn't talked about it, but the more time they spent together, the more *right* it felt for them to not just act like a couple, but to actually be one. *But is that what we want? What she wants?* Thankfully his thoughts didn't get to meander too far down the rabbit hole before Cass' voice brought him back into the moment.

"Nah, just about five or ten minutes. I was able to sneak out of work a few minutes early."

"Oh good. It's more crowded than I thought it'd be."

"Yeah, the rush followed me in."

They both took a minute to peruse their menus so that when the waitress found her way over, they were able to place their food and drink orders. When the waitress retreated, Alex looked over at Cass. "How was your day?"

"Oh, you know. The usual. Saving lives, one publicity stunt at a time. How about you?"

"Pretty awesome, actually. We apprehended a perp we'd been after for almost a year. I can't get into specifics, but this case . . ." Alex shook his head. "Let's just say it's a good thing he's off the streets. And our case is solid. We're going to nail this prick to the fucking wall. He'll never see freedom again. And I was there when we took him down. There's no better feeling than slapping cuffs on a guy who's destroyed the lives of entire families. Best part of the job." Alex sat back in his chair, feeling as though some of the residual anxiety of chasing a dangerous criminal had bled out of him as he spoke. Apprehending society's worst was nothing new, but he felt supremely satisfied every time he was able to close a case. It was a feeling that never went away: the incredible sensation of catching the bad guy and making him pay. *I definitely have a hero complex.*

Cass stared at him for a second.

"What?" he asked.

"You're really sexy."

Alex's eyes darted to the waitress, who'd of course chosen that moment to drop off their drinks. She smirked as she quickly put their drinks down and left. "Uh, thanks. Not that that isn't one of the hottest things anyone's ever said to me—and please, say it as often as you'd like—but what prompted it?"

"Just," Cass swirled her hand in front of him, "this whole badass–FBI agent thing you got going on. Taking down bad guys and keeping the rest of us safe. It's such a turn-on."

"Is it now?" Alex asked as he took a sip of his beer, willing his dick to behave.

Cass nodded slowly. "I think I may have to show proper appreciation on behalf of the good people of Virginia when we get back to your place."

"We could take our food to go."

"We could, but what would be the fun in that?" Cass teased.

"I can think of a lot of fun we could be having if we were somewhere more private."

"Good things come to those who wait," Cass replied as she sipped her gin and tonic. After she set the glass back down, she seductively ran her tongue over her lips.

"Why are you fucking with me?"

Cass laughed. "Because it's going to be a while before I get to talk about it *and* follow through on it. I plan to torture you for at least a couple more hours."

"Sadist," Alex grumbled, though his dick was very much on board.

Smirking, Cass said, "You love it."

Alex couldn't help but grin. He *did* love it. He was scared to admit how much.

Chapter 22

Integration

Alex grabbed some more of Nina's bags out of the trunk of Tessa's SUV. "How can a seven-year-old girl accumulate so much stuff?"

Nina shrugged, smiling proudly.

Cass stood on Alex's front lawn as he and Pete took the last of Nina's bags up to her room.

Nina followed them in, directing them to keep her art supplies downstairs and to put her stuffed animals on her bed.

Tessa had been standing near the car but took a few steps closer to Cass, giving her a small smile— one that Cass thought was probably difficult to manage, given the fact that Tessa wouldn't be seeing her daughter for two months.

Cass put her hands in the pockets of her shorts. "Thanks for this," she said. "It means a lot to Alex that you're letting Nina stay here."

Tessa lifted her sunglasses up onto her head, and

Cass could see her eyes were red with the tears she'd been holding back. "He's a good father. He deserves it." Then she shifted her gaze down to the ground and added, "They both do."

Cass gave her a small nod. "We'll take good care of her."

"I know you will."

It was a simple sentence, and one that could easily be interpreted as a polite reply. But Cass knew it was more than that. She looked toward the house when she heard the men's voices.

"I think she's all set," Pete called to Tessa.

Nina ran to Tessa's side, and she put an arm around her daughter. Pete went over and squatted down to say good-bye and give Nina a hug. Then he stood and moved away to open the driver's-side door, giving Tessa a moment alone with her little girl. Tessa wiped a hand across her eyes before pulling her glasses back down and saying something in Nina's ear. Nina nodded and then hugged her mother tightly. The two gave each other a kiss good-bye, and Tessa blew another on the way to the car. "I'll check in with you soon, honey. Have fun! Love you."

"Love you too." Nina waved as Tessa and Pete pulled out of the driveway, but Cass was glad that Nina didn't seem upset. She knew Alex had been worried she would be. "So, what are we doing first?" Nina asked, turning toward Cass and Alex once her mom was out of sight.

Alex raised his eyebrows at Cass, clearly looking to her for suggestions.

"Do you like Chinese food?" Cass asked her.

The three had spent the evening on the couch, watching some movie about a girl and a horse and eating

Chinese out of cardboard containers. Cass even taught Nina to use chopsticks, but not without a few soy-sauce carpet casualties. When the movie was over, Cass stood to clean up the trash from dinner and returned a few minutes later to a darkened family room.

She stopped in her tracks, guessing that Nina and Alex were hiding somewhere. "Hello?" she called, knowing that Nina was probably holding back a laugh. "Where did everyone go?"

"Shh," she heard Nina whisper.

Cass moved through the room, using the faint light coming in through the blinds to guide her. She saw that some of the couch cushions had been removed. They stood on their sides, propped up against the couch and the table with a blanket over the top of them, creating a fort. Cass slowly crept over and lifted the blanket to look inside. "Found you!" she yelled. But Alex and Nina were nowhere in sight.

That's when she heard a high-pitched laugh from behind her that made Cass nearly jump. She turned to see Nina and Alex pop up from behind the couch.

"Tricked you!" Nina yelled.

Cass laughed. "You really did."

"Daddy told me you'd think we were in there. Come on," Nina said. "Let's all get in the fort Daddy built."

Cass looked at the structure skeptically. "Is there room for all of us? I think your dad might need to make a separate one for himself." Cass stuck her tongue out. "This one's ours. No boys allowed."

Cass crawled inside and Nina followed. "Cass is right. You won't fit," Nina said to her father.

Alex lifted the blanket that hung over the entrance and shoved his large body inside, sprawling himself heavily across them. "I fit fine," he said as the fort caved in on them. "I don't know what you're talking about."

Nina squealed with delight and did her best to climb out from under Alex. "Now you'll have to make another one," she said. "Can you make one that's big enough for all of us?"

"For *all* of us?" Alex repeated. "I guess I'll see what I can do." He quickly moved about the room, pushing the coffee table farther from the couch and propping up cushions strategically against them. Then he disappeared and came back a minute later with a sheet, which he draped over everything and tucked in behind the cushions. "What do you think?" he asked, admiring his work.

Nina lifted the sheet and crawled inside. Cass and Alex followed her, flanking her on either side. "Perfect," she said. Then, after they'd all been quiet for a few minutes, she asked, "Can we sleep in here?"

"All three of us?" Alex's question was to Nina, but his eyes were directed at Cass.

"Yeah," Nina answered. "Me, you, and Cass. You can get some blankets and pillows, and we can go camping." Nina looked back and forth between the two adults. "I mean, not for real. It'll just be pretend."

Cass shrugged and gave Alex a small smile, letting him know that she was game if he was.

"Sure," Alex answered, his tone lighter than his expression. "We can pretend."

Alex awoke the next morning and crept stealthily out of the fort, hoping not to wake the girls. He gave them one last look before heading to the kitchen, where he put on a pot of coffee and got some bacon out of the fridge. As he expected, it wasn't long before Cass and Nina appeared at the entrance to the kitchen, sleep still fresh in their eyes as they rubbed them. Alex leaned against the counter, coffee cup in hand. "Morning. How are my two sleeping beauties?"

"Okay," Cass said, stretching. "I don't think I've slept on a floor since I was a kid."

Alex handed her a cup of coffee, and Cass thanked him.

"Can I have some?" Nina asked.

"Bacon and eggs? Yes. Coffee? No," Alex answered.

Nina tilted her head to the side as if his assumption that she would ask for coffee was dumb, and then grabbed a plate from the cabinet.

Alex finished cooking and then put scrambled eggs and bacon on all their plates. He added some sliced bananas to the side of Nina's meal and poured them each a glass of orange juice. Then the three settled into what had at some point become their spots at Alex's kitchen table, and dug in. None of them spoke, each too focused on eating to care about conversation.

Once all of them had finished, Nina asked to be excused to go to the other room to watch cartoons. Alex cleared the plates from the table and poured Cass another cup of coffee before heading to the sink to do the dishes. "What?" he asked when he noticed Cass staring at him, an amused grin on her face.

"Waking up to sizzling bacon and coffee?" she said. "I was just thinking I could get used to this."

Alex threw the dish towel over his shoulder. "Glad you liked it," he replied. Because he'd just been thinking he could get used to it too.

Chapter 23

Evidence

"Daddy, can I bury you?"

Alex directed his attention to Nina, who sat playing in the sand in front of him. "Wouldn't you rather go in the water?"

Nina shook her head. Ever since he'd made the mistake of letting her watch Shark Week a few days earlier, she'd had a newfound fear of the ocean. They'd been at the beach for almost two hours, and Nina had refused to do more than dip her feet.

"Are you sure? I'll hold you the entire time."

"So the sharks can eat us both? No way."

Alex heard a sputtering laugh beside him and shot Cass a glare.

"You only have yourself to blame," she said before turning her attention back to her magazine.

He rolled his eyes as he slipped out of his chair and lay down on the sand. "Bury away."

"Oh, I'm totally getting in on this," Cass said as

she knelt down beside him. "Maybe we should start with his head." She waggled her eyebrows playfully at Nina, who laughed.

Alex lay there and let them pour copious amounts of sand over him. It was oddly relaxing actually. The rhythmic patting of gritty sand was almost like getting a massage. Until Nina accidentally got some too close to his mouth.

"Sorry, Dad."

"It's okay. Just try to be a little more careful."

"You know what we need, Nina?"

"What?"

"Some buckets of water so we can make the sand wet. It'll pack in better."

"What a great idea," Alex said dryly.

"Yeah, let's go get some." Nina thrust two buckets at Cass before picking up two herself. "Don't move," Nina warned.

"Wouldn't dream of it."

Cass smiled at him ardently before taking Nina's hand and walking toward the water. Alex quickly lost sight of them, but the image of his two favorite girls walking hand in hand down the beach warmed him even more than the summer sun. He and Cass hadn't discussed labels or the status of their relationship, but his feelings were growing stronger. Nina had been with him for a week and a half, and Cass had spent a good bit of that time with them. They'd mostly hung out around the house or visited the park down the street. This was the first day trip they'd taken, and he was glad Cass had wanted to join them. It wasn't that he didn't think he and Nina would have fun on their own, because he knew they would. But spending time with Cass was always a perk.

It dawned on him that the girls had been gone for

much longer than was necessary to fill a few buckets with water. He tried not to disrupt the sand as he strained his neck to try to see where they could be. He had to lift himself up more, knocking most of the sand off his chest, to catch sight of them. Cass and Nina were in the water deeper than he'd been able to lure her all day, still holding hands as they tried to jump over waves. Sitting up all the way, Alex watched them for a little bit. Cass really was very good with Nina, and it was clear Nina adored her. Wanting to join in on the fun, Alex stood, halfheartedly knocking the sand off himself, and made his way toward the ocean.

Cass turned and saw him as he approached. "Hey, you moved."

"Of course I did. Why should you two get to have all the fun?" he asked as he took Nina's other hand and began jumping waves with them.

"Shit. I mean shoot," Alex was quick to amend as his eyes darted from his burned finger to a thankfully distracted Nina.

Cass smirked at him. "Maybe you should let me take over."

Alex stirred the taco mix with the ground beef. "Why? So I'll have to run out for takeout again when you burn everything?"

Cass walked over and flicked him in the arm. "Very funny. At least I'm able to escape the kitchen without third-degree burns."

"Maybe you are, but the food isn't."

He watched Cass' gaze dart to Nina before she replied. "You're lucky we have an audience, or I'd make you pay for that comment."

Alex couldn't help the barking laugh that escaped

him. "Oh yeah, lucky me." What was the worst she could do to him? Look at him harshly?

Cass scrunched up her face at him before turning back to help Nina add salad dressing to the vegetables she'd just put in a bowl with the care of a curator handling priceless art.

He smiled at the sight of his girls before turning his attention back to the sizzling food in front of him just as his cell phone rang. Snatching it off the counter, he answered it without looking at the display. "Walker."

"Alex. It's Don. We have a development that needs your attention."

Alex set down the spatula and looked at Cass, who was watching him with eyebrows raised in question. He gestured to the stove, and she nodded, quickly moving to take over. *Thanks,* he mouthed before leaving the room.

"What's going on, Don?"

"Travers has been running his mouth. Saying there are more bodies out there we don't know about. Says he'll tell us where the bodies are buried if we convince the prosecutor to take the death penalty off the table."

"Jesus Christ." Alex ran a hand through his hair. *More victims?* He didn't even want to imagine it. Travers had already left quite a body count. If there were more . . .

"It's your call, Alex. I thought you'd want to question him yourself, but it needs to be done immediately. We can't hand this case over to the prosecutor with a loose end like this."

Alex glanced into the kitchen, watching Cass and Nina laugh as they finished up cooking. He sighed. "I'll be right there," he said into the phone before disconnecting the call and joining the girls.

"Everything okay?" Cass asked when she noticed his approach.

He leaned against the counter. "Not really. My case . . . something came up. I have to go in."

Nina's smile faded from her face, and she looked down at the salad bowl in front of her.

Alex moved over to her. "I'm sorry, honey. If it's okay with you, I'd like to take some of the salad you made with me. It looks too good not to have some."

Nina raised her gaze to his and gave him a slight smile. "Are you going to catch a bad guy?"

"Yes." He wasn't *exactly* going to catch one, but the moment didn't warrant a full explanation of his directive for the evening.

Her smile grew. "Okay then. I'll get you a bowl to take with you."

Alex squeezed her shoulder. "Thanks, sweetie."

When she went off to find him a Tupperware container, he turned to Cass. "I'm so sorry that I have to leave. Are you okay to stay for a while? I don't really know how long it'll take, but I'll try to be as quick as I can."

Cass slid her arms around his waist. "Don't worry about it. I understand. And no rush. At worst, I'll raid your wardrobe for a T-shirt and shorts, and Nina and I will have a sleepover. I don't have any early meetings tomorrow, so I can always just run home in the morning to change. Do what you need to do."

Alex pressed a quick kiss to her lips. "You're the best. You know that?"

"Yup," she replied with a smirk before she moved back to the stove to finish dinner.

Alex was glad she knew.

* * *

Cass couldn't remember having so much fun. As much as she liked her job, she found that, more often than not, she looked forward to the day ending. Nina had been at Alex's for four weeks, and Cass had spent a lot of that time with them. Alex had settled into the role of primary caregiver quite well. And there had been only one time that he'd gotten stuck at work and needed Cass to pick up Nina from camp, so Tessa's worries about Alex not having time to spend with Nina were thankfully unfounded.

Despite worrying that she was intruding on their father-daughter time, Cass couldn't resist accepting Alex's invitations to go places with them. They'd taken a day trip to the beach, attended a baseball game, gone to the movies, and spent a day wandering around D.C. Today they'd driven to Bowie to go to Six Flags. Cass hadn't been to an amusement park in years, and she was probably more excited than Nina by the time they arrived.

They walked to the gate in what had become their usual pose: Nina between them as they each held one of her hands.

"This is going to be so much fun," Nina practically squealed.

"I know. I'm so excited," Cass agreed.

They made their way through the long line at the gate, grabbed a map, and entered the park.

"Want to hit the dry rides first, and then we can spend the afternoon in the water park?" Alex asked.

Cass looked over at Alex in his aviators and tank top. It seemed like he got more attractive with every passing day. Though maybe that was her libido talking. As much fun as they'd been having with Nina, the sex had definitely suffered. There'd been cuddling and innocent touches, even some hot-as-hell groping after Nina had gone to bed that had led to frantic sex, but they hadn't really taken the time to enjoy each other thoroughly in a while. However, judging by how she couldn't stop undressing him with her eyes, she thought that she might need to rectify that soon. "That sounds like a good idea. What do you think, Nina?"

"Fine with me." From the way she was fidgeting, it was clear that getting on rides of any type was her main objective.

As they walked deeper into the park, they were stopped by a young man with a camera around his neck. "Can I get a photo of all of you together?"

Cass looked over to Alex, who was also looking back at her. Then he smiled and pulled both Cass and Nina closer. "Sure."

The photographer snapped the shot and handed them a card with a number on it, explaining that they could purchase the picture at any point in the day. Alex put the card in his pocket, and they made their way toward the rides.

Nina's eyes were wide as she took in the attractions. They started on the rides that were geared toward younger kids first: teacups, bumper cars, and the carousel were her favorites. But Nina quickly grew tired of the kiddie rides, so they made their way into the rest of the park. They played a few games in between rides on the Tilt-A-Whirl, the pirate ship, the monorail, and the Scrambler. Cass found that she and Alex were actually perfect amusement park companions—she hated heights and he preferred to skip anything that spun excessively. So they each picked up the other's slack, with Cass accompanying Nina on anything that stayed on the ground, and Alex taking her on anything that went up high.

After about an hour and a half, Nina asked to go on a roller coaster. Alex consulted the map and chose the tamest coaster in the park. As they approached it, Cass decided that even though the height requirement would allow a five-year-old to ride, it was too much for her. She took hold of the stuffed animals they'd won for Nina and moved to the fence to wait for Alex and Nina to ride the steel death trap.

Looking up at the ride as it made its ascent, Cass wondered if Nina and Alex were aboard. She got her answer as she heard crying and Alex yelling for Nina to stop. Cass turned toward the entrance of the ride to see Nina running away from the coaster as Alex chased after her, though his larger body was having a difficult time getting through the crowd. Not knowing what else to do, Cass rushed forward and grabbed Nina before she got lost in the crowd. "Nina? Nina, calm down. What happened?"

"Let me go. I don't want to be here anymore. I want to go home."

Finally Alex reached them, and Cass directed the same question to him.

"I'm not sure. We got to the front of the line, and she just freaked out. Started crying and then took off." He lowered himself to one knee so that he was eye level with Nina. "Baby, what happened?"

"Nothing. I just want to go home," Nina wailed with a petulance reserved for those under ten.

"But we're having such a good day," Alex cajoled. "Why don't we find something else to ride?"

"No. I don't want to go on any more baby rides."

Alex looked totally confused. "Then we'll go on some big-girl rides."

"I don't want to," Nina whined.

"But why?"

"Because this ride's too scary." Nina started crying in earnest again.

Cass couldn't even pretend she knew what was going on in Nina's head. It didn't make a lot of sense to her. Clearly Cass was afraid to go on the ride, so it wasn't a big deal that a seven-year-old was put off by it. There were tons of rides they could go on. *This parenting stuff is exhausting.*

"Why don't we get changed and go to the water park then?" Alex asked.

"No. I'm a baby. I'll probably be scared of the water rides too."

"Nina, that's ridiculous. You love the water."

As Alex tried to coax Nina into downgrading from a category-four-sized tantrum to a more manageable category one, Cass finally thought she might be beginning to understand why Nina was so upset. "Nina," she said, as she turned the little girl gently toward her. "You don't need to be embarrassed that you didn't get on the ride. You're seven. I'm over twenty years older than you, and I had no intention of getting on there. It's not a big deal."

Nina sniffled. "Why are you scared?"

Cass smiled. "Like I told you earlier, I don't like heights."

"Just like I don't really like rides that spin around too much," Alex interjected. "We all have things we don't like, Nina. It's okay to not want to get on the ride."

"But how do I know I don't like it if I'm too scared to even get on?" Nina looked at Cass. "Have you ever been on a roller coaster?"

"No," Cass replied.

"Really? Never?" Alex looked shocked.

"Is now the best time for you to be judging my lack of coaster experience?"

"Then how do you know you won't like it?" Nina asked.

Cass sighed. The last thing she needed was a seven-year-old confronting her about her irrational fears. "I guess I don't."

Nina seemed to ponder that for a second.

Cass knew she was going to regret the next words out of her mouth before she spoke them. "Maybe we should both try it. Then we'll know if we really don't like it."

Nina looked both excited and apprehensive about Cass' suggestion. After thinking it over for a minute, much to Cass' dissatisfaction, Nina nodded. "Okay. Let's do it."

"Awesome." Cass tried to infuse some excitement into her response, but she was pretty sure she'd failed miserably.

Alex caught her elbow as they walked toward the ride. "You don't have to go on. She'll get over it."

Cass shrugged like it was no big deal, even though it was a *very* big deal. Cass had always imagined that her version of hell would consist of a roller coaster forever on the verge of its speedy descent toward imminent death. Though she guessed if she were already in hell, the threat of death would be less frightening. But none of that mattered as she waited in line to face her greatest fear. Or die from it. Whichever.

When they were next in line, Alex leaned into her to whisper in her ear. "I chose this coaster because it's pretty tame. It goes fairly high, but there's no loops or anything. It'll be okay." He put a strong, comforting hand on her back. "Thanks for doing this."

She turned to look at him, taking in the virile male beauty that was Alex Walker. She gave him a small smile. "No problem."

And there wasn't a problem. Until they boarded the rickety cart that Cass was sure hadn't been tested for safety since the early sixties. The fact that she had no idea when the park had opened or when the ride had been built made no difference to her assessment. She was obviously getting on a vehicle designed by Satan.

Nina sat between Cass and Alex, clutching at them both as the ride began its slow climb up the first hill. Cass wished she could clutch back.

As they approached what seemed to be the end of the track—the point that made it appear as though you were either going to soar into the sky or drop off the unfinished edge and hurtle toward the hard cement below, Cass did something she hadn't done in years. She prayed.

In truth, the hill wasn't very high. But the fear in Cass' head likened it to Mount Everest. And as they reached the top and hovered there for their final moments on earth, Cass thought about how at least she was facing the end with her favorite people. That thought was cut off by her own piercing scream as the ride flew down the hill and whipped around a turn. Once they disembarked the ride, Cass might admit that the terms "flew" and "whipped" were slight exaggerations, but for now her terror tended to blow things out of proportion.

Thankfully the ride was brief. Before Cass could even take inventory of all her body parts to make sure they were still where they were supposed to be, the ride was pulling back into where it started.

The safety bar lifted, and Nina jumped up. "That was awesome! Wasn't that awesome, Cass?"

Cass tried to get her shaking under control as she stood and climbed out of the cart. "It was something."

As Nina skipped toward the exit in front of them, Alex wrapped his arm around Cass' waist. "So, I'm going to go out on a limb and say that you haven't been converted into a thrill-ride enthusiast."

"The only way I'd get on one of those again is at gunpoint. Even then, it may be worth taking the bullet."

He tightened his hold and moved closer to press a kiss to her temple. "You're amazing. You know that?"

She curled into him, putting her own arm around him in return. "So you keep telling me."

They both laughed as Nina thankfully announced that she was ready for the water park. They spent the rest of the day riding water slides, eating junk food, and laughing hysterically. When Nina seemed to be struggling to keep her eyes open, they decided to call it a day. They changed back into their dry clothes and met outside the locker rooms. As they walked toward the exit, Alex put his hand in his pocket and pulled out the card they'd been given earlier. "I forgot all about this. Want to stop and see what it looks like before we leave?"

Cass *did* want to see the picture, but a glance down at a silent Nina made her reconsider. "Not sure this one is going to make it through any pit stops."

Alex looked down at his exhausted daughter. "Come here, honey," he said as he scooped her up.

Cass slid the backpack that had their wet clothes and towels in it off his shoulder so he could better carry Nina, who was already resting her head on her dad's shoulder with her eyes closed.

The photo center was right next to the exit, so they walked over. Alex gave the attendant the card and she cued up the picture on the screen. As it appeared, Cass couldn't help the smile that spread over her face.

"You have a beautiful family."

Cass was so wrapped up in the photo, she didn't even notice the older couple standing at the screen next to them until the woman spoke.

Cass smiled at the woman before turning back to their screen. They really did look like a happy little family. The thought made Cass proud. She shifted closer to Alex and wrapped her hand around his free arm, needing to feel close to him. "Thank you," she replied to the woman.

Alex looked over at her before pressing a soft kiss to her temple. To the attendant he said, "We'll take two copies."

Cass didn't let herself think about it for too long, but she recognized that moment for what it was. She'd known she had the feelings for quite some time, but right then, in front of the picture booth, was when she finally became okay with the fact that she was in love with Alex Walker.

Chapter 24

Bottom Line

Cass settled into the chair and began hitting buttons like she was preparing to land a space shuttle. "How do I get this to stop going up my ass?"

The girls leaned out a bit from their pedicure chairs and craned their necks to see her.

"What?" Cass asked, looking to the left and right at the three sets of eyes trained on her. "Are you gonna help me or not? This thing's gonna give me hemorrhoids."

"Just turn it off," Lauren said.

"Fine," Cass said, clicking the button. "But I like the shoulder part."

Simone eyed her suspiciously. "I'm sure Alex will give you a massage later if you ask him to." Then she sat back casually, as if she hadn't just called Cass out.

"Oh damn. Shade thrown," Lauren said.

Ignoring Lauren, Cass looked at Simone with feigned bewilderment. "What does that mean exactly?"

Simone kept her eyes closed, enjoying the part of the massage chair that Cass couldn't figure out how to work. "You know what it means."

And Cass did. Clearly Simone—and no doubt the rest of her crew—had figured out that her pretend relationship wasn't that *pretend* anymore. She just hadn't expected her friends to notice so soon; she'd just noticed herself not that long ago. Though she shouldn't have been surprised. Cass had been spending a lot of her free time with Alex and Nina. And her group of girlfriends had been close for fifteen years. If they could tell when she had her period, they could certainly tell when she was falling for a guy. Especially since she'd never fallen for one before.

Though Cass was a bit relieved that her friends had picked up on the change in her relationship status, she didn't know exactly how to explain what that change *was*. It was better to see what they thought first. "You'd better open your eyes and look at me before I close them permanently," Cass joked. "What is it that you think is happening between me and Alex?"

Simone's eyes opened again, and when they fixated on Cass, she immediately wished she could retract her question. Simone had a way of getting the truth from people like she was waxing someone's eyebrows; you didn't know exactly when it was coming, and it was usually painful. "It's not what I *think*," Simone said. "It's what I *know*. And what I know is that now you want more than just his dick."

The woman painting Simone's toes jerked her head up in shock, but Simone didn't seem to notice. Or maybe she just didn't care.

Cass rolled her eyes, mainly because she didn't know how else to respond.

"I'll take your silence as confirmation that I'm correct," Simone said.

Cass inhaled deeply, preparing to let go of some of the theoretical weight she'd been carrying around. "I'll talk to you about it. I've been meaning to anyway." *Just not today.* The girls' eyebrows lifted in what Cass guessed was surprise. "But I don't even know that I can explain how this whole thing turned into something . . . *real*. It's like one day we were faking our love for each other, and the next we were . . ." Cass let her voice trail off, unsure she wanted to continue. But she found her nerve. Admitting it to her friends couldn't be as hard as admitting it to herself had been. Cass let out a heavy sigh. "And the next we were *in* love," she finished quietly. "At least *I* am."

The girls' eyes widened even more in disbelief. Clearly, they hadn't expected her to say *that*. Lauren's jaw dropped as if she were about to speak, but no sound escaped it. Quinn spoke instead. "I'm happy for you, Cass. Really. I mean, I'm totally shocked you admitted to that," she added. "But I'm happy."

Cass offered Quinn a small smile.

"Does he feel the same?" Simone asked. Her voice was quiet, almost hesitant, but there was a steel behind it that let Cass know Simone had an opinion Cass probably wasn't going to like.

"I think so," Cass replied, meeting Simone's gaze.

"You *think* so? You guys haven't talked about it?"

Cass bristled at Simone's tone: a mixture of disbelief and recrimination. "Well, no. The feelings kind of just snuck up on me."

Simone sighed. "I know I'm probably coming off like a bitch. But just hear me out. You guys have been pretending to have feelings for a while now. I'm worried. Worried that you've spent so long pretending that you're confusing that with genuine feelings. I don't want to see you change your whole life around to accommodate a figment of your imagination."

Cass rolled her eyes. "Who said anything about changing my whole life around?"

"Come on, Cass." Simone didn't need to say anything else. Those words combined with the "don't bullshit your best friends" look Simone was aiming at her were enough.

Cass shrugged. "Okay, so loving Alex would change everything. But . . . it's how I feel. *Really* how I feel. Not how I've convinced myself to feel. I mean, seriously. You think I *want* to feel all turned inside out? I don't know how these two hookers survived it," she said, jerking her thumb toward Lauren and Quinn.

The girls laughed the tension away, and when Simone spoke again, she was smiling. "Then I'm happy for you too. Still a little worried. But happy." Simone paused for a second before continuing. "So what are you going to do now?"

"I'm not sure." Cass smiled, but she didn't feel it reach her eyes. "And that's the truth."

"What's wrong?" Lauren asked. "Tell us. That's what we're here for."

"Look, I know we haven't talked about any of the specifics, but I'm pretty sure he feels the same way about me—I hope so anyway." Cass let out a long sigh. "But I don't think now's the right time to discuss all this. Alex still has a few more weeks with Nina. And if our relationship isn't what I think it is . . . If he just wants to stay friends . . ." Cass knew she was rambling. But now that she had verbalized her feelings—though unfortunately not to the person they needed to be verbalized to—she couldn't stop the stream of consciousness.

Cass and Alex had come this far with their plan, and she didn't want to fuck that up by discussing their feelings, especially if Alex's weren't the same. *But they are.* The voice inside her head came out of nowhere, but she knew why it'd spoken. What she'd felt that night after Alex's dinner with Nina, what she'd felt . . . Alex *had* to have felt it too.

"You need to tell him," Quinn's voice was calm but certain.

"I know," Cass agreed. Looking down at her hand, she noticed the ring on her finger. She'd gotten so used to it, she wore it more often than not now, even when she didn't have anyone she needed to convince of their fake nuptials. It just . . . felt right on her hand. The clarity of the diamond shining at her gave her clarity as well. "I will. When all this is over and Nina's back at Tessa's. I'll tell him then"—she shook her head absentmindedly—"when we can focus on *us* and what this all means."

Lauren's face was impassive. "I'll tell you what it means," she said. "It means you're getting married before me."

Chapter 25

Complaint

Something wasn't adding up. Alex looked back through the stack of paperwork in front of him and pulled out an arrest record. *How the fuck could this guy have been arrested in Miami if he was already serving time in Halifax?* This was the kind of shit this case didn't need: dumb clerical errors that made his team look incompetent. Combine that with the fact that the bodies Travers promised he'd lead them to didn't even exist, and his team's work on this case was nothing short of embarrassing.

He'd turned over the file on this case to the federal prosecutor two weeks ago, but they'd sent it back a few days later with a note that outlined the discrepancies they'd found. Now Alex needed to fix what his team had overlooked the first time. Usually he was more of a perfectionist than this. He'd never let mistakes like this past him before. But with having to drop off and pick up Nina from camp, as well as keeping her entertained once they got home, he'd let some of the other guys pick up his slack. And he'd paid for it with a snarky note from the prosecutor and an ass-reaming from his boss.

It wasn't that he regretted taking time away from work to spend it with Nina—that was all part of being a father. But he also had a responsibility to his job, and he needed to see that responsibility through. He was thankful that Cass had been around to help. For the past week, she'd met them at his place a few times after she'd finished work so she could keep Nina occupied while Alex retreated to his office so he could get some things done. She'd been a lifesaver.

Alex continued shuffling around papers in an attempt to piece together the past ten years of this guy's life. He'd lost track of how long he'd been in there when he heard a throat clearing behind him. He turned to see Cass standing in the doorway.

"Dinner's ready," she said.

"Oh, uh, thanks." He turned back toward his desk. "I'll grab some in a bit."

"Why don't you take a break and eat with us?"

"Sorry, can't right this second. I'll be out soon."

"Yeah, right," Cass muttered.

Alex turned back to her. "What does that mean?"

"You know what it means. You've been totally consumed by this case for the past week."

Alex scoffed. "I think you're exaggerating just a little."

"Oh really?" Cass stepped into the room and closed the door behind her. "What meaningful time have you spent with Nina since you brought this case home?"

"What are you talking about? I've only worked from home on this case a few times since it landed back on my lap. I've done all sorts of things with Nina since she's been here. When you take in the scope of the entire summer, what do a few days matter?"

"Yeah, you pulled all kinds of grand gestures when she first got here, but now you're getting complacent. Baseball games and trips to the beach are all well and good, but she doesn't need a father who can fill a high-light reel. She needs someone who will sit down at the dinner table with her and ask about her day."

"How the hell do you know what *my* daughter needs?" Alex couldn't keep the anger out of his voice. *Where the hell does she get off?*

"Well, seeing as I'm the one currently attending to her needs, I figured I had some insight." Cass' words were biting, and Alex felt the sting.

"You're way out of line. Nina and I have gone to dinner, watched TV, played outside. You're acting like I've been holed up in here for the past six days, completely ignoring her."

Cass sighed, relaxing her posture slightly with the exhalation. "Alex, I don't want to fight with you. Honestly I don't. It's just . . . you wanted this time. We went through a lot to get her here. And now you're wasting it. You're here, but you're not really *present*. Sure, you've retreated to your office only a couple times, but you've been preoccupied all week. It's been obvious that your mind has been elsewhere, even if you're physically sitting right next to her."

"I have a job to do. You, of all people, should understand that. What I do is important. If this guy goes free, there are lives at stake. Don't act like you wouldn't be the same way if one of your clients broke a nail or posted a selfie taken in poor lighting."

"Okay, first of all, you're being a real dick. Second of all, do you have any idea how much I've sacrificed at work to be here for you and Nina? I've turned down two weekend events my boss requested I attend, I've ignored phone calls from clients that came outside working hours, and I even had to pass on a major project because it would take up too much of my time. None of this," she said as she gestured around her, "is my responsibility, but I'm here anyway."

"Then go."

"What?" Cass narrowed her eyes. Alex could tell she'd heard what he'd said, but she'd asked him to repeat it anyway.

"You said it wasn't your responsibility. And you're right; it isn't. It's mine. All of it is mine: my job, Nina, the house—all of it. None of it was what you signed up for, so if it's such a burden to you, just leave." He heard his voice rising, but he did his best to keep it down. Despite his anger, the last thing he wanted was for Nina to hear them fighting, especially when the fight had something to do with her.

Cass crossed her arms over her chest. "I never said it was a burden. Don't put words in my mouth. Don't try to make this about me. This is about *you* and *your* responsibilities as a father. You're the one who said life's about showing up, remember? You've said you learned your lesson, that you won't make the same mistakes you made with Tessa—"

Alex tossed the pen he'd been holding across the desk and stood at the mention of Tessa's name. "Don't bring her into this."

"I'm not bringing her into anything she isn't already a part of. Like it or not, you were married to her. Tessa is Nina's mother. I know you hate what she did to you, what she did to your family. But I also know you hate what *you* did to your family just as much."

"You don't know anything about my family." Alex

heard the tension in his voice, the anger. He could feel how cold his stare was, but he didn't care. He wasn't going to stand there and let Cass talk about something she knew nothing about.

Cass took a step toward him, but then stopped as if the proximity to him caused her physical pain. "Really, Alex? I don't know what I'm talking about? Because I'm just repeating what *you* told me. You weren't there as much as you should've been. Your mind was elsewhere. *You* told me that. I didn't make it up. And now you're doing it all over again. Don't you see it? Same shit, different day."

Alex felt his jaw tick as his mind formulated what it wanted to say.

Then Cass' voice softened. "Your job is important. I get that. Believe me—I do. But it's not more important than that little girl sitting downstairs who thinks her daddy hung the fucking moon. This is one of those things that's not going to be about how you started. It's going to be about how you finish. And Nina is going to go home in two weeks, feeling disappointed that her dad didn't pay more attention to her." Cass stared at Alex, her gaze heavy on his as she shook her head slowly. "You say you've changed," she said quietly. "So fucking act like it."

Alex looked at her for a second, unsure of what to say. All of the words that had been circulating in his head as she'd spoken seemed to vanish. It wasn't that he couldn't see where she was coming from, but his anger at her insinuating that he wasn't the father he should be overruled any rational thought. He glared at her for a moment before finally speaking. "Thanks for the speech. I love getting unsolicited advice."

Cass laughed humorlessly and spun around to walk toward the door. She hesitated with her hand on the knob. "I get that you may think my advice is meaningless. But I know what it's like to have great parents. And you know what I remember most about my dad, growing up? The times he let me help him repair things around the house, and when he let me stay up to watch scary movies with him even though my mom would've ripped him a new one if she'd known, and when he threw me pop-ups outside for hours, even though his arm had to have been hurting like hell. He probably had work to do too, but he never made me feel like he had better things to do than spend time with me." Cass pulled the door open. "I'll eat with Nina, and then I'm heading home. That should buy you another half hour." And with that, she left.

Alex looked at the empty doorway for a minute before glancing back at the papers strewn across his desk. He'd known that Cass had sacrificed in order to help him. But where did she get off acting like a martyr when it was her own fault she was involved in the first place? If she'd kept her mouth shut, they wouldn't be dealing with this whole fake-wedding nightmare, not to mention the fallout that would eventually occur from it. If she thought Nina would be upset because he had to spend a few nights focusing on work, just wait until she saw the devastation Nina would experience when he told her the wedding was off. *Oh wait. Cass won't need to see that, because she won't be the one who has to break the news to Nina.*

Alex willed himself to calm down. So many emotions were rolling through him, he was having a hard time pinpointing exactly how he felt. Did Cass have a point? Or was she unnecessarily attacking his parenting? Was he angry at her or angry at the damned-if-you-do, damned-if-you-don't situation he found himself in? He let himself marinate in his feelings for the half hour Cass had told him he had before she left, and then decided to head downstairs. He glanced out of an upstairs window first to make sure Cass' car was gone before he went to find Nina, telling himself it was because he didn't want to have an awkward encounter in front of his daughter. Though he knew the truth: he'd rather face Hannibal Lecter than a hundred forty pounds of irate female.

He found Nina sitting on the couch, watching some Disney movie about princesses. "Hey, baby. Whatcha doin'?" He slid in next to her and put his arm behind her on the couch.

"Just watching TV. Cass left."

Alex ignored the comment, opting to change the subject instead. "Did you have a good day at camp?"

Nina shrugged. "I guess."

Alex hoped he was just overanalyzing the situation in light of his argument with Cass, but Nina seemed reserved around him. "You really into this movie, or do you want to go for a walk with me? Maybe we can hit the playground and then grab some ice cream on the way back?"

Nina didn't look at him. "That's okay. I know you're busy."

Ouch. "Hey." He bumped Nina's shoulder and waited until she looked at him. When she did, he smiled at her. "I'm all done being busy. I want to go play at the park with my favorite daughter."

It was faint, but Alex saw a smile begin to form on Nina's face. "I'm your *only* daughter."

"Okay, with my favorite *person* then. You in?" Alex stood and held out his hand.

Nina looked at it for a second before putting her hand in his. "I'm in."

As they walked out of the house together, Alex told himself that he wasn't spending this time with Nina because of Cass' scolding, but because he was a good dad. He didn't need a self-proclaimed bachelorette for life to tell him to how to do right by his daughter. And for the next couple of hours, Alex forgot about the people who might be transient in his life and focused on the constant in front of him.

Chapter 26

Indictment

Less than nine hours. That's how much total sleep Cass had gotten over the past three nights. She'd tossed and turned so much that she'd skipped the gym, deciding that her sleep—or lack of sleep—habits were exercise enough.

And it hadn't just been her body that had gotten a workout. Her mind had too. She had so many thoughts running through it, she wasn't sure how to even make sense of any of them. As she sat at her desk, staring at her computer screen, she thought back to her fight with Alex, if it could even be called that. It was more of a conversation—a request even—that, in her opinion, Alex had gotten irrationally defensive about. And then it had just escalated from there.

She hadn't meant to imply that he wasn't a good father. She knew he was. But Cass also knew that as much as she didn't want him making the same mistake again, Alex didn't want that either. And if Cass were honest with herself, she *had* been a little unfair. Accusing Alex of putting work before his daughter and then connecting it to the very thing that had ultimately been the catalyst for the split between him and Tessa had been a shot below the belt that she'd taken in anger.

Split. She let the word bounce around in her mind for a moment, its echo an unwelcome visitor there. But that thought was what she'd needed to finally put the whole thing in perspective. Maybe this was *not* a big deal. Maybe it was *not* a deal breaker. Maybe it was just a minor disagreement—one that was common in any relationship. There was no avoiding that. It was hopefully just a small ripple in what Cass saw as a much larger sea. And just because they'd encountered their first wave didn't mean their boat would capsize and they would drown out there.

Sure, she'd had a right to say what she'd said. No matter how much she loved someone—and she *did* love Alex—she would never censor herself. But Alex had a right to his reaction too. He was as much a part of this relationship as she was, and that meant having a voice in it. Even if it wasn't a voice she wanted to hear at that particular moment.

Maybe that's what set her relationship with Alex apart from others she'd had in the past: she might not have wanted to hear his voice at the time, but that didn't mean she never wanted to hear it again. Whatever anger had existed in her a few days ago had evaporated now.

Cass saw it for what it was: their first fight as a real couple. The only problem was that they still hadn't talked about how real their coupling *was*. So despite the fact that she'd promised herself she'd wait until Nina left to come clean about her feelings, she couldn't stop herself from sending a Can we talk? text to Alex before putting her phone back in her purse and opening her e-mail so she could actually get some work done.

But what she saw surprised her: an e-mail from Alex. Maybe he wants to let this go too. She smiled as she opened the e-mail and read the first line.

Hey, take a look at this when you get a chance. The band sent over a list of the covers they do. Let me know what you think.

Cass was relieved he hadn't mentioned the fight. Though the text of his e-mail had been straightforward, there hadn't been any edge to it.

Cass scrolled down, quickly realizing that it was a chain. But as her finger moved over the mouse, her eyes involuntarily scanned the blurred words as they passed by rapidly on the screen. And what she saw confused her. The e-mail chain wasn't from the band at all. It was a conversation between Scott, Xavier, and Alex from the past few days. Cass laughed internally at Alex's mistake, figuring she'd be getting a glimpse at some ridiculous male nonsense. But she quickly sobered when she realized that the topic of Alex's "mistake" was her. Though Cass knew she should read from the bottom up to get the full context, words and phrases like "hypocrite" and "some nerve" jumped out at her as the text passed her line of vision.

Cass' blood pressure rose as she skimmed the bullshit in front of her. But as she got to the bottom and finally calmed down enough to read Alex's entire first e-mail, the anger she'd initially felt had dissipated.

All she felt now was hurt.

Alex had been responding to Xavier's simple e-mail of, What's new? I haven't talked to you assholes in a few days. And I'm at work. And bored as shit. So give me something good.

It was a simple question, innocent. But Alex's response was anything but.

Hmm, let's see. Oh yeah. Cass jumped down my throat last night about being "present" when I'm present or some bullshit like that. I don't need that shit again. And I definitely don't need it from someone who has openly admitted that her job is more important than a family. Where does she get off judging someone's parenting when she's not a parent and doesn't want to be? She doesn't know how hard it is to juggle two full-time jobs because she'll only ever have one. She admits she doesn't have a maternal bone in her body and then she goes and calls me out on how I'm an absent father? Yeah, okay. That makes a lot of fucking sense. She's not a mother, and she'll never be one.

Xavier essentially had the same reaction Cass did. Though his had probably been without the tears that she felt stinging the corners of her eyes before one finally fell. She didn't even bother wiping it away.

Wow! was all Xavier had written in his next e-mail. It wasn't until Scott wrote back a few hours after that, asking Alex to slow down and explain what happened, that his angry rant got a little less angry. He detailed what had taken place between him and Cass. And though the tone of the rest of Alex's e-mails seemed to have softened as time passed, the message hadn't: Cass had no room to critique who he was as a father when she wasn't a mother and had no interest in being one.

She closed her laptop slowly, pulled her purse out of her desk, slung it over her shoulder, and headed to her boss' office to tell him she felt sick and needed to go home. It wasn't a lie.

And as she pulled her keys from her purse in the parking lot and caught a glimpse of Alex's text back to her, the nausea she'd been trying so hard to quell came back in full force. He'd asked if she wanted to come over later.

She left the phone in her purse, knowing that she shouldn't respond in anger, and turned the key in her ignition. Cass drove home in silence. Well, not actual silence; the thoughts running through her head were louder than any radio would've been. And they were all saying the same thing: Alex was right about her. Cass *wasn't* the maternal type, and she never would be. She'd been delusional to try to convince herself otherwise. She'd hoped that their fight was something they could work through. She'd hoped that they'd both just said some things in anger that they hadn't meant. But all of that hope was gone now. And in its place was the realization she'd been trying so hard to ignore since she'd read the e-mails: Alex meant what he'd said that night. Every word of it. He could never see her as a wife or mother because he viewed those roles as nothing but a burden to her. And if Alex didn't see her as capable of motherhood after the past few months, no amount of time or effort would rectify it. The only person she would ever be capable of being anything to was herself. And maybe she'd be okay with that again. Eventually.

But that didn't change the fact that what Alex had

written to the guys had hurt her. And Cass was never one to bow out when something needed to be addressed. So when she pulled into her space outside of her apartment, she took out her phone and replied, I can be there around 7.

Alex was nervous. Once he'd had time to calm down, he realized that the lingering annoyance he'd felt after his argument with Cass was because of how much he'd hated having her mad at him. It was also helpful to have friends who called him out on his bullshit. When he'd told Scott and Xavier about what had happened, neither had pulled any punches in basically telling him he was an idiot. And he was—for a lot of reasons. That's why he'd invited Cass over. He set Nina up with popcorn and a movie in his room so he and Cass could have some privacy, and they could finally lay it all out on the table: his feelings, her feelings, where they'd go from here— all of it. He was fucking petrified.

He smoothed his T-shirt and ran a hand nervously through his hair as he scanned the room for something that would keep him occupied until she arrived. But a soft knock at the door kept him from having to look long. He walked over to the door and took a deep breath before pulling it open. And there she was. She didn't look happy to see him.

"Hey," he said softly, flashing a small smile.

"Hi." She didn't smile back, nor did she hold his gaze.

Shit. "Come on in." He moved back from the door and then closed it behind her. "Want to sit in the living room?"

"Sure." She followed him silently. He hadn't even known Cass could be that quiet.

They both sat down on the couch, but she was as far away from him as she could get without toppling over the armrest. "I-I wanted to talk about the other night. I didn't like how we left things, and I wanted to—" Alex began.

"It's fine. You really don't have to explain."

"No, I do. I mean, I *want* to. I got defensive, and some of the things I said to you were uncalled-for. You've been a big help, and—"

"Alex, please just stop. We don't need to do this."

"I think we do. You said you wanted to talk, and you agreed to come here. Can you please stop interrupting me so I can apologize, and—"

"No. I can't stop interrupting you because I've already heard how you feel. Or *read*, I guess would be the more appropriate word. And as for agreeing to come here, I shouldn't have. I don't want to be here if you're going to give me some bullshit apology that isn't even honest." Cass rose from the couch and picked up her purse, which she'd set beside her on the floor.

"Cass, wait. I'm totally confused. What do you mean, you've already heard how I feel?"

She let out an audible sigh before turning to face him. "You have your phone on you?"

"Yeah." He fished it out of his pocket.

"Look in your Sent mail for the message you sent me earlier."

He unlocked his screen and opened up his e-mail. He pulled up the band information he'd forwarded her, and . . . *Oh fuck.* "I can explain that. I was angry, mostly at myself."

"Really? Because I don't see a ton of self-recrimination there. Sure, the guys manage to calm you down a little, but you said what you said. And you're not wrong. I never wanted a family, never wanted to be a wife and mother. I'm married to my job, and that works for me. If our little experiment here has taught me anything, it's that I should stick with my strengths. And playing house isn't one of them."

"That's not true. You're great with Nina. I see the way you look at her. It's not an act. And . . . you're great with me too. We're great together. Please don't let my bitching to the guys ruin what we've started here."

"Save it, Alex. When I texted you that I wanted to talk, I thought we could work things out—that our argument the other night was just a little bump in the road. But it's not. I see that now."

"Cass." Alex let her name hang in the air because he wasn't sure what he could say that would explain what he'd written. He'd initially felt like she was judging him, so he'd immediately gone on the defensive. But she hadn't been judging him—she'd been trying to help him because she gave a shit.

Cass' face was completely blank, just as it had been since she arrived. "I know you're used to being able to fix things—that if you try hard enough, think long enough about something, all of the pieces will just fit together." Cass dropped her eyes to the floor, and Alex could see the moisture on them when she brought her gaze back up to his. "But the two of us," she shook her head, "we don't fit together. We never did."

Alex couldn't believe what she was saying. He'd actually had a chance with Cass, and he'd fucked it up before it had even begun.

"I care for Nina," Cass continued. "She's an awesome kid. And I was happy to give up my time for a few months to hang out with her. I promised when this all began that I'd be there for her. And I'll keep that promise. It's not fair to her to have it any other way. But as for us being great together—" Cass shrugged. "We're friends who made a good team for a few months. But I was never big on team sports. I'm a solo act, Alex. I like my life that way. It's not fair of you to ask me for more than I want to give. I've given you enough already."

And she had. He couldn't argue with that. Cass had done more for him in the past four months than he could ever repay. But it couldn't have meant as little to her as she was implying. He understood that he'd hurt her, but he could explain. He could fix it if she'd just give him a chance.

But the expressionless look on her face, the detachment in her words—nothing he could say right now would get through to her. Maybe if he gave her some time she'd come around. Hear him out. But not now. "You're right. I've definitely asked you for enough. I didn't mean to take advantage."

"You didn't. I offered to help, and I was happy to do it. I also promised I wouldn't disappear from Nina's life, and I won't. We're friends—we just need to get back to acting like it."

Alex could only nod as he followed her to the front door. She pulled it open but hesitated briefly in the threshold before murmuring, "Bye, Alex." And then she was gone.

Chapter 27

Admission

"So, you fucked things up pretty bad, huh?" Xavier said before taking a sip of his beer.

When Alex had asked the guys to get together for a drink so they could talk, he was thinking he'd get a little more moral support. Evidently that wasn't going to happen. "We *both* fucked up."

"Yeah, but you *really* fucked up. First, you treated the girl like she was a glorified nanny. Then you blasted her via e-mail. And to think I used to consider you the smooth one." Xavier tried to lighten his words with a wink.

"Please. When did you ever consider me smooth?"

"Never. I was just trying to be nice."

Alex snorted. "Try harder."

Scott, who had been toying with his pint glass as Xavier and Alex spoke, cleared his throat. "How do you feel now that she's gone?"

Alex wasn't sure how to answer. A lot of feelings

had been flowing through him over the past week since Cass had walked out of his house: anger, confusion, guilt, regret. Sadness. But he didn't want to cop to those emotions. Admitting them made them more real, more painful. However, he'd been the one to call on his friends to help. The least he could do was share what he was feeling. "Like shit."

"Why?"

"Why? What do you mean, why?" Alex was beyond confused by the question. They knew about the fight and the e-mail disaster. Scott knew why.

Scott stopped playing with his glass, set both hands on the table, and leaned in a little. "Why do you feel like shit? Is it because you lost the best sex you ever had?"

Alex hesitated as he tried to wrap his brain around Scott's question. "You really think that's it? I'm mad because I lost a good lay?"

Scott shrugged. "So what is it then, if it's not that?"

Damn it. Alex stared at him, thinking that he should have just agreed with Scott. It would have been easier than explaining what was really wrong. Now he had no choice but to share what was going on in his mind. "I feel like shit because I hurt Cass' feelings. I didn't mean the things I said. I was just pissed. And now I'm gonna hurt Nina too."

Scott sat up straight, effectively backing away from Alex. "Then it's just as well it's over."

"What? What the fuck do you mean?" Alex sputtered.

"Listen, Alex. I love you like a brother, man. You know that. And I've only ever wanted you to be happy. But I can't want that at someone else's expense. Especially not Cass'."

Alex just stared at his best friend. Then, turning to Xavier, he said, "Do you have any idea what the hell he's talking about?"

Xavier shook his head. "No, but I have a feeling it's going to be deep."

Alex turned back to Scott, who continued. "You should feel bad for hurting Cass' feelings. Anyone with a conscience would. And the whole Nina thing . . . that sucks on a lot of levels. You're a good dad, so it makes sense that you feel bad."

Alex waited for him to finish his explanation. When he didn't, Alex prompted him with, "But?"

"But neither of those are good enough reasons for someone to dedicate their life to you. You're upset because of how your actions made *other* people feel, not because of how they made *you* feel. If you don't feel anything on behalf of yourself—other than maybe missing out on some orgasms—then you were just wasting her time."

Alex wanted to be insulted. But if he wasn't going to be fully honest with his friends, how could he legitimately hold their opinions against them? "It's not just that."

"Then what is it?"

Alex couldn't take it. His best friends were staring at him expectantly like he was supposed to have some magical answer. The truth was, on top of all the other emotions whirling around in him, there was something else there: relief. Relief that Cass left before things had gotten even more serious. Before he'd gotten irrevocably attached. He'd had the clichéd rug pulled out from under him before, and he didn't know if he could risk it again. He hadn't been enough for Tessa—not as a husband—so how would he ever be enough for Cass? How could he be, when he was making all the same mistakes? He was doing the right thing by letting it lie, but he needed to be absolved of the pain. He didn't want to hurt anymore. He needed someone to cauterize the goddamn wound. "Can you just be on my fucking side?" Alex growled. "I know I fucked up one of the best things I had going for me. I don't need you to rub it in. I just need you to sit there and offer empty words of sympathy like best friends are supposed to do."

Xavier clapped him on the shoulder. "How can we do that when there's still time to fix it?"

Alex moved, causing Xavier's hand to fall from his arm. "What if I don't want to fix it? What if this was how it was meant to be?"

"You want to know what I think?" Scott asked.

"No," Alex replied.

Scott smirked. "Tough shit. I think that since you divorced Tessa, you've been acting like you've wanted to settle down again, when the idea really scares you shitless. You've gone on tons of dates, but the women you picked, they weren't even close to being your type. That was intentional, wasn't it?"

Alex shrugged. "I honestly don't know. Maybe."

"Maybe," Scott repeated with a shake of his head. "I think you do know. I think when Tessa left, it did more damage than you ever admitted. Because the truth is, no matter how horrible what she did was, you didn't exactly fight for your marriage either. Not before the affair, and sure as hell not after. You just walked away. Which is what you're trying to do now. And you want us to support you in that, like we did when your marriage to Tessa fell apart. But Cass isn't Tessa. Cass didn't betray you. She helped you.

She was there for you. She probably even loves your stupid ass. Why would you walk away from that?"

"Because according to you, it's what I do best," Alex snarled.

"Don't do that. That's not what I was trying to say."

"What are you so scared of?" Xavier questioned.

"Alex, come on, man—" Scott started.

"I'm afraid I'm not enough," Alex yelled, causing the other patrons to turn and look at them curiously. He lowered his voice before continuing. "Cass is . . . larger than life. And what I feel for her is deeper than what I ever felt for Tessa. You want to know what I feel? I'm fucking devastated. Because I found someone who was perfect for me, but I fell right back into old patterns. I got caught up in my job and in my own arrogance, and I pushed her away because she dared to call me on it." Alex took a shuddering breath. "And then when she showed up at my house to confront me about the e-mail, when it became clear that she was going to leave too, I didn't even try very hard to explain. You don't need to be Freud to figure me out. All of the important women in my life have left in one way or another. It's the story of my life."

Both Scott and Xavier stood there gaping at him, clearly at a loss for what to say. At least initially.

Xavier was the first to break the silence. "Wow. For such a smart guy, you really are a dumbass."

Finally . . . wait . . . what? "Did you just seriously call me a dumbass? After all that?"

"You bet your ass," Xavier snapped. "It's not some giant cosmic conspiracy to force you to be alone for the rest of your life. If that happens, you'll have only yourself to blame."

Alex scoffed. "I didn't say it was a conspiracy. I just—"

"Stop. Please. Stop and just listen. You are a good guy who messed up. But it's not like you caused a complete and utter disaster. You're letting dumb shit ruin your chance at a really good thing. Knock it the fuck off." Xavier punctuated his final words by taking a long drink of his beer.

"That was quite a pep talk," Alex said.

Xavier shrugged. "What can I say? I have a way with words."

Alex shifted on his stool uncomfortably. "I'm pretty stupid, huh?"

"Yup," the other men replied in unison.

"I should try to fix it, right?"

Xavier and Scott looked at one another before saying, "Yup."

Alex took a deep breath and straightened his posture. "Okay."

"Hello?"

"Hey, it's me. Alex."

"Hey. What's up? Nina okay?"

"Yeah, yeah, she's fine. I was wondering . . . can we meet up for lunch Monday?"

Cass was silent for so long, he looked to see if the call had disconnected. "Why?" was her eventual reply.

"Because you said we'd be friends but we're not acting like it. I just want to try to get some of *us* back."

"The 'us' we were before all this started?"

I fucking hope not. "Whatever us there can be."

She took a deep breath and exhaled it slowly. "Sure. I guess I can do that."

"Great. How about noon at that tavern we ate at a few weeks ago?"

"Okay. See you then." She hung up, leaving Alex with an overwhelming dread that tomorrow wasn't going to go well.

Cass pulled back the shower curtain and leaned out. *Is someone knocking on my door?* She quickly shut off the shower and grabbed her robe. There was definitely someone pounding on her door. Relentlessly, in fact. She rushed toward the racket. "Who is it?" she asked as she looked through the peephole. *Shit.*

"It's us," Lauren yelled.

Cass sighed heavily and unlocked her door before pulling it open. "Ever hear of calling?" She stepped back from the threshold to let them in.

"We're staging an inter*friend*tion. These things work best when they're surprises," Quinn explained.

"You've been watching too much A&E," Cass retorted. She walked into the living room silently cursing the day she let these girls know the code to get into her building. Flopping down on the couch, she waited for her friends to join her before she spoke. "What's up?"

"You tell us," Simone countered.

"The sky. Airplanes. Birds. Clouds. Dirk Diggler's dick."

"Funny," Simone said with a look that distinctly showed that she did *not* think Cass was funny at all.

"You've been avoiding us for over a week. We're worried," Quinn said.

Cass would've felt bad if she hadn't been so numb. "Sorry. I've just been busy."

"Busy trying to heal a broken heart without your

best friends. And without this." Quinn reached into a bag she's brought and pulled out a carton of chocolate chip cookie dough ice cream.

"And these," Lauren added as she pulled a stack of chick flicks out of her purse.

Simone got up and came to sit beside her. "And, of course, this." Simone wrapped her arms around Cass.

Cass tried to stop it. Tried to hold it in. But as Simone's arms tightened, Cass' resolve weakened. The tears came silently at first, but then broken sobs weren't far behind. Cass had kept all of these emotions locked up for eight days. It took her friends less than eight minutes to set them free. She felt Quinn and Lauren join them, their arms twining around her. Holding her tightly in an attempt to put back together what had just broken.

Cass let herself have that movement. Allowed herself to get it all out—to unload it on the people she knew would gladly carry the burden for a while. God, she loved these girls. When her tears slowed, she pulled back so she could wipe her face. "How did you know?"

"The boys are horrible gossips. They make us look like the CIA," Lauren explained.

"What happened, Cass?" Quinn asked.

So Cass told them. She didn't leave out a single detail, and by the end they'd devoured the ice cream and two bags of popcorn, and were currently working through a box of cookies. "And now he wants to meet for lunch tomorrow. I agreed because I told him that we'd always be friends and I didn't want to seem like I was welching on that. But . . ."

"But what?" Simone prompted.

"But I don't want to go. There's nothing left to say. And I'm afraid that seeing him will cause it to hurt even worse."

"Oh, Cass," Quinn said as she moved closer and took Cass' hand. "I'm so sorry that you're going through this." Quinn stopped and bit her lip, seemingly conflicted about what she was about to say. "Are you sure there's nothing to say though? Maybe it was all just a big misunderstanding."

Cass shook her head. "He was pretty clear. And honestly I don't have it in me to even contemplate that we could work it out. False hope is worse than no hope at all."

The girls exchanged a look that conveyed that they wanted to disagree, but they refrained from voicing any further concerns. Cass had never loved them more.

Alex had shown up early so he could get a table before the lunch rush poured in, which proved to be a mistake, since it gave him time to stress about how their meeting was going to go. Cass was right on time, and he stood to wave her over.

She approached him with a polite smile. "Hey," she said with a cheer that was characteristically *not* Cass.

"Hey." They sat down and grabbed menus. Cass scanned it like she didn't have a care in the world. He was totally thrown. "So, how ya been?"

"Good. Busy with work. You?" She never looked up from her menu.

"Same."

They sat in silence until the waitress came to take their order. Once she left, the silence continued. Cass finally broke it. "Tessa comes back Friday, right? You and Nina have anything special planned for the last few days?" Cass was fiddling with her nails, still avoiding eye contact, but her voice was light.

Alex couldn't take it anymore. "What's going on, Cass?"

Her eyes flitted up briefly to his. "What do you mean?"

"I mean with the fake-happy act you have going on."

She huffed. "It's not fake. You said you wanted to go back to how we were before. So that's what I'm doing."

"I'm pretty sure we could maintain eye contact before. I also think we didn't need to pretend to be happy to see one another."

Cass flipped a piece of hair behind her shoulder. "Okay, fine. So I thought I'd try to fake it until I could make it. Guess I'm a shitty actress."

"You *are* a shitty actress. Which is how I know that you felt more for me than friendship."

"So?"

Alex spluttered. He hadn't expected her to admit it. "So? What do you mean, 'so'? That's important. Because I feel that about you too."

"I *felt* more. Past tense. Now that I've had some distance and time to think, I can see what those feelings really were with more clarity. I got swept up in the fairy tale. I forgot myself for a little while. We were spending all of our time together. Of course we got confused."

"I'm not confused."

Cass laughed, but the sound was hollow. "Oh, come on, Alex. We were faking an engagement, fabricating an entire life. It makes sense that we'd get caught up in that. But the charade is coming to an end, and we need to come back down to reality if we have any hope of salvaging a friendship."

"I don't want a friendship. I want you—*us*. Cass, I know I screwed up—on so many levels. The things I said in those e-mails, I said them because I was mad at *myself*, not at you. I didn't mean any of it. I just . . ." Alex felt like he was talking so rapidly, he wasn't sure if Cass could understand what he was trying to say. He took a deep breath before continuing, his eyes making contact with hers as he spoke. "You were right. I was making the same mistakes I made with Tessa all over again. I don't want to do that. I want this to be different. I want *us* to be different." Alex reached his hand across the table, but Cass didn't take it. "Please. Just give me a chance."

Cass dropped her gaze to the table. "You had a chance, Alex." And with Cass' words, any hope of repairing what he'd broken disappeared completely. "I know it's going to be hard to break the news to Nina," she continued. "I can be there if you want—if you think it'll make it easier—so she knows that we may not be getting married, but she can still count on me to be around. You're her dad. I defer to you to decide what's best." Cass blurted out her little speech like she'd prepared it in advance. He was sure she had. "Oh, I almost forgot," she exclaimed as she dug into her purse. "I figured you'd want this back." She slid the ring he'd bought her across the table.

Alex was stunned. Seeing the ring passed to him like the prop she clearly thought it was hurt. "What am I supposed to do with it?"

"Return it? Sell it? You're out a lot of money for the other stuff we booked. I figured you should make some back where you can."

"I don't care about the money."

Cass looked at him, holding his gaze for the first time since she'd walked in. Then she blinked, seemingly shaking off whatever had been running through her mind. "Well you should. Our fake wedding isn't worth going broke over."

He wanted to disagree. Wanted to tell her that maybe the fake wedding wasn't worth it, but the *real* feelings they'd shared were worth more than anything. But there was nothing more he could say. Because it had all been tainted now. The things they'd said and done couldn't be taken back. Their relationship was over. And fuck if it didn't break his heart.

Alex sat at his kitchen table, his body slumped and his hands supporting his head. He was about to do the very thing that he'd been dreading since all of this had started—the very thing that he would've had to do anyway. Only it seemed harder than he imagined it would be. Maybe because, for a brief moment in time, he'd thought he wouldn't have to tell Nina that the wedding was off. He'd put off telling her for three weeks after his lunch with Cass, hoping like hell there was still a chance for them and she'd come around. Because at one point, he and Cass hadn't been just fake fiancés. They'd been something else. Something more. They'd been *something*.

But then he'd gone and fucked up everything that *could have been*. And now all that was left was what *was*. And as he ascended the stairs and leaned against Nina's doorframe, watching her paint her nails peacefully, the last thing he wanted to do was disrupt that peace. From the moment she was born, all Alex had tried to do was love her with everything he had, protect her from anything that could hurt her.

And now he'd be the one causing the hurt. And no amount of love could counteract that. At least not right now.

Nina was sitting on the floor, her head down as she carefully brushed the purple nail polish over her toes. It was the same polish Cass had used when she'd painted them. "Hey, Daddy," she said happily, her head turning up toward him.

"Hey," he replied. He could hear how broken his voice already sounded, and he cleared his throat to try to correct it. He entered her room cautiously, as if his presence alone might shatter the happiness he'd worked so hard to maintain. "Can I talk to you for a minute?"

Nina put the nail polish down on her small plastic table and took a seat in the chair that went with it. "Sure. Is it about going horseback riding?" It was the only thing Nina had asked to do in the summer that they hadn't done. So he'd promised her they'd go at some point in the fall, now that Nina was back with Tessa and he had her only three weekends a month.

Alex pulled out the other chair and took a seat. The tiny piece of furniture beneath him was another reminder of just how fragile children were. His body felt huge in comparison, like his weight alone might crush it. It could. "No," he said. "I didn't come to talk about horseback riding. I need to talk to you about the wedding." He figured it would be better to just get to it than to drag things out any longer than necessary. And though Cass had offered to be here for this, he knew this was something he needed to do himself. He snuck a glance at his daughter, and she looked concerned.

"What about it?" she asked.

Alex leaned forward, clasping his hands together tightly and resting his forearms on his thighs. His thumb massaged the palm on his other hand nervously as he spoke. "We decided not to have the wedding, honey. Cass and I . . . We talked about it, and we think it's better if we don't have a wedding . . . if we don't . . ." his chest tightened and his voice trailed off, but he was able to recover it. "We thought it would be best if we don't get married."

Though he wanted to look away, bring his gaze anywhere but to Nina's, he didn't dare avert his eyes. This wasn't about him. It was about his daughter, who was now an innocent victim in another one of his failed relationships. Again. He swallowed hard, waiting for Nina to say something. Anything.

There was an uncomfortable silence before she finally spoke. "I don't get it," she said, shaking her head in confusion.

Alex wasn't sure if her response was the only one she could think of or if she was actually unsure of what was happening. He reached across the table and touched her hand gently, but just as quickly as he'd touched it, she jerked it away.

Nina's posture deflated. "Cass isn't going to live here then?"

Alex shook his head. "No, but she'll still be around. She'll still—"

"But she won't be my other mom anymore?" Alex could hear the anger starting to come out in Nina's voice, and he didn't try to stop it. He was sure it was only masking her pain.

That's when he realized why all of this would be so difficult for Nina to accept. It always made Alex proud when he thought about how smart, how perceptive, his daughter was. But not this time. He wished Nina hadn't realized the implications of what the wedding cancellation meant. She didn't just think of Cass as someone she hung out with, someone she had fun with from time to time. She'd begun to think of her as a mother. "No," was all he could say in response, and he'd said it so softly, he wondered if Nina had even heard him.

Nina jumped up suddenly, the chair she'd been sitting in falling back behind her. "So you and *Cass* just decided this?" She said Cass' name in disgust, and it only furthered his guilt. Cass had only been trying to help, but she'd now likely carry more than her share of the blame.

He nodded.

Nina's eyes reddened until they nearly matched the color that her face had turned in anger. "So when do *I* get to decide?" she asked, a few tears falling from her eyes. Alex wanted to wipe them away, but he knew he probably shouldn't try to touch her again. "When do I get to talk about what happens? You and Mommy decided you didn't want to be married anymore, and you didn't ask me what I wanted then either!" Nina was yelling now, her body nearly shaking in what Alex was sure was a cocktail of emotions: hurt, frustration, anger, and sadness. "And now you decide that you don't want to be married to Cass either. What about what I want? When do I get to tell you what *I* want?"

Nina was waving her hand around frantically, tears flowing freely from her eyes. Alex couldn't take it any longer. He reached out to grab her and pulled her tightly to him in a protective hug. "It's okay. It'll be okay." Alex said the words, but he wasn't sure he meant them.

"Don't touch me!" Nina screamed, spilling the nail polish onto the rug when she knocked into the table.

Her fists smacked hard against Alex's chest. But he didn't let go. It only made him want to hold her tighter.

"I'm sorry" was all he could manage. He was crying now too. Not to the extent that Nina was, but he felt the salt stinging his eyes as he tried to blink back tears. But he was too late. A few had already fallen. And something told him they weren't just for Nina, but for everything they had all lost. "I'm so sorry," he repeated, not knowing what else to say.

"No, you're not! You only think about yourself. You only think about what *you* want. *You* didn't want to get married, so now you're not. But I wanted to be your flower girl. I wanted to wear the pretty dress Cass got for me, and I wanted us to be—"

"You can still wear your dress, Nina. I promise. We'll get dressed up and I'll take you out. Just you and me, baby." He could hear how desperate he sounded. He was pleading with her now, begging her to give him any indication that he didn't just break her heart completely.

Nina pushed away from him, and this time Alex loosened his grip enough for her to escape it. He knew there was nothing he could say or do in that moment that was going to make her feel better. He just needed to let her process things, deal with them in her own way.

With blurry vision, he watched his daughter storm across the room toward the door. But before she walked out, Nina turned back to him one last time. "I don't want it to be just you and me," she said quietly. And just like that, Nina's heart wasn't the only one that was broken. Before Alex had time to respond, Nina rushed down the stairs.

When he heard the back door slam, he looked toward the window and watched her run into her playhouse. Alex closed his eyes for a moment, defeat spreading through every inch of his being. When he was finally able to move, he stood. But before he left

Nina's room, he went to her dollhouse, where their little pretend family still remained. He reached in and took out the Barbie doll that Nina had said was Cass, and looked at it for a moment before placing it gently inside Nina's toy box with the others she wasn't using.

Then he looked back at the Ken and Skipper, who remained in the dollhouse alone. "I don't want it to be just us either," he whispered before turning toward the door and walking away.

Chapter 28

Tonality

The month and a half that followed Cass' lunch with Alex made her feel conflicted. On the one hand, they'd agreed to be friends, and that was a good thing. Or at least it should be. But on the other hand, for some reason it didn't feel that way. Instead, it felt . . . maybe "ridiculous" was the word she'd been searching for. Alex wasn't even her ex—at least not in the traditional sense—and things were strained between them. He'd said that he had real feelings for her. And his words had been hard to ignore. But with the echoes of those e-mails still ringing clearly in her ears, it was nearly impossible to believe him.

Nearly.

In the time since their breakup, she'd seen Alex a few times, mostly in passing or out with their whole group. She'd made an effort to act like things weren't different between them, but it proved an impossible task. And from the way Alex always avoided her eyes, she could tell he was struggling too.

"Cass, you there?"

Lauren's voice pulled Cass from her most recent bout of self-pity, and she adjusted the pillow under her head so she could shift her phone to her other ear. "Yeah, I'm here. Sorry. I was just putting some laundry away."

Lauren hesitated as if she knew Cass was lying, but thankfully Lauren didn't press her further. "I just think you should consider going to the party. That's all. Just consider it. You and Alex agreed to be friends."

"I can't even believe he's still having that damn thing. I mean, I know he spent money on it, but we had trouble finding enough people to go when we were inviting people from my side too." She realized how weddingish "my side" sounded, but she chose to ignore it. "He should just cancel it and save himself the embarrassment."

"Don't be mean."

"Oh yeah. He tells his two best friends that I'll never make a good wife or mother and to keep my mouth shut, and I'm the mean one."

"I doubt he said it like that. That doesn't sound like Alex."

"I should show the e-mails to you sometime, Laur." Cass sat up and pulled her nightstand drawer open to withdraw the e-mails. She'd deleted them from her in-box, not wanting the memory staring her in the face every day. But she couldn't let herself get rid of them completely. So she'd printed them, thrown them in the drawer, and hadn't looked at them since. "You'd be surprised who the real Alex is. I thought I knew him too."

"Cass . . ."

"Just leave it alone, Laur." Cass' voice was more pleading than angry.

Her best friend let out a defeated sigh. "He's miserable without you, Cass."

"Yeah? Well, he brought that on himself." Cass huffed out a disgusted laugh through her nose and shook her head. "And *he's* not the only one who's miserable."

Lauren remained silent on the other end of the phone.

"I'll talk to you later, okay?" Cass knew Lauren would understand when she hung up without waiting for Lauren to say good-bye.

Cass tossed the phone onto the bed and the stack of e-mails followed. She didn't even know why she'd kept them. Memories? Ammunition? A reminder of why she'd chosen the single life over a married one? She had no idea, but she decided that none of it fucking mattered anyway.

She sat on the edge of her bed, closed her eyes, and collapsed her head into her hands. She needed to get past all of this somehow, find a way to maintain a friendship with Alex—if only for Nina's sake—no matter how difficult that might be. Despite how hard she tried to let go, she still couldn't sever the connection she had to the little girl. She missed her. And she wondered if Nina missed her too.

Cass opened her eyes and shifted them to the drawer she'd left open. Next to where the e-mails had been was a picture Cass didn't want to see. But she couldn't help but look at it anyway. She reached in and pulled out the photo Alex had bought for her at the amusement park. The three of them were smiling,

Alex's arm around Cass' waist as he pulled her close to him, his other hand on Nina's shoulder in front of them. Their "beautiful family," as the woman at the photo counter had said.

But she knew how misleading pictures could be. They are only glimpses into people's lives—snapshots of happy moments that are often, unfortunately, fleeting. It isn't the moments themselves that matter; it's what happens in between those moments that tells the full story. Dealing with the death of a loved one, working your ass off in college, realizing for the first time that who you thought you were isn't who you are at all. *That's* the shit that makes a difference, not some isolated moment when she felt happier than she'd ever felt. Any idiot can stand in front of a roller coaster and say "Cheese."

Cass ran her thumb over where the frame's glass had shattered. She might have thrown it into her drawer, but she hadn't thrown it away. For whatever reason, she'd felt the need to keep it. She set the picture down next to her and then turned her head back toward the e-mails strewn across her bed.

She gathered them together and with as clear a head as she decided she was ever going to have, she started at the beginning. Lauren had said Cass' paraphrasing didn't sound like Alex. So she had no choice but to look back at the words themselves—try to look at things in a new light. Maybe she and Alex would never be together in the sense that she'd once hoped, but if his words weren't as harsh as she had initially interpreted, then maybe they had a shot at staying friends.

She focused on the first e-mail he'd sent, the one she knew had the most negative tone. Reading with a lack of bias—a skill she'd learned during her public relations courses—she studied the e-mail closely.

> Hmm, let's see. Oh yeah. Cass jumped down my throat last night about being "present" when I'm present or some bullshit like that. I don't need that shit again. And I definitely don't need it from someone who has openly admitted that her job is more important than a family. Where does she get off judging someone's parenting when she's not a parent and doesn't want to be? She doesn't know how hard it is to juggle two full-time jobs because she'll only ever have one. She admits she doesn't have a maternal bone in her body and then she goes and calls me out on how I'm an absent father? Yeah, okay. That makes a lot of fucking sense. She's not a mother, and she'll never be one.

When this whole wedding agreement had begun, she'd been the one giving the lesson on perception. And she was just now realizing that the teacher had become the student. Alex had told her that he'd never said she wouldn't make a good mother, that he actually felt the opposite. He'd said he was just defensive because some of what she'd accused him of was true: just because he was there didn't mean he was present.

Cass let out the breath she'd realized she'd been holding as she reread Alex's words. Though his tone was harsh, Alex was right. He hadn't written that she'd make a poor mother. He'd just said that she wouldn't ever become one. With a clearer head, she could see his intended meaning. Not becoming a mother was *her* decision, not his. It was how she saw *herself*, not how *Alex* saw her.

And as Cass was slowly beginning to realize, Alex was never the one who had doubted her. The only person who'd ever doubted Cass could do something she put her mind to was herself.

And with that thought, she picked the photo back up again, taking one last look at it before she carefully propped the frame up on her nightstand where it had once been. Then she reached for the phone and shot Lauren a simple text. I'll go.

This had been a bad idea. When Alex had promised to take Nina horseback riding, he'd clearly been so focused on ensuring that she had been excited to spend the summer with him that he'd forgotten one crucial piece of information: he fucking hated horses. The last time he'd been near one was at Tessa's parents' place, and he was still convinced to this day that her father had given Alex's horse meth before letting Alex ride him. The fucker had taken off at a gallop, jumped a fence, and then dumped him in a creek. Of course, Tessa's dad said he'd never behaved that way before, but Alex wasn't buying it. That man had never liked Alex and had clearly tried to kill him that day.

Nina had spent enough time at her grandparents' small farm over the years to have learned how to ride proficiently. Which meant that Alex was told to stay close to the guide while his seven-year-old trotted ahead of them down the trail. The place he'd taken her had initially resisted allowing Nina to ride—their policy prohibited riders under eight—but they'd made an exception when he'd assured them of her riding experience. They'd still made her prove her mettle by having her show command of her horse in an enclosure before allowing her out on the trails.

They hadn't made him prove a damn thing, which was probably a serious oversight on the ranch's part. Despite his anxiety, he still found himself enjoying watching Nina. It had taken them a little while to bounce back from the wedding cancellation. Nina had even asked to go home after he'd broken the news to her. Tessa, thankfully, hadn't asked too many questions. She'd seemed genuinely sad for the loss of Alex's relationship.

"You doing okay up there?" Alex called to Nina.

"Yup," came the reply.

The trail was beautiful. A stream ran along one side, while the other was covered in thick forest. The foliage had begun to change and swayed softly in the gentle October breeze. It was picturesque, really, and Alex would've tried to snap a shot with his phone if he hadn't been too terrified to take one hand off the reins.

"Keep right," instructed the guide. "Another group is moving past."

Alex steered his horse to the right of the trail while holding his breath and praying the horse complied. Once he got the horse where it needed to be, he looked up to see the approaching group. Though as they neared, he guessed "family" would be the more accurate term.

"Mommy, why do we have to go back to camp already?" he heard the little girl ask.

"Because we have to get the fire going again so we can cook the fish you and Daddy caught earlier."

"Oh yeah," the girl said with a bright smile.

The woman smiled as she passed. "Excuse us."

Alex nodded at them before turning his attention back to the trail ahead of him. He saw Nina looking at the family as they passed, her neck craned around to watch them ride away. She eventually turned so much that her eyes caught Alex's, and she quickly diverted her attention back to the trail. The look on her face broke his heart all over again. She had been watching the family with a kind of longing—a sadness—that reminded him of how badly he'd hurt her.

He knew she missed Cass. He'd seen Cass a few times since she'd called things off with him, and they'd been civil to each other, but he had never chanced bringing Nina with him when he knew Cass would be there. Because while they both tried to act like nothing had changed, the truth couldn't be ignored. Something had been fundamentally broken between them, and he didn't want Nina to have to endure their *pretending* anymore.

Nina's posture atop her horse was slightly rounded now. God, he hated that he'd done this to her. The guide must have noticed—though she probably chalked it up to Nina growing tired—because she suggested they dismount for a few minutes and allow the horses to get a drink. Nina got down, as did Alex, and the guide steered the horses toward the stream. Nina also walked toward the water, picking up some stones on her way, and began throwing them into the stream.

Alex walked up and stood beside her for a moment before speaking. "It's okay to miss her, Nina."

Nina dropped her hands to her sides. "You said I'd still get to see her sometimes. But I haven't. She just left us." Nina's chin fell to her chest. "Why doesn't she miss me?"

Alex sank to one knee to look into Nina's eyes. "I'm sure she misses you. It's just . . . She's staying away because it's difficult for her to see *me*. She left *me*. You aren't the reason she's staying away, sweetie. I am."

Nina sniffled. "What'd you do?"

Alex sighed. How the hell did he explain this to a seven-year-old? How did he explain it to anyone? "I messed up. I said things I didn't mean, and I hurt Cass' feelings."

Nina looked up at him. "Did you tell her you're sorry?"

"Yeah, baby. I told her."

"Didn't she forgive you?" Nina looked like she couldn't imagine not forgiving someone who'd asked for it.

He didn't know what he should say. Alex had no desire to paint Cass in a bad light, but he was also done lying to his little girl. "No. She didn't. Not really."

Nina pursed her lips and furrowed her brow. "You should try again," she finally said.

"What?"

"Sometimes my friends make me mad. And even if they say they're sorry right away, it doesn't matter. I'm still mad. But after a little while, I miss them and I decide not to be mad anymore. Maybe Cass just needed time to not be mad anymore. Maybe if you said you were sorry again, she'd forgive you."

Alex kneeled there, trying to figure out how to explain that adult problems were a little more complicated than not wanting to share toys at recess. Finally, he answered with the only truth he had. "I don't know. I'll think about it, okay?"

Nina didn't look happy with his reply, but she nodded anyway and walked back toward her horse. They climbed on and rode the trail a little farther before turning around.

Despite the peaceful landscape, Alex felt anything but at peace. Even though he'd verbally dismissed Nina's advice, his brain couldn't let it go. *Could it really be that simple?* The truth was, Nina wasn't the only one who missed Cass like crazy. Alex woke up thinking about her, went to bed thinking about her, and thought about her off and on throughout his days. Maybe the old adage of time healing all wounds applied here. If there was even the slightest chance that he could fix things, didn't he owe it to all of them to try?

Alex debated with himself all the way back to the ranch, then all the way home. When they arrived at his house, he'd finally made up his mind. He sent Nina to take a shower, and then called Scott. "Hey. I need a favor."

Chapter 29

Confession

Cass hadn't realized how much she'd needed a night out with the girls until they'd forced one on her. She suspected that they were trying to get her mind off things. Her "wedding" was supposed to be in two days, and she had to admit that she was struggling a little bit. Even though there was never going to be an actual marriage, there was still supposed to be a solid friendship—and maybe a promise of something more down the road. But that was all gone now, having evaporated with one misinterpreted e-mail that she wished she'd never laid eyes on. *Ignorance is bliss and all that crap.*

They'd all gone to dinner and then barhopped for a while. The girls drank, danced, and laughed their way through the evening. Cass had never been more grateful for them. Until they turned up at Nothing Gold. How could the girls have overlooked the difficult memories this club would dredge up? Looking up at the building, her mind flooded with thoughts: when she'd first seen Alex, the immediate attraction she'd felt, the food tasting where Alex had told that other couple about his meeting her here, how he'd felt about her. And while she hadn't been sure at the time whether the feelings he discussed were real or not, she knew better now. He'd felt it—they both had—and now it was gone.

"You coming?"

Cass' attention snapped back to the girls in front of her. She wasn't even sure which one had spoken. "Yeah. Yeah, I'm coming." Because even though she didn't want to go in, she had to. It almost felt like a penance she'd assigned herself. She'd forced herself to walk away from Alex, but she wouldn't walk away from the good memories this place held—even if they'd hurt her like hell.

They walked into the crowded club after showing the bouncer their IDs. Cass started to turn toward the bar, thinking that was where they'd logically start.

Until she heard Quinn say, "The guys are over there."

Um, what? Cass whipped around and grabbed Quinn's arm. "What do you mean, the guys are here?"

Quinn's eyes widened. She raised her hand to point at Scott, Tim, Xavier, and Alex. "I mean, the guys are here."

"What the hell? Why didn't any of you tell me they'd be here?" Cass was pissed. The club she could handle. The club and Alex, she couldn't.

The girls all looked at one another before Simone shrugged and said, "I guess we all thought that one of the others had mentioned it. Why? What's the big deal?"

"What's the big deal? Are you kidding me right

now? I was supposed to have a fake wedding with the real love of my life on Saturday. We talked about coming here for a joint bachelor/bachelorette party to celebrate the nonimpending nuptials. And you're really asking me what the big deal is?"

The girls looked at her like she was one precarious step away from toppling off a high-rise. She probably was. Lauren was the first to try to talk her back from the edge. "We didn't know the whole thing about the joint parties. When I told Scott we were all hanging out, he said for us to meet him here later. I'm sorry. I really didn't think anything of it. Do you want to go somewhere else?"

Cass rolled her eyes. How could they go somewhere else? She'd tried so hard to act normal around Alex the few times she'd seen him. She couldn't go running out of the club like it was on fire now. It'd make the strain between them even worse. "No, I just . . . wasn't prepared. I'm fine. Really. Let's go over."

The girls looked like they didn't believe that she was truly okay, but they kept their mouths shut and led the way to the table. Once they arrived, hellos were exchanged, and even though Tim and Scott were there, Quinn and Lauren made no move to go to them. Instead they remained firmly on either side of Cass. Her little army was flanking her, and she felt some of her annoyance at them melt away.

Conversation flowed naturally, though both Cass and Alex remained mostly quiet. A few drinks helped loosen her up, and she felt her posture relax. It also gave her the courage to steal a few glances at Alex. *Jesus, he looks good.* He wore dark-rinse jeans and a hunter green henley that hugged him in all the best places. She wanted to touch him. Or lick him. Or hump him. *Maybe I need to slow down on the drinks.*

Especially since the alcohol was beginning to convince her that Alex was looking at her too. Each time she snuck a peek at him, it seemed as though he quickly diverted his gaze from her. The game of is-he-or-isn't-he-looking started to wear on her already frazzled brain. "Let's go dance," she basically commanded before walking toward the dance floor.

The girls wisely followed. Cass wasn't sure how long they stayed out there, but it was long enough that she felt her buzz begin to burn off. Even as she sobered, she couldn't help but look over at Alex from time to time as she swayed to the music. At one point, he looked like his hands were fiddling with something, his brow furrowed in concentration. As his hands stopped moving, so did Cass' body. She stood stock-still in the middle of the dance floor and stared at Alex. Who was now staring back. The look that passed between them was the realest and rawest moment they'd had in almost two months. So much so that it caused Alex to leave the table and stalk toward her. *Wait. He's coming toward me. Shit.*

Alex invaded her space, his eyes seeming to search hers for . . . something. She wasn't sure whether or not he found it, but he grabbed her hand and led her off the dance floor anyway.

And she went.

They ended up in a corner of the club where it was slightly quieter. Alex lifted the hand that he'd been holding and opened her palm. He placed a knotted straw wrapper in it.

She looked down at it, then up at him, utterly confused.

"Nina told me that if you tie a straw wrapper in a knot and it doesn't break, someone you love is thinking about you. Since I'm pretty sure Nina is asleep, dreaming of ponies right now, that only leaves one other person who could be thinking about me." He moved closer to her. "After I tied it, I looked up, and you were the first person I saw." He smiled and ran a hand across her cheek before cupping her jaw. "And since you're the only other person besides Nina who I love, I need to know: were you thinking about me, Cass?"

Cass was pretty sure her brain was short-circuiting. "Did you just say you loved me?"

He rubbed his thumb over her skin. "Yeah. I should've said it a long time ago. Because even though you hate me, you still deserved to know."

"I don't hate you." Cass' voice was so low, Alex probably barely heard her. But from the way his eyes brightened, she knew he did.

"Answer my question, Cass."

It took her a second to remember what his question had even been. "You could've tied that stupid knot at any point over the past months, and it always would've been me who was thinking of you."

Alex's expression softened at her admission. "I've been thinking about you too." He somehow crowded even closer to her, bringing his other hand up so that he cradled both sides of her face. "I can't stop thinking about you. I know I fucked up. I know I hurt you. And I can't promise that I'll never do it again, because sometimes I'm an idiot. But I swear, if you can forgive me, I'll try my best to be everything you deserve. I love you, Cass. With every fiber of my being. Please give me another chance to get it right."

Cass was speechless. She knew this was one of those moments that would change the trajectory of her life. And she was scared. Because admitting what she *really* wanted and allowing herself to have it could result in more pain than she'd be able to survive. But . . . *Fuck it. Some things are worth the risk.* "We both screwed up. We both got so much so wrong. But I love you, Alex. More than anything. And I want to fix it. I want us to finally get it right."

The kiss he pressed to her lips was full of passion and promise. She allowed herself to get swept up in it, despite the very public setting they were in.

But all too soon, he was pulling back. "That night when you told me I needed to be more present with Nina, you said that I was trying to win her over with grand gestures."

"Alex, I didn't—"

He pressed a finger to her lips. "One second. Just let me get this out." He lowered his finger and replaced it on her jaw. "You were right. And I realized the other day that while I was quick to offer those gestures to Nina, I never offered any to you. And while I don't want to be a highlight reel–only guy with you, I think you deserve at least one truly memorable and over-the-top display of my feelings for you." He gave her a quick kiss before dropping to one knee.

Is he doing what I think—

"Cassidy Mullen, I love you. I'm not entirely sure when it happened, but at some point all of our pretending became real for me." He had one of her hands clasped in his, and with the other he dug into his pocket and withdrew a ring. *Her* ring. "When I bought you this, you told the salesman that my proposal was a spur-of-the-moment decision I made because you were sick and I was scared of losing you. And while I did have to have a little bit of a plan in order to get you here, I *am* still scared to lose you. I need you, Cass. My life just doesn't feel right without you in it." He smiled at her, and it was full of love and honesty. "So, what do you think? You wanna marry me in two days?"

She took a deep breath in an attempt to keep the emotions from overtaking her. "Put that on my finger and get up here."

Applause erupted around them as he put the ring back where it belonged and stood to kiss her. Cass had forgotten people were even there, and she forgot again as soon as Alex took control of her mouth with his.

"Is that a yes?" he asked in between kisses.

"Yes, it's a yes."

They probably looked ridiculous as they stood there, kissing one another's smiles, but that didn't matter. Eventually they separated and rested their foreheads together. "Are we really going to get married in two days?" Cass asked.

"I think it's only fitting."

"How are we ever going to get everything organized in time?"

He smoothed his hands down her back. "Most of it's already planned. And the rest will come together. Even if it's not perfect, it'll be perfect for us."

"We should probably get out of here and make a list of things we need to do. We need to get a license, and, shit, I need to tell my parents. That's going to be an interesting conversation. And I need flowers and a dress and—"

"Cass?"

"Yeah?"

"Can we worry about all of that tomorrow? I think our night is better spent getting reacquainted."

Cass hugged him closer. "What the hell are we waiting for?"

* * *

They were barely inside Cass' apartment before they were ripping clothes off each other. Alex couldn't believe Cass had actually agreed to marry him. Sure, he'd obviously gone in there with that hope, but he wasn't sure how she'd actually respond. And now here he was, about to make love to her. He was a lucky son of a bitch.

In their haste to leave, they hadn't even said good-bye to their friends. He bet they were as shocked as Cass by what had transpired at the club. When he'd called Scott to see if he would help arrange a get-together with the girls, he'd made Scott swear to not tell anyone else about his proposal plans. He wanted to make sure Cass knew before any of the other girls. He now also wanted her naked beneath him. "I can't believe you're going to marry me. I want to taste every inch of this body that's going to become mine on Saturday."

"I've been yours for months."

Impossibly, her words made his dick get harder. He wanted to consume her. To burrow inside of her and never leave. They fumbled their way to her bedroom, shedding the last remnants of clothing before falling onto the bed. His hand kneaded her breast roughly as his lips nipped along her neck.

Cass moaned. "Don't tease me, Alex. I need you."

"I need you too. Always." And with that, he thrust into her. What was happening between them wasn't quite the lovemaking he'd imagined. It was a claiming. He put his arms beneath her knees and pushed her legs back so he could drive deeper into her. His eyes locked with hers as he pumped into her wildly.

She tilted her hips so she could meet him thrust for thrust. "Mmm, I'm close."

So was he. As much as he wanted it to last, his

cock had other ideas. He sucked one of her nipples into his mouth and lowered a hand so that he could massage her clit.

She let out a guttural moan as her body shook with her release. He continued to fuck her through it, teasing her clit until she rode out her climax. He followed soon after. And as he emptied his release inside of her, he felt all the pain and uncertainty drain out of him too. *This* was where he was supposed to be. With Cass, he was home.

Sliding onto his side, he pulled her to him. He pressed his nose into her hair and breathed her in. She melted against him, and her breathing evened out before he spoke. "You'd better not fall asleep. I said I was going to taste every inch of you, and that's a promise I intend to see through as soon as I recover."

"I'll hold you to it," she murmured. Suddenly she turned to face him, burrowing her face into his neck. "I love you so much. Thank you for not giving up on me."

He let his hands roam all over her body. "There's no giving you up. You're it for me."

She pulled back slightly and looked at him as though she were trying to memorize him. "You're it for me too," she whispered.

He took her mouth in a kiss that was sweet and filled with love.

"We should probably get some sleep. We have a busy couple days ahead. Plus, you're going to need to be in top form tomorrow."

"Why's that?" he asked as he settled more comfortably.

She chuckled. "Because I'm taking you to meet my parents."

Chapter 30

Benchmark

As Cass stared into the full-length mirror to fasten her earrings, she thought back over the whirlwind that had been the past day and a half. Yesterday morning, Cass and Alex had gotten up and eaten breakfast, and Cass had outlined a battle plan for the day.

First on the list was getting a marriage license and wedding bands, which they were able to do without any major hassle. But that was where Cass and Alex's joint effort had ended. The girls had descended on Cass' apartment by noon, each with a cell phone to her ear as Simone contacted a woman who could do Cass' hair and makeup, Quinn called her parents to arrange for flowers, and Lauren said she would handle the dress. Cass had no choice but to put her trust in her friends' abilities to help her pull this off. For her part, Cass had a very important call to make—to her parents. She asked if they were home, and if she could bring someone by in a couple of hours. Her mom sounded curious, but invited them over immediately. Cass also placed a quick three-way call to Amy and Rachel. They were confused, but since they'd at least heard of Alex, the conversation wasn't as difficult as she was sure the one with her mom and dad was going to be. Her sisters had assured her that they'd be present at the wedding—after multiple questions that were all variations of "Are you sure you know what the hell you're doing?"—and that Cass was to let them know if she needed anything.

Alex had left when the girls arrived, telling Cass that he would procure an officiant, buy himself a suit to wear, and call his sister. She texted him to see if he could be back by two-thirty so they could head to her parents' house. He sent back a simple Sure, which did little to calm her nerves.

Cass wasn't stupid. It was no parent's dream to have their daughter wander into their house with a stranger and pronounce that she was marrying him the next day. But by three o'clock, that's exactly what Cass was doing.

"I don't understand," her mom said.

"I *hope* I don't understand," her dad added firmly.

Cass tried for lighthearted. "But I'm pretty sure you both do."

"No offense, Alex," Tom said, "but we don't even know who the hell you are. And you expect us to accept that you are not only marrying our daughter, but that you're doing so tomorrow?"

Alex looked at Cass and took her hand in his before turning back to her father. "I know how crazy it sounds. I have a daughter of my own, and I can only imagine how I'd be feeling if she came home in twenty years and told me what we just told you. But I love your daughter. I know I haven't earned your blessing, but if you can support us tomorrow, I promise that I'll spend the rest of my life earning it."

His words hadn't fixed everything, but they'd thawed the Mullens enough to where they promised to be present the next day. Her mom had even given Alex a hug when they'd left forty-five minutes later. Gloria had wanted them to stay for dinner, but they still had one more stop to make.

Alex called Tessa and gave her the rundown on what had happened over the previous twenty-four hours, and she'd reluctantly invited them over. Cass understood her hesitance. The dissolution of their "engagement" had taken a huge emotional toll on Nina. And even though Alex and Cass both hoped this would fix it, there was a big chance that their news would make it worse.

Tessa opened the door before Alex and Cass had a chance to knock. The look on her face was filled with resolve. "I need to know it's for real, Alex. Before I call that little girl down here and let you tell her this, I need to know that it's something you both intend to see through. Because I have to tell you, this back-and-forth bullshit isn't very encouraging."

Alex pushed a hand through his hair. "Tessa, I get it. Believe me—I get it. Hurting Nina is the *last* thing I ever wanted to do. You know me, and you know how much I love Nina. Hurting her once nearly killed me. I could never do it again."

Tessa's gaze shifted from Alex to Cass, and Cass got it. Tessa *did* know Alex—knew that he wouldn't hurt their daughter again. But she didn't know if the same could be said for Cass.

"I know you have no reason to trust me. You put

your faith in me—that I would take care of your little girl when you weren't there—and then I walked right out of Nina's life and left all of you to pick up the pieces." Cass took in a ragged breath and tried to get her emotions under control. "I love Nina. With everything I have. And I promise that I'll make sure she knows it every day."

Tessa looked at Cass for a moment longer before turning and calling Nina.

Cass watched as she happily bounded toward the stairs and took two steps down before coming to a halt, the smile slipping off her face. "What's going on?"

Cass sighed and stepped forward, hoping her next words would be the right ones. "It turns out that I'm in need of a flower girl after all. I was wondering if you were still willing to take on the job."

Nina looked back and forth between Alex and Cass. "Really?" The wariness in her voice nearly brought Cass to tears.

"Really," Cass replied.

And then a bright smile lit up Nina's face. She rushed down the steps and flung herself at Cass. "Yes!"

Cass hugged her back tightly. "Good. Because there was no way I was getting up there tomorrow without you next to me."

They talked a little more and worked out the logistics. Nina wanted to come with them immediately, but Tessa managed to convince her to allow Cass and Alex a few more hours to prepare for the next day. Tessa would drop Nina off at Alex's after dinner, and then Cass would take Nina back to her apartment so they could pamper themselves properly before the wedding.

And now here she was, looking at herself in the

mirror as her best friends, mom, sisters, and Nina bustled around behind her. She wasn't having bridesmaids, since getting dresses for all of the women who were most important to her would have been an added nightmare that no one had time to deal with, but they were all here anyway—bridesmaids in spirit.

Cass lightly fingered the large curls that were pulled to one side of her head, and surveyed the makeup that had been applied. The woman Simone had hired had done a wonderful job. She'd even gotten Nina to sit still long enough to French braid her hair. Cass smoothed her hands down the dress Lauren had shown up with earlier that afternoon. Cass hadn't been able to hold back her tears when she'd looked at the dress—*her* dress—the one she'd tried on in the store that day. When Cass had asked Lauren how she'd gotten it in Cass' size, Lauren had simply hugged her and said she preferred not to say anything that could be used against her in a court of law. Cass let it go.

She watched in the mirror as her mother approached her with a bag in her hands. "You didn't give me a lot of time to get things together. But I did my best." Her mother reached into the bag and withdrew a white piece of fabric. "This is the bonnet Amy wore at her baptism. When you remove the straps, it doubles as a handkerchief that you can use for your wedding. It has blue flowers on it. So you have something old, something blue, *and* something borrowed. We can just pin it under your dress so you don't have to carry it. As for something new . . ." Gloria looked over her shoulder at Nina, who was talking excitedly with Lauren, before turning back to meet Cass' eyes in the mirror. "I think you already have that covered." Gloria put her hands on Cass' shoulders and squeezed. "You're going to be a great wife and mother, Cass. And even though I wish the circumstances were slightly different, I'm so very proud of you for following your heart."

Cass brought a hand up to rest on one of her mother's. "Thank you," was all she could manage without ruining her makeup. Cass' mom withdrew her hands to fasten the handkerchief beneath Cass' dress. When she was done, she fussed with the dress for a minute before stepping back, allowing Cass to admire herself in the mirror one more time. The last time she'd worn this dress had been an eye-opening experience for her. But she found that this moment was equally as special. When she'd last put on the dress, the girl staring back at her had been surprised, unsure. But the woman she saw now was neither of those things. Her new self was confident, certain. She'd found the man she wanted to spend the rest of her life with. But what's more, *he* had found *her*—or a version of her she never knew existed.

"You look gorgeous," Amy said.

Cass smiled shyly, turning to see the back of her dress. "Thanks. For everything," she added. "I can't tell you how much it means that all of you came through at the last minute like this. I'm so happy you could all be here today." The women stayed quiet, returning her comment with nods and sweet smiles. Then Cass turned to Nina. "Especially you," she said quietly, her hands on Nina's shoulders. "I'm so glad you decided to be our flower girl again."

Cass could see how excited Nina was at the mere mention of being their flower girl. "I'm glad too," Nina said. "I missed you."

Cass sat on the bed so she could be at Nina's level, and put her arms around the little girl who would become her daughter. "I missed you too," she said. "But you know what?"

"What?"

"We never have to miss each other again, because I'm not going anywhere." Cass put her forehead against Nina's and then gave her a quick kiss between her eyes before standing so she could put on her shoes. Then she inhaled deeply and gave the girls a confident nod. "I'm ready."

Alex hated being the center of attention. But as he stood under the trellis, the crisp October air enveloping him and the guests, he felt all eyes on him. It wasn't that he was nervous. He wasn't. Everything was ready to go, and there was no doubt in his mind that this was the right decision. But Alex was a private man, and the attention made him fidget under the scrutiny. He was also overwhelmed with the desire to make this the perfect day for Cass. After all they'd been through, they both deserved to have the moment they became man and wife be as flawless as possible.

Finally he saw Nina come down the aisle. He could tell she was making every effort to slow her pace as she tossed yellow rose petals onto the grass—Alex's idea—to represent that the core of his relationship with Cass was friendship. Nina beamed as her eyes locked with Alex's, and she nearly ran to him. Soon he'd have both his girls by his side.

He knew it would be only another minute or so before he'd get to see Cass, and once he saw her, he wouldn't be able to look at anything else, so he used the moment to take in his surroundings. Cass had been right the day of the food tasting; the outside ceremony was beautiful. The leaves on the trees surrounding the grounds had just started to turn, their colors decorating the landscape naturally.

Alex looked into the white seats, which were filled with their family and close friends. Some of the guests would have been in attendance even if it had just been a party. But there were others who'd found out last-minute and had still been willing to put their lives on hold just to take part in *their* day. It meant a lot.

Finally, Alex heard the song that signaled Cass would be walking down the aisle. The guests stood, blocking any early view he might have gotten of her. Alex's heart fluttered with a movement he'd never felt before, even the first time he'd gotten married. This felt different, better, more . . . right. As soon as he saw Cass making her way toward him, her arm locked with her father's—Alex immediately relaxed. Her presence alone calmed him.

She walked slowly down the aisle, her blond hair shining even more brightly in the late-afternoon sun. A few soft curls fell into her face and she swept them to the side casually, her gaze never disconnecting from his. Her smile was small. It was the kind that looked like she was trying to hold back tears. As she approached him, Alex finally let his eyes drift down the length of her, over the lace of her dress that hugged her breasts and hips perfectly. Suddenly the small distance between them was too much. He wanted to touch her right then, wanted to feel her hands in his as he stared at her.

"Please be seated." Cass whipped her head toward Scott in what Alex immediately identified as confusion. They'd been so caught up in staring at each other as she approached him, Alex was sure this was the first time she noticed Scott was standing in front of them.

Cass' eyes were still narrowed at Alex.

"Scott got a onetime officiant certificate," Alex whispered. "Which means I had to tell him I was proposing before I actually proposed. I hope you're not mad."

"I'm not mad, but are you sure we're actually gonna be legally married?"

"Yeah. The certificate was issued by Fairfax County, so we're all good."

Cass' eyes widened, and Scott cleared his throat, signaling that he was ready to begin the ceremony. "We're gathered here today to celebrate the marriage of Cassidy and Alexander. We'll also be their witnesses and supporters as they celebrate their commitment to one another. Everyone they've invited here today is special to them, and Cass and Alex want to thank you for being here to take part in this important day. They would also like to recognize everyone who could only be with us in spirit." Scott paused for a moment, and when Alex closed his eyes, Cass knew he was thinking of his parents. "Or those who couldn't make it today because Alex and Cass decided to give people only a day's notice."

Everyone laughed, including Alex and Cass, immediately lightening the mood.

"And speaking of important people, who gives this woman away in marriage to this man?"

Mr. Mullen spoke. "Her mother and I do." Then he gave Cass a kiss before turning to Alex to shake his hand. "Take good care of her," Tom said. "You're a lucky man."

He wanted to disagree, to tell Cass' father he wasn't just *a* lucky man. He was *the* luckiest. He'd somehow gotten the girl of his dreams. And now that he had her, he planned to never let her go. But instead, he just nodded and answered, "I will" before turning back to Cass so he could make the same promise to her.

Surprisingly, Scott did a decent job with the ceremony, which had been short and sweet. Cass thought it was fitting, since their real engagement had been pretty much the same. It was hard to believe that only a few days ago they'd been miserable without each other. And now here they were, sipping champagne to the soft melody of Eric Church's "Like a Wrecking Ball." *What a difference forty-eight hours can make.* "I still can't believe you got Cockfeather," Cass said, smiling.

"Consider it your wedding gift." Alex laughed and put an arm on Cass' back, rubbing his hand lightly across the sheer fabric. "And they *are* pretty good," Alex admitted. "They even dressed up for the occasion," he said, referring to the matching tuxedo T-shirts they were sporting. Even Slim—whose real name, Alex found out, was Slimberly—was wearing a halter top that looked like a fitted suit jacket with nothing underneath.

The guests seemed to be enjoying their meals, tapping their silverware on their glasses every now and then so Cass and Alex would kiss. It should have been annoying. But seeing Alex dressed in his tailored suit and no vest made her want to keep her lips on him permanently.

Gradually the plates were cleared and it came time for their first dance. Cass leaned against Alex's chest as Cockfeather began to play "My Wish" by

Rascal Flatts. The two swayed slowly to the rhythm, feeling each other's hearts beat as they danced. Cass lifted her head to look into Alex's eyes, and then the two stretched out their arms, signaling to Nina that it was time for her to join them. And just like that, two became three—or maybe it had been that way from the beginning—and the three of them moved to a beat that was all their own.

They wouldn't want it any other way.

Acknowledgments

We're going to make this simple this time.

Sarah Younger, thank you for always believing in us and helping steer our sometimes off-course ship toward its destination. And thanks for still loving us even though sometimes we bother you incessantly.

To everyone at Penguin, we appreciate all of your hard work throughout this entire journey. Thank you for getting this book to what it is today.

Amanda, thanks for being a sounding board when we were struggling with plot issues.

To all our padded roommates, thanks for participating in the craziness and for sticking by us.

To our families, thank you all for being unconditionally supportive of us and our insane hobby. Sometimes we really don't deserve you.

Love,
E and H

Don't miss the first book in
Elizabeth Hayley's Strictly Business series

THE BEST MEDICINE

Turn the page for a sneak peek!

Chapter 1

Temporary Insanity

"If one more douche bag gets handsy with me tonight, I'm going to go 'Kung Fu Fighting' on his ass," Lauren yelled over the blaring techno and raucous crowd.

"Tell me about it," Simone agreed. "I haven't been groped this unappealingly since I was in the back of Todd Grady's car in eleventh grade."

"Doesn't he go by 'Tina' now?" Cassidy asked.

Simone widened her eyes and slowly nodded her head. The girls instantly broke out in hysterics.

Lauren relished these nights with her girlfriends— casually drinking in Mickey's Bar and Grill and flouncing around the dance floor like deranged *Riverdance* rejects. The four of them—Lauren, Simone, Cassidy, and Quinn—had been the Fantastic Foursome since middle school, though Lauren had known Quinn since kindergarten, when she'd dragged Quinn out of the lunch line so they could go outside for recess early. They'd been friends ever since.

Lauren took a sip from her glass and tasted diluted Malibu. "I'm getting another drink. Maybe the alcohol will kill the STDs that are seeping out of these cretins. Anyone else need anything?" Her friends all shook their heads, causing Lauren to say "Lightweights" over her shoulder as she pushed her way toward the bar. With school starting in two weeks, Lauren intended to take full advantage of the last few days of summer before she'd have to buckle down and get into student mode.

Eight years ago, Lauren had thrown her small crew for a loop when she'd announced that she was going out of state for college. But that sojourn had only lasted two years before she'd returned to Virginia, taken some time off from school, and ultimately gotten her life back on track. Now, at twenty-six, she was about to finish her last year of graduate school at George Mason University and couldn't wait to join "adulthood"—a place her friends had entered years ago.

Once she arrived at the bar, she smoothed down her canary yellow halter top, which had ridden up as she pressed her way through the multitude of men. Lauren flagged down Sam, one of the bartenders she knew, and held up her glass to him. He gave her a swift nod and set about mixing her drink. Lauren and her friends had been coming to Mickey's since they were twenty-one. Her parents had known Mickey since they were kids, so she'd always felt comfortable there despite the influx of drunk, horny guys.

"Can I buy you a drink?"

Lauren cringed as soon as she recognized the voice. She took a deep breath before turning around to face the man who had shamelessly been trying to get into her pants since tenth grade. "Hi, Josh," she said, feigning a small smile. Lauren had always been good at reading people. It was part of the reason she had changed her major from marketing to psychology when she enrolled at George Mason. And she knew *exactly* what kind of man Josh was, which is why she had no interest in being around him.

"Hey, beautiful. So how about it? Can I get you a drink?" Josh winked at her, which reminded her of her great-uncle Thomas, who had an odd tic that caused his eyelid to spasm constantly.

The image made her laugh abruptly, which earned her a curious look from Josh. *Great, now I've suddenly become the weird one*, she thought. It wasn't that Josh was unattractive: he was tall, well-built, and had a handsome face. No, the real problem was that his dick had been buried in more holes than a homeless dog's bone. And since he was an arrogant prick, those holes didn't always belong to Virginia's classiest bachelorettes. Lauren regarded him with the same wariness a child would a party clown: he was fun to laugh at, but the last thing you wanted was to find yourself alone in a room with him.

"Sorry. You just reminded me of something really funny."

Josh smiled, thinking her words were a compliment. "Oh yeah? What would that be?"

"Uuuh." Lauren dragged the word out, trying to think of the right way to phrase her response. "My uncle used to wink at me a lot. Well, not just me. It wasn't like some creepy thing where he'd wink at his young relatives. He had this spasm problem. Not that you looked like you were spasming. I just don't see a lot of people wink, so when you did it, that's what I thought of." Lauren was rambling and from the bemused smirk on Josh's face, she could tell he thought he was flustering her. Which he was, but not for the reason he thought. "Anyway, we have a tab running, so I'm all good on the drink. Thanks, though." Lauren turned back toward the bar just as Sam set the Malibu and 7-Up in front of her.

"Anything else?" Sam asked, glancing quickly at Josh and then back to Lauren.

"You got an exit strategy back there anywhere?" Lauren asked quietly so Josh wouldn't overhear.

"I can pull the fire alarm," Sam joked.

Lauren smiled widely. "I'll keep it in mind."

Sam wiped the bar between them with a wet dish towel. "Well, I'm here if you need me," he said before walking away to help another customer. Lauren smiled again. Sam had been best friends with her older brother, Cooper, and always looked out for Lauren when she was at Mickey's. He had become a sort of surrogate older brother over the years, even if it was only between the hours of ten p.m. and two a.m.

Lauren turned back around to face Josh, hoping to quickly give him the brush-off so she could return to her friends. But, not expecting him to be standing so close to her, she nearly collided with him. Her drink sloshed over the side of her glass and splashed onto Josh's gray T-shirt.

"Shit, sorry," Lauren apologized as she reached toward the bar to grab some napkins, putting her drink down so she could help dry Josh's shirt.

"No worries. It'll dry. Though if you were feelin' like you needed to make it up to me, I'd accept a dance as payment."

The thought of dancing with Josh made Lauren's stomach flip. She felt her lips turn down in disgust before she had time to stop them. She noticed his eyes narrow at her reaction and desperately tried to recover.

"I, uh, think I've done enough damage to you for one night. God only knows what would happen to you if you tried to dance with me." She let out a small laugh that sounded as halfhearted as it was.

Josh leaned even closer, causing his torso to connect with Lauren's chest. She silently cursed her size B breasts. If they'd been larger, they would've kept Josh farther from her face. "I think I can handle myself," he replied.

Lauren hoped that was true since she had *no* intention of handling any part of Josh. The very thought made her shiver in repulsion. Of course, Josh took the slight movement of her body as an invitation. He began leaning down toward her, eyes closed. Lauren suddenly understood why women in horror movies never ran until it was too late. It took her brain a while to accept that this nightmare was actually a reality. Just as his lips were about to connect with hers, she threw her hand up, causing him to kiss her palm.

His eyes jerked open. "What the hell was that?"

"Uh, my hand?" Lauren wasn't sure why it came out as a question, but it had.

"Yeah, I figured that much out." Josh backed up a bit, heat radiating off of him. He was pissed. "You're a real fucking tease—you know that?"

Lauren's back straightened. If this douche bag wanted to start name-calling, then he'd found a willing adversary. "And you're a fucking misogynist. Since you're clearly an idiot, let me take the time to spell something out for you: I'm. Not. Interested. Now get the hell out of my way so that I can go back to people whose company I actually enjoy." She sidestepped Josh quickly and began walking toward her friends, not even bothering to pick up her drink.

Josh stood stock-still for a moment, clearly stunned by Lauren's words. But that didn't last long. Lauren hadn't made it more than five steps before she felt a firm grip on her biceps and was pulled toward a small alcove off to the side of the bar. Once the destination had been reached, Josh spun her around and thrust her roughly against the wall. The impact caused her breath to leave her momentarily, but she recovered quickly.

"Don't you ever put your hands on me again!" Lauren yelled in Josh's face. If he thought she was going to back down, he was sorely mistaken. When it came to fight-or-flight situations, Lauren always fought. Her brother had taught her how to handle herself when she'd grown boobs, and she'd been ever thankful for it.

Josh pushed against her, putting his arms on the wall on either side of her head in an effort to use his size and proximity to intimidate her. And while the situation did cause fear to bubble within her, she'd never let it show.

"You're so sexy when you're mad," Josh rasped into her ear.

"Josh, I'm giving you one last chance to back up before I seriously lose my shit." Lauren's voice was strong and laced with a warning that she had every intention of following through with.

"Stop playing hard to get, baby. I know you want it. I can see how hard your nipples are through your shirt. And I bet if I touch that sweet pussy, I'll feel how wet it is for me. Maybe I should prove it to you." Josh's hand quickly skated down the wall and landed on the button on Lauren's jeans. He fumbled for a couple seconds before all hell broke loose.

Lauren might have been more than a little tipsy, but that didn't make her more tolerant of Josh's inappropriate behavior. It made her rail against it with a fervor she'd only felt a few times in her life. Reflexively, she brought her fist up in a lightning-fast move and connected with Josh's windpipe. He staggered back, gripping his throat, but Lauren wasn't done. She brought her heel down hard on the top of his flip-flop-clad foot, then brought her knee up to connect with his balls, causing Josh to double over with a pain that she was sure radiated through his body.

Lauren stepped closer to him, needing to make sure he knew that she wasn't scared of him. She'd just kicked his ass, and she'd do it again. *Anytime.* "Fuck with me again, and a broken dick and a sore throat will be the least of your problems."

ALSO AVAILABLE FROM

Elizabeth Hayley

THE BEST MEDICINE
A Strictly Business Novel

A gig at Trinity Hospital isn't exactly Lauren
Hastings definition of a good time, but Dr. Scott
Jacobs quickly changes her mind. He's straight-up
gorgeous, and he always gets what he wants.
And that includes Lauren. It's an ideal
arrangement for both of them. No strings.
Just fun—at least at first.

But feelings quickly begin to run deeper than
either Lauren or Scott is willing to admit, causing
issues neither of them want to confront. After all,
who wants to risk the perfect relationship on
something as terrifying, as messy, and as
unpredictable as love?

S0633